EndLess CrossRoads

EndLess CrossRoads
The End to All Roads

BLOSSOM CARTER

© 2019 Blossom Carter

All rights reserved. This book or any portion thereof may not be reproduced or used in any manner whatsoever without the express written permission of the publisher except for the use of brief quotations in a book review.

ISBN: 9781798405482

ACKNOWLEDGMENTS

When I think about acknowledgments this time around, I asked God to give me a different perspective on who and what should be acknowledged.

For starters, I would like to thank God for all "It" has done for me. For months I went back and forth with God about this novel. I had so many ideas for part two that I ended up giving myself writer's block. Writing *EndLess CrossRoads* and *UnExpected CrossRoads* has taught me so much about myself. Whoever knew something as simple as writing could help build your faith, teach you patience, motivate you, and give you peace of mind? I could never thank God enough for allowing me to CrossRoads with my gift to write, because every novel I write is attached to my "Fruit of Life."

To my big brother Durrell: Thank you for all your support and for showing up to every event I had. I know at times dealing with me isn't so easy, but I swear I'm thankful for you. Anything I've ever needed for the Blossom Carter brand, you were on it like it was your own brand. I never had more fun in my life than when we both hit the block and started pushing *UnExpected CrossRoads*. Epic. If I don't tell you this enough, I love you to death. You're beyond a genius, bruh. You're gifted.

Erica: When it comes to you, cousin, LOL. You just need to be a motivational speaker, because you motivate the hell out of me. Whenever I need you, no matter what, you're always there for me. You show up to all my events. No matter if they're in the city or in a different city, you're there at all of them, supporting me. I remember bitching one day about not having a support system and you telling me, "Fuck everybody! If you don't have nobody, cuz, you got yourself, and most important, you have God! This is your dream. Get out there and make it come true, even if all you have is you." Ever since then I've been on to "something." Thank you.

I want to give the biggest THANK YOU to every last person/reader who bought or supported *UnExpected CrossRoads*! You guys are the reason why part two is here. You all are the reason why I didn't give up, even with all the setbacks I was having. Every day I thought I wanted to quit, I'd get a DM or an email asking about this book! And every time I'd read a DM from one of you, it motivated me to keep going. Thank you.

PROLOGUE
UNEXPECTED CROSSROADS

Malik

You would think with all the bullshit a nigga been through in the last forty-eight hours that God was trying to get my attention, or a nigga is just catching karma for all of the shit I've done over the years. How did I go from finding out I had a seed on the way to being unstoppable and unnoticed? To all my traps being burned down, my shipment being hit with all my money and product in it, Cinnamon and my nigga Zilla being shot up, being interrogated for hours only to be released to find out Cinnamon had lost my seed. Not to mention crossing roads with the muthafucka responsible for all this shit.

Then when you think things couldn't get any worse, you find out that the nigga you got tied up in the chop shop is the feds. Shortly after being released from Cook County and finding out Cinnamon lost our baby, my auntie Porsha hit Dominique up, saying she needed to meet up with us ASAP. When we finally met up with her, she gave us the whole rundown on that nigga Meech and exposed that he was the feds. You would've thought a nigga was about to drop dead the way the air left my body at once as I tried to let everything she just said register in my mind.

I knew from the first conversation I had with that nigga that he wasn't who he said he was. I kept saying he was too pressed to cop them bricks from me. I should've known when Dominique couldn't dig anything up on him that something was wrong, but at this point I could give a fuck about how much this nigga knew about me. Only thing I needed to know at this point was who threw me and my team under the bus because with all the connects we had and the way we moved, I knew for a fact this pussy didn't catch on to us on his own, I said to myself as I cleared my throat.

"Aye, Choppa! Take that duct tape off that nigga's mouth," I said as I continued to watch the blood run down his face, body, and open wounds from the torture we put him through, I thought to myself as I watched Choppa hit the blunt a few times before snatching the duct tape off his mouth.

"Please, I've told you everything I know. Please don't kill me," he said in between slow breaths as he spat blood onto the floor.

"You told me everything except the name of the muthafucka who paid you to set us up," I said as I held the .45-caliber in my hand while waiting for his response.

"I told you, I don't know his name. Only that he wanted you gone but not dead. Please, I have a wife and kids that need me," he said, causing me to smirk at that comment.

"Aw yeah? Well, I got a wife too. She was pregnant with my seed but miscarried behind all this bullshit. So, you see, we're both in the same boat. I lost my seed because of the choices I made. Just like you will never see your seeds again because of a choice you made," I said right before I pulled the trigger, hitting him in the head, causing his body to jerk before his head fell forward.

"Got damn!" Choppa yelled as he wiped the blood and brains from Detective Knight off of his face.

"Damn, you coulda warned a nigga to get the fuck out of the way before you started letting shit loose," Choppa said as he walked past me and out of the room right before I looked over at Markese, who was breaking down his weed into a Backwood. "Aye, call the cleanup crew. Tell them I need two cars washed and the inside detailed," I said, referring to the two dead bodies that were still tied to the table and the chop shop that needed to be cleaned, I said while looking over at Dominique, who seemed to be zoned out or plotting on the low.

"You good, fam?" I asked as I walked toward him while sitting the .45-caliber on a table that I was passing by.

"Yeah, I'm straight. I'm just tryna to make sense of all this shit," he said as he sat there, still zoned out.

"That makes two of us," I said as I let out a deep breath before telling him I needed him to get rid of Detective Knight's body. It wasn't that I didn't think Corey or Brandon couldn't get the job done. I just didn't need anyone outside this room to know that I'd just body bagged a fed.

"If I knew I'd end up with that nigga's blood all on me, I woulda squeezed that trigger myself," Choppa said, bringing me out of my thoughts as he walked back into the room with a towel in his hand that was cover in blood.

"My bad, fam," I said as he walked over to where I stood and gave me some dap.

"It's all good, but I do wish I could have body bagged that nigga, though," he said as he looked over at Detective Knight and shook his head.

"Shit, I think we all do," Markese added as he stood up while lighting his blunt before I began to tell them our next move.

"All right, y'all," I said, and everybody look over at me. "As of right now, we going to have to shut down shop until we come up with a plan to move our product without being seen," I said as I watched Choppa and Markese shake their heads back in froth in disapproval of my decision. "In the meantime, we gotta keep a low profile with this case still pending against us, not to mention now they know we all rotate with each other." Well, all of us except for Dominique. Right before the paramedics and police pulled up, he, my auntie Porsha, and my mother hit ghost.

Dominique had made it clear way before we ever jumped off the porch that he'd never allow the feds to get a hold of his prints or take his freedom from him. So him fleeing the scene didn't surprise me at all, I thought to myself as I continued to run down the plans.

"As of right now, we only contact each other for business through our burnouts. We gotta play this shit smart from here on out, especially now that we know the feds is watching. And if they haven't already noticed that this nigga is missing," I said, pointing to Detective Knight, "then I'm sure they will soon. And when they can't find him or figure out what happened to him, they'll start investigating the last case he was working on, which was us. So we gotta appear to them like we're legit businessmen until I can figure out a way to move these bricks without being seen. Until then, we're going to have to appear at work every day," I went on to say before telling them the rest of the plan.

"Choppa, I'm putting you in charge of my restaurant on the North Side. Just show up every day and stay for a few hours. You know, make it look like you're at work. It's not like you're not already on the payroll list," I said, because when I opened up all my businesses, I made sure to add everyone to the list of employees or business partners, except for Dominique, just so we all would have some type of paper trail in case some shit like this were to ever happen, I said to myself as I continued to tell Choppa his part.

"Don't worry about shit. I already got somebody to take care of all the paperwork and anything else that needs to be handled. I just need you there for the act," I said as he gave me a head nod letting me know he got it.

"Markese, you gonna run the strip club," I said, causing Choppa to shake his head back and forth before looking over at me.

"You really about to leave this nigga in charge of the strip club, fam?" Choppa asked, still shaking his head. "You know this nigga about to be knee deep in everything up in there," he went on to say as Markese let out a slight laugh.

"Shit. It's a little too late for that, fam," he said as he put the end of his blunt out.

"You know that nigga wild, fam, but it makes sense for him to run the strip club, seeing that we're business partners. And besides, I don't need Brittany coming up there every day fucking shit up," I said while flashing back on the last time she popped up at the strip club tryna fight Choppa because she heard he was up there fucking off with one of the strippers, I thought to myself before looking over at Dominique, who was still sitting where I had left him.

"Dominique, all I need you to do is find out who paid this nigga to step us up, and to get me any info on the driver of the van and that nigga who survived the shooting. I would tell you to go grab that bitch-ass nigga, but that's easier said than done with all the pigs guarding his room at the hospital," I said as I ran my hands over my head, then let out a deep breath. "Last but not fucking least, that nigga, the Grim Reaper or whatever the fuck he wanna call himself, is our main priority. I don't give a fuck what it costs or how long it takes or where he's at. Any and everybody affiliated with him, I want body bagged."

"Fasho," Choppa added as he threw his head back to get his dreads out his face, and for the next thirty minutes, we continued to go over everything that had gone down a little over forty-eight hours ago to see if we had missed or overlooked anything or anybody. That was, until Dominique said he need to holla at me about something, and moments later I was following him toward the doors. Once we got outside, he walked over to his car, opened the door, and pulled out this big brown envelope.

"I know you got a lot of shit on yo plate, fam, and I'm sure this is about to add more," he said while holding the envelope out for me to take it.

"Your moms told me to make sure you get this. And before you just say fuck it, I advise you to read what's inside. I know how you feeling right now, and I also know, whether you wanna hear this or not, you're gonna eventually need to speak with her, especially after you read everything that's inside," he said as I held the envelope in my hands before telling him I'd look at it once I get a chance and to let everyone know I was leaving, then gave him some dap and told him I would get back with tomorrow before walking toward all-black SUV, where I hopped inside and drove back to the hospital before Cinnamon's ass woke up and realized a nigga was gone.

1

CINNAMON (REGRETS, A FEW WEEKS LATER)

"I'm sorry, Ms. Jones, but you miscarried at ten weeks and three days," I began to think to myself as I repeated those words in my head over and over again, wishing that I'd never heard them or that this was all a dream, one I'd soon wake up from, I thought to myself as I continued to reminisce on how happy Malik and I had been hours before my life took a turn for the worst.

Whoever knew losing someone you'd never gotten a chance to meet but had grown to love so much would have such a big impact on your life? I thought to myself as I lay in bed and began asking God the same question I'd been asking since I woke up from surgery and found out that I had lost my unborn child, and that was, How could he give me something so precious and pure, only to take it right back before I could even get a real chance to enjoy it? I asked myself as I wiped the tears that were beginning to fall down my face as I continued to think about everything that had happen to me.

If you asked anyone else, most would say I should be grateful to be alive after being shot twice, once in the shoulder right above my heart and again in my arm, causing me to have a blood transfusion due to all the blood I'd lost from the gunshot wounds and the miscarriage. Don't get me wrong—I was more than grateful to be alive, but overall, I felt empty and confused, and being stuck in the house, trapped in my own thoughts, didn't help one bit.

All it did was push me further into depression and further away from Malik. Ever since the loss of our baby, things between us had been different, and we'd become distanced from one another, mainly because of me. All I'd wanted since the incident was to be left alone so that I could cope with everything that had happened to me, but that was easier said than done. And as far as Malik, he'd been in the streets every day since the shooting happened. Most of the time, I believed he stayed gone all day just to avoid our problems or to avoid talking about the incident.

I knew deep down in my heart I couldn't blame Malik for everything that had happened, but somehow I did. sometimes i even find myself contemplating back and forth and forth if being with Malik was what was best for me, but no matter how much I tried to convince myself that being with him was just too dangerous, the love I have for him just wouldn't allow me to walk away, especially at a time like this when I knew he needed me the most, even though I knew deep down that I should, I began to think to myself but snapped out of my thoughts when I heard my phone begin to ring.

I knew it couldn't be anyone other than Stonie, Chyna, Mariah, or my mother calling to check on me, I thought to myself as I looked at the screen to see who was calling. To my surprise, it was Malik's mother calling. Instead of answering her phone call, I sat the phone back down and allowed it to ring all the way through. Truth be told, I didn't have shit to say to her. Just like Malik, I blamed her for everything that had taken place that evening.

The last time I spoke with her was at the hospital, when she came to apologize for everything that had happened to me and the baby that she knew nothing about until after the miscarriage and promised to make things right, but I couldn't understand how she or Malik felt like they could ever make what had happened to my unborn child right, because there was no fixing or reversing this shit, I thought to myself as I sat up in bed before putting my Fendi robe on and then headed down stairs to see where Malik was at. But before I could make it past the living room, Martha stopped me.

"Good morning, Cinnamon," she said in her thick accent.

"Good morning, Martha. Have you seen Malik?" I asked.

"Yes. He left early this morning. He said he had some business to take care of, and if he wasn't back before you woke up, then I should take you to your doctor's appointment," she said, causing me to roll my eyes at the reply she'd just given me. I felt that it wasn't her responsibility to make sure I got to my doctor's appointment. It was his, and the fact that he thought something else was much more important than this pissed me off even more, I said to myself before taking off upstairs, where I dialed his number only to get sent straight to voice mail, I thought to myself as I threw the phone on the bed before finding me a Nike jumpsuit to put on for the day, then took off for the bathroom, where I stood in front of the mirror and began looking at myself while wondering how my life had gotten so fucked up overnight or how I had allowed myself to fall into a deep depression the way I had.

My hair was all over the place. My eyes were bloodshot red from all the crying I had been doing late last night and early this morning. I had bags that were starting to form underneath my eyes from the lack of sleep I'd had lately, and now I was starting to lose weight, I thought to myself as I let out a deep breath before reaching for my toothbrush and toothpaste and then began brushing my teeth before taking my Fendi robe off while walking toward the shower and cutting it on as I stepped inside, letting all six shower heads wet my whole body and wash away the tears that were now falling down my face.

How had I gone from being the happiest woman on earth to my whole life being torn apart and flipped upside down? I asked myself, as if I had the answer to my own question as I stood there lost in my own thoughts before finally reaching for the Dove soap. And fifteen minutes later, I was out of the shower and putting on the jumpsuit I'd pick out to wear.

"Do you need help?" Martha asked as she walked in the room and noticed I was struggling to get dressed due to the gunshot wounds. A part of me wanted to be a bitch and say no, but I knew deep down I needed her help if I was going to make it to my appointment on time. Once I was dressed and Martha was done helping me with my hair, I grabbed the keys to my all-gray 2019 G-Wagon Malik had gotten me as a Christmas gift and headed back downstairs.

"I'm going to drive myself," I said to Martha, who was putting her coat on so that she could take me to my appointment.

"Oh no, Ms. Cinnamon. I can't let you do that. You're in no condition to drive yourself. Malik would be very upset with me," she said in stern tone that I'd never heard before.

"Well, you can tell Malik I sunck out, because I'm driving myself. If he gave a fuck, he would be here taking me, but he's not," I went on to say as I walked out the door before she could get another word out, I thought to myself as I opened the door to my G-Wagon and got inside, then pulled off toward the doctor's office while taking a look around my car that I hadn't stepped foot in since I'd gotten it. I can't even lie; this muthafuck is nice as hell, I said to myself as I continued to drive until I reached the hospital my doctor's office was in, then waited about fifteen minutes until I was called back.

"Cinnamon Jones," one of the nurses said as she stood in the doorway waiting for me to get up so I could follow her to the back, where she got my weight and blood pressure, then told me the doctor would be right in. And five minutes later, she was walking in with a big smile on her face, and I could tell by the way she hugged me she was happy to see me, I thought to myself as she released me from her embrace.

"How have you been?" she asked as she took a seat in front of me.

"I guess I'm doing as good as I can—you know, with everything that has happened."

"That's understandable. The reason I ask is because most women fall into a deep depression after a miscarriage or a tragic event such as yours. I just want to make sure that if you're feeling like you may be depressed, let me know so we can get you the proper help that you need," she said, causing me to swallow the lump that was beginning to form in my throat, because I knew deep down I was depressed and beyond heartbroken behind everything that had happened to me, I thought to myself before taking a deep breath and reassuring her I was OK.

"Well, let see how you're really doing," she said as she stood up and began checking my wounds right before telling me that my stitches were due to come out as she began putting gloves on and pulling them out one by one. I guess she could tell by my facial expression and the way I took a deep breath every time she pulled one out that it hurt.

"Just a few more. I know it's uncomfortable, but I'm almost done," she said as she took the rest of my stitches out, then began going over my treatment for physical therapy so that I could regain strength back in my left arm and shoulder.

After scheduling to have a therapist come out to the house and to be seen back in the office in the next two weeks, I headed out to the car, where I pulled my phone out that wouldn't stop ringing as I looked at the five missed calls I had from Malik and a text message that read, **"Where the fuck you at!"**

But instead of responding, I put my phone back in my Gucci purse. I didn't feel the need to explain shit to him, especially since he was the one who was supposed to take me to my appointment. I said to myself, "Right" before pulling off and heading back home to do what I'd been doing for the past few weeks, and that was lie in bed and think.

DETECTIVE BROWN

You have to know that when you're dealing with anything in life, that you have to have both feet in. You can never have one foot here and anther foot there, because that's when things get difficult. Out of all my years as a detective and using my badge to rob, extort, and take from the local drug dealers, I never thought I'd see the day when my badge couldn't get me out of a jam, I thought to myself as I looked at the clock while awaiting the phone call that was highly anticipated, and right on cue, the phone began to ring.

"Hello," I answered as I sat in my patrol car outside of Cook County and listened to my pregnant wife on the other end crying as she told me she was fine and that she had finally started to feel the baby move as I swallowed the lump that was began to form in my throat, then began promising her that I'd get her and my unborn child out of this situation even if it cost me my life, I said right before the call ended at the forty-five second mark so that I wouldn't be able to trace the call.

"Shit, shit, shit," I yelled as I hit the steering wheel over and over again and began to beg God to not allow my wife or my unborn child to be held accountable for my mistakes or my sins, as I began to flash back on that day when I walked into my office and an envelope was on my desk with a small box sitting next to it.

When I went to open the envelope, there were photos of me and all the drug dealers that I had stolen from and set up to either be killed or sent to prison. You would have thought I saw my whole life flash by me when I saw everything that was inside the envelope. When I went to open the small package, there was a phone inside and a note that read, "Call the last number dialed." When I called the number, the man on the other end demanded that my partner and I meet with him ASAP. Before I could get all the way off the phone, my partner was walking into my office with the same envelope with photos of all the dirt he done as well. After telling the unknown caller we would meet up with him, I ended the call and headed to the location that was given to us.

Once we met up with him, he basically gave us an ultimatum: to either help him bring down Chicago's most feared kingpin or serve a lifetime in prison. But that was easier said than done, seeing that Malik had most of the Chicago's police force on his payroll. Bringing him down would mean bringing down every officer that was tied in with him, but this guy didn't see it that way and wouldn't take no for an answer. You would have thought he had some type of obsession with him, the way he talked about destroying his life and everyone close to him, I thought to myself as I continued to flash back on that day and began regretting everything I'd ever done in my life up until this point.

I was just a detective looking for a better way to take care of my family, not knowing that I'd end up in a situation like this or that I'd be tied in with the devil himself. After I took him up on his offer, he gave me and my partner $100,000 in return for any information we could get on Malik as well as everyone affiliated with him. I knew we wouldn't be able to pin anything on Malik or catch him in action, so my partner, Brian, went undercover to try to get some real evidence on him. But that didn't go as planned, because he wouldn't take the bait and practically dismissed Brian, leaving us to come up with a different approach. And the odds of us catching him red-handed were slim to none.

That was, until I got a call from the sick fuck who started all of this saying he had somebody working underneath Malik's nose and would have the evidence we needed to take him down. Hearing that was a relief for me.

Once I got word of that, I called Brian to let him know the good news. But when he didn't pick up the phone or return any of my calls, I began to think he had run off. That was, until his wife began calling me looking for him. Now here it was, weeks later, and there was still no sign of Brian or his whereabouts. It was like he had disappeared without a trace, but I wasn't a fool. I knew that Malik must have found out he was an undercover detective and killed him. Why else would he go missing and leave his wife, kids, and job behind?

After two weeks of no sign of Brian, I began to panic, and everyone began to ask questions about his whereabout and called in for a search party, in hopes of finding him. Once I saw this was getting out of hand, I went to the man who had started all this and told him I wanted out and returned all the money that was given to me to take Malik down. But that didn't go well, I thought to myself as I tried to fight back the tears that were trying to come out as I thought back on the day I came home to find my wife missing and a letter that read, "You're done when I say you're done."

At that moment I knew I'd fucked up, and now my wife and unborn child were missing, and I didn't have the slightest idea where they were. And I couldn't report them missing, or else he would kill them and expose me for everything I'd done over the years. I'd get a call twice a day, one at 9:00 a.m. every morning and one in the evening to let me know they were still alive.

I knew my wife and my unborn child life solely depended on me taking down Malik and his team. Not only did I have a maniac who had kidnapped my family until this is over, I still didn't know how this muthafucka knew so much about me. Not to mention I had Brian's wife and every detective and cop in Cook County and Chicago pressuring me to find Brian or to figure out what had happened to him, I thought to myself but snapped out of my thoughts when I walked into Cook County and Derick, this detective Brian and I had gone through the academy with, began asking me questions as I walked toward my office.

"Aye, any leads on Brian's whereabouts?" he asked while stepping into my office as I placed my jacket on the back of the chair before taking a seat behind my desk.

"No, I haven't come up with anything yet. It's just strange that he would up and disappear like that," I said as I looked up at him.

"Yeah, that's what I said. I know me and Brian weren't as close as the two of you, but he was my friend too, and I hate to see him go missing the way he has. I asked the chief to get someone to look into his personal files and computer. Maybe that could give us some kind of lead to what might have happened to him," he said, causing my hands to sweat as I wiped them on my pants.

"That's good, but I already have someone looking into that," I lied as I sat and waited on his next response. But before he could give me one, the chief walked in.

"Derick, I need you at this address. A homicide has been reported. This is your case, and I need you on it now," he said before looking over at me.

"Any updates on Brian?" he asked.

"We were just talking about that when you walked in. I'm looking into his personal files and computers as we speak. I'm just waiting to see what they find," I said before he told me to keep him updated. And they both left, leaving me to raid Brian's things in hopes that I wouldn't find anything in his files or computer that could lead back to me or anything we were doing, I said to myself as I grabbed my jacket off the back of the chair and headed out of Cook County and right into the strong January wind.

DOMINIQUE

"Sit the fuck down," I said to the man who had just walked into the house as I sat off to the side in all black, with a Smith & Wesson M&P45 that had a silencer on it so that when I shot, no one would be able to hear it.

"Who the fuck are you, and how the fuck you get in my crib?" he asked with a mug as he stood not too far from me.

"Ima ask you one more time to sit the fuck down before shit goes left way before it has to," I said, sitting up a bit in my chair while I waited on him to sit down. But it was obvious this nigga was hard at hearing, and I wasn't the type of nigga that liked to be taken as a joke, I said to myself right before shooting him in the right shoulder, causing him to yell out in pain before he hit the floor, where he tried to pull his gun from his waistband. But I was already up and standing over him with my gun pointing to his head, causing him to stop reaching.

"What the fuck you want?" he asked as he lay there, still holding his shoulder, right before I knelt down and gave him a shot in the neck, putting him into a deep sleep until I got him to the chop shop, I said to myself as I began dragging his body to the car, where I popped the trunk and threw him inside with the other nigga I'd grabbed right before him, then jumped into the car and pulled off while dialing Malik.

"Wassup," he answered on the third ring.

"That package just came in. I'm about deliver it now," I said in regard to the two niggas who were involved in the shooting a few weeks ago.

Once the one who was hospitalized was released from the hospital, he was taken to Cook County and booked, then hit with a $50,000 bond. When I got word of that, I sent this white bitch I had fucked with a while back to bond him out. Once he was free, I waited about a week and then went and grabbed both of them niggas so that they could face the real jury, I thought to myself as I listened to Malik on the other end tell me he would meet me in an hour, before hanging up the phone.

Ever since the shooting, a nigga's been working overtime tryna keep shit on our end straight, from the hits I was still doing on the side for my auntie Porsha to Malik being on my ass every day for updates on that nigga the Grim Reaper's whereabouts, to figuring out just what the fuck we were really up against, because shit wasn't adding up.

The day Malik's pops showed up at my auntie Yvette's spot, he said something about her not being loyal while he was locked down. Even if she had left him to rot in prison, that still wouldn't be enough to come back and try to take everyone out, especially his kids. It wasn't until the police were about to arrive that me, Porsha, and my auntie Yvette ran back into the house. I peeped my auntie Yvette putting superglue on her hands and fingertips right before we hit the back door. Only reason someone would do that is if they didn't want anyone to get a hold of their prints if they were to get caught up.

When I saw that, I knew the reason behind why this nigga the Grim Reaper was here was much deeper than what they wanted us to know. And I'm not the type of nigga that likes being left in the dark, so I began digging into our family history, especially since my auntie said our great-grandparents were drug dealers and paid hit men. But when I looked up Porsha, Yvette, and my mother's name, I got nothing. And that was strange, so I dug even deeper to get at least a death certificate for my mother. But not even that was available, and that part fucked me up the most, because that's public record.

It wasn't until I paid a muthafuck to hack into Detroit records from the late seventies early eighties that I came across a picture of Detroit's most dangerous criminals, and there they were—my mother, Porsha, and Yvette. But their names weren't what they are today. It stated in the file that they all were killed in 1987 in an explosion in an attempt to get away from the police a few years before they came to Chicago, which makes sense because when my mother was murdered, my auntie kept asking what all I had told the police. She must have asked me that a million time before I stopped speaking altogether. But the real question was, Why did they fake their deaths? I was willing to bet that played a part in why this nigga was back in town, I said to myself as I pulled up to the chop shop and parked the car around back before taking both bodies inside and tying them down to chairs. And thirty minutes later, Malik and Markese walked into the chop shop.

"This shit better be good, Fam. I was knee deep in some pussy when this nigga hit me up saying meet him here," Markese said as he gave me some dap, causing Malik to let out a slight laugh as he shook his head and then gave me some dap.

"Shit, that ain't new," Choppa said, walking in with his dreads hanging, with the chopper in his hands and Zilla right behind him.

"Wassup, fam," Choppa asked while giving us all some dap.

"I heard you got them pussy-ass niggas. Where they at?" Zilla asked as he walked up, smoking a blunt.

"Still on that ape shit, I see," Malik said while giving him some dap and at the same time hugging him.

"Come on, now. You know it gonna take a lot more than a few shots to the stomach for them pussies to slow me down," he said as we walked to the next room, where I had them niggas tied up at. And from the looks of things, one of them niggas was trying to wake up, I thought to myself as I watched Malik walk over toward the one who was waking up and slap him a few times.

"Wake the fuck up, nigga. It's Judgment Day," he said as the nigga began to open his eyes.

Once his eyes were fully open, it was like he had seen a ghost as he sat there looking at Malik and the rest of us, I said to myself right before my phone began going off nonstop with missed calls and text messages from Chyna going off on a nigga. And I could tell by the way shorty was texting and calling that it was about to be some shit whenever I made it back home.

2

MALIK (BROKEN PROMISES)

I'd be lying if I said a nigga wasn't fucked up behind the loss of my seed or the fact that Cinnamon almost lost her life behind me and my family, I thought to myself as I sat in the living room smoking a blunt while taking shots of Henny as I flashed back on the day when I promised her I'd never let anything happen to her behind the shit I had done in the streets. Not only had I failed at that, but I had failed at making sure my seed was straight.

The moment I saw Cinnamon at my mother's house, I should have told shorty to leave. But I wasn't thinking shit would go left the way it had. A part of me felt like I oughta be grateful, because things could have been way worse than they were, and Cinnamon could have died along with my seed. And another part of me felt like, fuck being grateful, because this shit should never have happened at all. So you can only imagine how this situation is taking a toll over a nigga, I said to myself as I exhaled the smoke from the blunt and then began regretting not offing that pussy when I had a chance. But every dog has its day, and his was sooner than knew, because I was about the paint the city red with his blood and anybody who had anything to do with what had happened, I said to myself right before my phone began to ring.

"Wassup?" I said into the phone as I listened to Dominique tell me he had picked them two niggas up who were involved in the shooting and to meet him at the chop shop. After telling him I'd be there in an hour, I dialed Markese.

"Yo?" he said into the phone when he answered.

"Meet me at the shop. I got two cars that need taking apart," I said right before hanging up the phone and calling Choppa, and on the third ring he answered. And from the sounds of it, he was knocked the fuck out, I said to myself as I looked over at the clock that sat on the wall that read 6:00 a.m. before I told him the same thing I'd just told Markese.

Once he told me he would be there, I hung up and told Martha I was leaving, and if I wasn't back in time to take Cinnamon to her doctor's appointment, then I needed her to take her for me before walking out of the house and jumping in my pickup truck, where I pulled off and headed toward the chop shop while bumping Lil Poodie's song "I Ain't Goin'." Shit, I felt like him. I wasn't going for the shit these bitch-ass niggas or the feds were tryna pull, and I definitely wasn't about to let some hoe-ass nigga by the name Grim Reaper come and take everything I'd worked hard for or let him get away with what had happened to Cinnamon's and my seed.

I could give a fuck about that shipment that got hit. That shit can be replaced. But I could never get my seed back. And although it wouldn't change the outcome, it damn sure would make us even, I said to myself as I pulled up to the chop shop at the same time as Markese and parked my pickup truck next to his before getting out of the truck and giving him some dap as we walked into the chop shop. And moments later, Choppa was walking in, and to my surprise he had Zilla with him.

I can't even lie. Seeing my little nigga bounce back from the shooting the way he did made a nigga happy. Last thing I ever wanted was for him to leave Baby Zilla behind without a father, I said to myself as I gave him some dap while hugging him at the same time before we walked toward the other room, where Dominique had both them niggas who survived the shooting tied down to chairs, I thought to myself before slapping one of them a few times so that he could wake all the way up.

"Wake the fuck up, nigga. It's Judgment Day," I said as he sat there trying to fully wake up before looking directly at me. And if looks could kill, well, let's just say he wished he would have taken a nigga out that first time, I said to myself but snapped out of my thoughts when this nigga began to speak.

"What the fuck y'all niggas want?" he asked, causing Markese to answer the question as he and Zilla sat off to the side rolling a blunt.

"What the fuck you think we want, nigga?" he asked, and by this time the second nigga was tryna wake up.

"Fuck you niggas. I ain't telling y'all shit," he said, causing me to smirk because he couldn't tell me shit that I already didn't know, I thought to myself before speaking.

"What makes you think we need a statement from yo bitch ass?" I asked, confusing him as he sat there looking puzzled by my response.

"Ahh shit," the other nigga moaned out, causing me to look his way. And for the first time since we had entered the room, I realized this nigga had been shot, I said to myself, as I looked over at Dominique, who obviously didn't deny it or give a fuck about shooting him.

"The nigga has a hearing problem, fam. He better be lucky that's all he got," Dominique said right before Choppa began to speak.

"Can we off these pussies already? Shit, a nigga ain't had no sleep since these muthafuckas came through with the oops, i'm ready to dirt all these pussies and get back to this paper," he said as he hit the blunt Zilla had just passed to him.

"You know I with you when you right, fam," Markese added as he stood up and handed me the blunt he'd rolled for me as I listened to the two niggas who were tied down begin going back and forth with each other. That was until I walked over toward a closet and grabbed an apron, some gloves, a face shield, and some rubber high-top boots so I wouldn't get any blood on me. Then I walked back over toward Markese, Zilla, and Choppa who faces read.

"What the fuck is this nigga on?" I thought to myself as I continued to smoke my blunt.

"Y'all niggas need to suit up," I said while putting the apron on.

"What you on, fam? You need all that shit just to off a nigga?" Markese asked as I sat down and began putting the boots on.

"I never said we was gonna give these niggas an easy way out," I said, referring to just shooting them. "Everybody we toe tag from here on out, we going about it like the mob," I said, causing Zilla to shake his head back and forth before speaking.

"You saw what happened last time you got to cutting niggas up," he said, referring to the last nigga, whose dick I cut off and stuffed in his mouth, causing him to throw up, I said to myself as I watched him hold his stomach while still shaking his head. And moments later everybody was suited up with chain saws and machetes in their hands, as I placed the two of them in front of each other so one of them could watch the other one die before it was his turn, I began to think to myself as I started the chainsaw and watched them hoe-ass niggas begin to pray as I walked closer to them. But at this point, God himself couldn't help them from what I was about to do to them, I said to myself as I walked up on the one who woke up first and wasted no time sawing his head off. You would have thought the other nigga was the one who was getting killed, the way he screamed at the sight of me sawing off the other nigga's head, I thought to myself as I watched all the blood squirt out right before his head fell off and began to roll.

"Ah, hell nah," Markese said as I took a towel and wiped the blood off my face shield so I could see.

"Untie that nigga and cut off his arms and legs. I want that nigga in pieces," I said, and moments later we were cutting down his whole body until we reached the other nigga, who had damn near passed out from the sight of everything he was seeing before we did him the exact same way. Once we had both their bodies cut up, we placed their heads in a box to be shipped to their families.

"Put them niggas on ice until it's time to deliver them to their families," I said to Dominique before calling the cleanup crew to come detail the chop shop and get rid of the remaining body parts, I said to myself as I let out a deep breath while running my hands over the top of my head because this was only the beginning, and I was saving the best for last, I said to myself as I sat and thought about my next move but snapped out my thoughts when Brandon and Corey walked into the chop shop.

"Got damn, what the fuck y'all muthafuckas do? Turn this into a slaughter shop?" Brandon asked as he walked in and took a look around the room at all the blood and body parts that were lying around.

"Yeah, something like that," I said as I stood up to give them some dap.

"Aye, real shit, fam. This is probably one of the worst crime scenes I've ever seen," Corey said as he gave Markese, Zilla, Dominique, and Choppa some dap.

"I doubt that," Choppa said right before they began cleaning the room, and we all walked to the next room to discuss our next plans.

"All right, y'all. Once these niggas' heads show up on their families' doorsteps, they going to look at us for the blame, seeing that one of them just been released a week ago, and he's already dead. Not to mention he's tied in to the case that's still pending against all of us. But that's neither here nor there. We're still gonna send a message until we get to the sender himself," I said referring to that nigga the Grim Reaper.

"Y'all already know we got the feds watching, so make sure y'all's alibis are straight. As of now, everything stays the same. We're gonna keep making it look like we're legit businessmen until this shit is over with and this case is thrown out," I said, and for the next hour, we sat and talked about our next target. That was until Dominique had to leave, because Chyna kept blowing his phone up. Come to find out, this nigga ain't been home since yesterday morning. I don't know when that nigga planned on telling shorty about his second life, but one thing I did know was that disappearing shit could only last so long, I said to myself right before telling Markese I had to go and to hit me up once Corey and Brandon were done with the chop shop.

Then I headed out to my pickup truck, where I had missed calls from Cinnamon and Martha. But when I went to call Cinnamon back, I got no answer. So I dialed Martha, and when I did, a nigga was beyond heated when she told me Cinnamon had left without her. Shorty was in no condition to be driving, and with all this shit going on in the streets, she damn sure didn't need to be out alone, I said to myself as I tried calling her a few more times. But just like before, I got no answer. So I sent her a text asking, "Where the fuck she was at?" before pulling off and heading home.

Once I pulled up to our spot, I saw that Cinnamon's G-Wagon was parked out front, like she had plans on leaving again. But she could hang that shit up, I said out loud to myself as I walked into the house and upstairs to our room, where I spotted her sitting on the bed talking on the phone, not caring that I was standing right in front of her. That was until I reached out and snatched the phone, causing her to jump up.

"What the fuck is wrong with you?" she yelled as I threw the phone across the bed, not giving a fuck about what she was saying.

"If you wanted to talk on the phone, you should have answered the phone when I was calling you back to back! And I thought I told you while all this shit was going on in the streets that it wasn't safe for you to be out alone," I said as she stood there looking at me with a mug that could kill.

"Then you're out here driving and shit with all the meds that you're on. Like come on, Cinnamon, what the fuck is you on, shorty?" I asked as she stood there looking at me like she could give a fuck about what I was saying.

"I'm just confused as to why you're going off. You knew I had a doctor's appointment to go to this morning, but yet you left and did what you wanted to do and think Ima make Martha do something my man is supposed to do. How the fuck is Martha supposed to protect me if some shit pops off?" she yelled. "You're so fucking wrapped up in the street and getting even that you have been neglecting everything at the home front, including me!" she yelled again, but this time it was directly in my face. "You're more worried about these niggas than you are about your bitch, who just had a fucking miscarriage and was shot multiple times," she said, causing me to rub my hands across my face and to let out a deep breath, because a nigga knew more than half of the shit she was saying was true.

I had been gone a lot lately, trying deal with all this shit in the streets. It wasn't like I was purposely leaving her at home or that I didn't care. A nigga just had to tie up some loose ends before they tied me up, I thought to myself as I continued to listen to her go off.

"If you want to be mad at somebody, be mad at your damn self," she went on to say before snatching her phone off the bed and brushing past me, leaving me standing there in my own thoughts for a minute before taking off toward the bathroom, where I showered and got dressed. I still had business to handle at the restaurant, and with Cinnamon being pissed off the way she was, this would give her enough time to calm down before I got back, I said to myself as I headed out the door.

CHYNA

If it's one thing my last relationship taught me, it was to pay attention to the signs when they were given, I said to myself as I rolled over to see that Dominique still hadn't come home yet, as I looked over at the clock, which read 8:00 a.m. in the morning before I reached for my phone and dialed his number over and over again, only to get sent straight to voice mail. And that alone pissed me the fuck off more than I already was. You would think after the last incident we had when he didn't come home that we had an understanding about this shit, but now I see that we don't.

I mean, don't get me wrong. I knew what I was getting myself into when I got involved with a street nigga, but what real nigga that claims he loves his bitch doesn't come home unless he's with another bitch or the feds picked him up. And even if they did, I couldn't look him up in the system if I wanted to. After almost a year of being together, I still didn't even know this nigga's last name. Everything about Dominique was starting to seem weird to me. He didn't get any mail sent to the house. I don't know his full name or if his birthday is really even his real birthday because just last month he couldn't even remember that it was his birthday. Who the fuck doesn't know when they were born? I asked myself as I continued to think about all the weird shit he was doing.

He had left the crime scene when the shooting popped off. He sneaks around the house unnoticed like some fucking creep, not to mention almost a month ago, this nigga drugged and kidnapped me. And I still wasn't over that shit, I said to myself as I reached into the top drawer for the jar of weed and began rolling me a blunt to calm my nerves, because at this point I was beginning to question our relationship. And there wasn't anything he or anyone else could say to make me feel OK about my man not coming home. Hell, even James's dog ass didn't have the balls to stay gone all day and night, and that nigga was doing everything underneath the sun plus some, I said to myself as I continued to roll the blunt.

Once I had my blunt rolled, I headed toward the bathroom, where I began brushing my teeth before I lit my blunt and got inside the shower, where I began to think about putting some space between me and Dominique because it was clear that me talking with him wasn't getting the job done. Only way a nigga gonna get the picture is if you up and leave. I made a vow to myself after James to never stick around and let another nigga play me, I said to myself as I let the water run down my body while I smoked my blunt, and fifteen minutes later, I was out of the shower and higher than a Delta pilot, I thought to myself as I grabbed my pink silk robe and headed out to get dressed for the day. But before I could get halfway out of the bathroom, I was stopped by the sight of Dominique sitting off to the side like the creep he was.

"What the fuck?" I yelled out as I stood there holding the front of my robe to keep it from opening.

"You could have at least told me you were here. And where the fuck have you been?" I asked as I walked up on him, invading his personal space.

"I had a lot of shit going on," he tried to say, but I cut him off.

"You weren't that muthafucking busy where you couldn't pick the phone up and say hey baby, I'm coming home late, I'm good—anything!" I yelled.

"But let me leave and stay gone until the next morning, Ima end up drugged and brought back home," I said as he sat there letting me get everything I had to say out. "I'm really starting to get fed up with this shit. I told you when we first got together I wasn't up for being made out to be a fool, and here you are doing the same shit my last nigga did. But even James's bitch ass had enough courtesy and respect to come home," I said as I watched his facial expression begin to change because I had compared him to James once, again knowing he hated that shit. But I could give a fuck because that was who he was acting like, I said to myself as I let out a slight laugh and threw my hands up in the air right before he asked me in a calm voice, "Are you done yet?" Then he stood up and gently grabbed me by my face and forced me to look at him.

"I told you one too many times to stop comparing me to that hoe-ass nigga. But it's obvious you can't fucking comprehend, so let help you out, shorty. The next time I hear that bitch-ass nigga's name or you compare me to him again, Ima take a trip to Indianapolis and grab that bitch-ass nigga off Morris Street—you know, the white house he lives in with his grandmother," he said, causing me to look at him like he lost his fucking mind and leaving me to wonder how he knew where James or his grandmother lived. Hell, I didn't even know he'd moved back with his grandmother.

"And then you will see the big difference between me and that nigga," he went on to say right before I slapped his hand off my face and took a step back.

"You know what? I don't have time for this shit. I'm going to stay in a hotel until I can get my own place. It's obvious you need some space to figure out what you want and who you want, because I'm not going to deal with no disrespectful-ass nigga who can't respect our relationship or come home like he's supposed to," I tried to say, but that shit backfired quick.

"Let's get some shit straight, Chyna. If you wanna leave a nigga, you can, shorty, but it won't be until this shit in the streets is over with. So I suggest you get that shit through your head. I don't need to remind you what happened the last time you called yourself trying to pull a stunt like that. And because I know how hardheaded you can be, I'm giving you a fair warning," he said. And at that moment, I knew everything I felt about him being weird and crazy was real, I thought to myself as I stood there looking at him, wondering, *Who the fuck did I fall in love with?*

"You're fucking crazy," I said, still standing there looking at him.

"Yeah, crazy about you," he said with a smirk right before I turned for the closet to get dressed. But he stopped me halfway into my walk.

"Aw, yeah, Shorty, and make that the last time you accuse a nigga of fucking off. I don't need to fuck off when I got the Queen of Chess at home," he went on to say, but I ignored that comment and continued to walk toward the closet, where I picked out some Fashion Nova pants that fit my body better than the skin I was in, a Gucci shirt with a matching Gucci belt, some all-black Moncler boots, and an all-black mink coat, and then walked out of the closet and threw what I planned to wear on the bed next to my phone, which was now ringing, I thought to myself as I reached down to pick it up.

"Wassup," I answered as I walked toward the dresser and pulled out a black bra-and-thong set and began putting it on.

"Nothing much. Heading into town to see Cinnamon and to shop," Stonie said on the other end of the phone, causing me to roll my eyes as I reached for my pants.

"That's nothing new," I said.

"Yeah, yeah, yeah, whatever. But I'm about an hour away. Ima come get you when I touch down. I need somebody to go shopping with, since Cinnamon can't leave the house," she said as I looked over at the clock before responding.

"Yeah, I'll go. I'll see you in two hours, because I know for a fact you're farther away than what you're saying," I went on to say as I listened to her let out a little laugh before I hung up the phone and continued to get dressed.

Once I was fully dressed, I put my Rolex on along, with my Cuban-link chain and then began walking back toward the bathroom, where I began doing my makeup and running the flat iron through my blunt-cut bob that was giving me life, I thought to myself as I stood there giving myself one last look in the mirror before walking back into the room and grabbing another blunt to roll, along with my mink coat and Gucci bag, and then headed downstairs, where I began rolling another blunt while waiting on Stonie's slow ass to arrive, I thought to myself as I watched Dominique walk into the living room. As much as I hated to admit it, he was looking good as hell in all that Dolce and Gabbana he was rocking, I thought to myself as I lit the blunt I'd just rolled and watched him take a seat across from me.

"You look good, Ma. Where you think you're going?" he asked as I blew some smoke his way.

"Out," I said, keeping it real short with him, causing him to let out a slight laugh before pulling a gun out of his waistband and setting it on the table.

"I gotta make some runs. If you gonna be out without me, take this. It's a .40 Glock. It's already one in the head, so be careful," he said as he stood up while pulling his pants up a bit before walking out, leaving me sitting there in my own thoughts. That's until Stonie called, saying she was out front.

STONIE

The last thing I ever thought would happen was me getting a phone call saying my cousin had been shot and was now fighting for her life or that she was pregnant and lost her unborn child because of the nigga she had chosen to fall in love with, I thought to myself as I flashed back on the day when I arrived at the hospital to see Chyna covered in Cinnamon's blood along with Mariah as I listened to both of them tell me the story on why she had gotten shot in the first place. And all I could do was cry and thank God that Cinnamon made it out of surgery alive, because the way Chyna and Mariah told the story, I knew for a fact it wasn't anyone other than God watching over her.

Shortly after talking with Cinnamon, I ended up staying in town for a week and a half to make sure she was good and to be there for Markese prior to the shooting. We had been on some low-key friends-with-benefits type of shit for about two and half months. Every other weekend I'd drive to Chicago to visit him and, of course, my cousin. I'd be lying if I said during that time that I didn't catch feelings for him. I loved everything about him and our friendship. I also loved the fact that he didn't try to change me and accepted all my rules and didn't allow sex to come in between our friendship. He was definitely my twin, something like my best friend. Shortly after I made sure he was good, he up and disappeared on me. A part of me wanted to be mad, but then another part of me was relieved knowing that I didn't have to break it off with him.

I wasn't a fool, and I damn sure wasn't tryna end up in the middle of some shit that had nothing to do with me. Hell, Cinnamon almost lost her life behind a nigga she was in love with. I was only fucking Markese. Who was to say I'd be as lucky as she was if some shit was to go left again, I said to myself as I continued to flash back on that day and then shook my head and continued to drive. After staying in chicago for a week and a half, I went back home to Indianapolis. When I got home, I noticed that I hadn't had a period that whole month and that I was very tired—to the point I had to cancel two of my appointments because I couldn't get out of bed. When I finally gained the strength to get up, I went and bought a First Response pregnancy test and took it.

I damn near dropped dead when it came back positive. There was no way in hell I could be pregnant, I kept telling myself over and over again as I contemplated whether to call Markese and tell him about the pregnancy. I mean, damn, how did I go from not wanting a relationship to feeling like I loved him? To being pregnant? I must have asked myself that question a hundred times, along with, Should I keep the baby or get an abortion? Don't get me wrong. I know kids are a blessing, but the last thing I was about to do was have a baby by a nigga I wasn't with and was in the street as deep as Markese was, not to mention all the bullshit that was still going on. I wasn't trying to end up a single mother if something were to happen to him, so you can only imagine what I was going through right now. It had been two weeks since I found that I was pregnant, and I still hadn't told Markese yet, mainly because I still hadn't reached a decision about the baby. And if I did decide to get an abortion, no one could know about it—not even him, I said to myself but snapped out my thoughts when my phone began to ring.

"You saw me calling you all morning," I said as I answered the phone and then rolled my eyes as I listened to Cinnamon tell me she was at her doctor's appointment and couldn't answer my calls. "Umm huh. Tell me anything," I said before asking her how the appointment had gone. After she told me everything had gone great at her doctor's appointment and reassuring me that she was fine, I told her I was coming into town to visit her. But before I could get the rest out, the phone hung up. "Hello," I said into the phone a few times before calling back, but I got no answer. "She'll call back," I said out loud to myself before dialing Chyna's number, and on the fourth ring, she answered.

"Wassup," she said into the phone." As I swerved in and out of traffic while telling her I was on my way into town and that I was coming to get her so we could go shopping. After agreeing to come, I hung up the phone and continued to drive until I reached Chyna's gates. I was just about to press the button so she could let me in, but the gates open and Dominique came driving past me in an all-black tinted SUV, I thought to myself as I drove through the gates before they closed and then called Chyna to let her know I was out front. And moments later she was coming out dressed cleaner than the Board of Health I said to myself right before giving her a compliment and pulling off.

"So where we going first?" she asked as she smoked the little piece of blunt she had in her hand.

"We're gonna stop by Cinnamon's place first," I said as she passed me the blunt. At first I was going to turn it down, but if I did that, she would know something was up. So I hit the blunt a few times just to play it off, I thought to myself, and I hit the blunt a few more times before passing it back to Chyna. And for the rest of the ride to Cinnamon's place, we talked and caught each other up on what been going on in our lives. Once we pulled up to Cinnamon's house, I pressed the button to get in the gates and then waited.

"Who is it?" Cinnamon asked through the intercom.

"Open the gate," I said, and instead of her replying back, the gates opened. And moments later, we were pulling in and parking next to this all-gray tinted G-Wagon.

"Damn, that muthafucka's sexy," I said as I grabbed my Louie bag and walked to the front door, where Martha was waiting for us. "Thank God," I said to myself, because Cinnamon's ass was known for leaving a muthafucka standing at the door, I thought to myself as I walked in with Chyna right behind me.

"Cinnamon's down in the basement. It's your third door on the left."

"Thank you, Martha," Chyna said before we took off for the basement, where we spotted Cinnamon sitting on this big-ass fluffy couch drinking some wine and watching movies on the Fire Stick, and from the looks of it, she was tipsy or on her way to being there, I said to myself as I walked over and took a seat on the couch.

"What's up with you?" I asked as she took a sip of wine.

"Nothing at all. Watching movies on the Fire Stick," she said, looking over at me with bags underneath her eyes from either too much crying or not enough sleep.

"Really, Cinnamon, you look tired, like you haven't been getting any sleep," I said, and Chyna agreed with me. And moments later Cinnamon broke down and started crying.

"I just don't understand," she said as tears began to run down her face, and both Chyna and I moved closer to her and began to hug her.

"I just don't understand why all this happened to me," she kept saying in between her cries, and before you knew it, me and Chyna both were crying along with her. I felt bad for Cinnamon. She was normally the one wiping our tears and making us smile when things were going wrong. I couldn't even remember the last time I had seen her cry or this hurt, I thought to myself right before telling her that this situation wasn't meant to break her but to make her stronger than she already was, and when it came to the loss of her baby, God makes no mistakes, I said as Chyna went on to tell her how blessed she was to still be alive and that all things work together for the greater good.

"I know, but it still hurts," she went on to say as she shook her head back and forth, but she should know better than anyone that time heals all wounds. Nothing happens overnight. She used to tell me that all the time when I was frustrated about my salon not opening when I wanted it to or when I was heartbroken behind a bum-ass nigga, so now it was my turn to remind her of that, I thought to myself before Cinnamon began talking again.

"What are you doing here anyway?" she asked as she wiped her tears that were still falling and so were we.

"I came to see you, and of course I need a shopping spree," I said, causing her to smile a bit.

"Typical Stonie."

"Same thing I said," Chyna added before Cinnamon asked where I was staying while I was in town.

"Girl, it was supposed to be this hotel downtown, but you know I'm last minute to do everything. I ended up missing my check-in time, so whatever hotel I'm closest to when I feel like calling it a night," I said causing Cinnamon to shake her head while Chyna rolled a blunt.

"You can stay at my condo," she said, causing me and Chyna to look at her like, What condo?

"Now y'all know damn well I wasn't about to give up nothing I had before I met Malik. I bought the condo from the owner and kept it in case I'd ever need it," she said, shrugging her shoulders as she grabbed the blunt Chyna had just passed to her.

"That was smart. I shoulda done that shit," Chyna added. And for the next few hours, we talked and passed blunts back and forth until I began to get hungry. Then me and Chyna left, and for the rest of the day, we ate, shopped, and got facials until I couldn't stay awake any longer and ended up going to Cinnamon's condo to take a nap. But before I fully dozed off, I texted Markese and told him to give me a call when he got a chance, because I wasn't sure how much longer I could hide this pregnancy without knowing what I really wanted to do.

3

MARKESE (BOTH SIDES)

I had just dropped dick in this bitch name Erica when Malik hit me up saying meet him at the chop shop so that we could handle them hoe-ass niggas from the shooting. When I got there, I thought it would be a quick situation and I'd be able to get back to shorty—not because I wanted to finish what we'd started but because I wanted that bitch to take a Plan B pill. Right before Malik hit me up saying meet him at the chop shop, the condom broke while we were fucking. I thought I would be able to get right back to shorty, but that didn't go as planned because when I got to the chop shop, Malik was on some straight mob shit cutting niggas heads and body parts off. I always knew that nigga had a dark side to him, but damn, I'd never seen him go this far, I thought to myself as I shook my head back and forth.

    I can't say I blame him, though, because I'd be on the same shit if my shorty was shot up and lost my seed behind some shit that had nothing to do with her, I said to myself as I took a look around the room at all the blood and body parts on the floor before looking over at Malik, who looked like he hasn't had sleep in days. No matter how hard he tried to cover that shit up, I knew my brother well enough to know he was fucked up behind everything that had gone down with Cinnamon, the baby, our moms, and our drug operation. It was like he couldn't get a break even if he paid for one, I said to myself as I listened to him go over the rest of our plans before leaving me to wait on Brandon and Corey to finish cleaning shit up, I said to myself as I rolled a blunt and dialed Erica, and on the third ring, she answered.

"Hello," she said into the phone as I continued to break down all the weed into the Backwood.

"Aye, shorty, I'm almost done handling this little business I had to take care of. But before I hit the club, Ima need you to take that Plan B pill," I said, as I lit the blunt and hit it a few times as I listened to her on the other end tell me she had already taken the pill before she left out for work. But that wasn't good enough for me, because I didn't see her take it myself, I told her right before she began going off about how she doesn't have to lie and damn sure didn't have to trap a nigga. That last part I could believe, though, because shorty was paid and had her own. I learned a long time ago not to fuck with bitches that didn't have their shit together. I wasn't about to be no bitch's come up or retirement plan, so all the hoes I fucked with were paid and had something going for themselves.

I was just about to tell shorty it wasn't that I thought she'd try to trap me, a nigga just didn't want no kids by a bitch I couldn't see myself with, but Corey walked in, causing me to end my call before I could explain that to her. "Aye, Ima hit you right back," I said In between hitting the blunt. "Y'all niggas done?" I asked Corey as I passed him the blunt.

"Just about. Y'all muthafucks really painted the shop red, didn't y'all?" Corey asked as he hit the blunt a few more times before passing it back to me.

"Shit, happens every day, B," I went on to say, causing him to let out a slight laugh before telling me he had to run to the van to get some shit to remove all the blood that couldn't be seen if you just looked at it but could be seen if the feds or anyone else put a special light on it, I thought to myself as I continued to smoke my blunt. And an hour later, everything was cleaned up and I was heading out to the strip club to sit for a few hours just to make everything seem legit, I said to myself as I continued to drive while I bumped Young Dolph's *Thinking Out Loud* album until I reached the strip club. Once I had pulled up at the strip club and was inside, I headed upstairs to Malik's office, where I poured me a shot of Hennessey and pulled out my phone to call Erica's ass back but stopped when I received a message from Snapchat.

"What the fuck is this?" I asked myself out loud, but then it dawned on me that I had let Mariah download an app on my phone the other day when we met up. I was just about to delete it when I got a text message from Stonie, I thought to myself as I took a seat behind Malik's desk. I ain't gonna lie. Stonie had been on my mind a lot lately. The last time I'd seen shorty was a little after the shooting happened. I can't even stunt. A nigga really fucked with shorty, especially after she was there for me when I needed her the most. But a nigga's head was so fucked up after everything that went down that I hit ghost on shorty without so much as a goodbye, I thought to myself as I opened her text message and read it.

I could honestly say, out of all the bitches a nigga had, none of them made me feel the way she did. Everything about her was real. Plus, I respected the fact that everything she got, she got it on her own. I couldn't say the same for most bitches, but no matter how shit left off between us, I was still going to give shorty a call, I said to myself right before I heard a knock on the door and my favorite white bitch walked in dressed in a blue thong with blue stars on the nipples, I thought to myself as I pulled out a stack of ones I'd stopped to get on my way upstairs when I first came in, and I watched her cut the music on before dancing for me. A nigga was feeling like Moneybagg Yo when he said, "Ice Tea swag bitch look like CoCoa," I said to myself as I began throwing ones up in the air until the floor was covered and then let her polish my dick until I released all my seed down her throat. And for the rest of the day until it was time for the strip club to really start jumping, I chilled out until it was time to head out.

MARIAH

When you're stuck in between your mother and brother's beef, it's hard to choose a side when everyone wants the same person dead but no one want to compromise.

There are no sides. You have to do what's best for everyone, even if that means playing both sides, I said to myself as I lit my blunt and waited on my mother to pull up to my new condo I'd just moved into a week ago because it would be a cold day in hell before I ever went back to my mother's house. Besides, it was time for me to move out and experience life on my own, I said to myself as I hit the blunt a few times before walking toward the front door, where I came face to face with my mother, who I had only spoken with over the phone a few times since the shooting. And I could honestly say I was beyond happy to see her, I thought to myself as I moved out of the way so that she could come inside.

"Very nice," she said while giving me a hug, and I could tell by how tight she hugged me and how long that she missed me just as much as I missed her. I couldn't tell you even if my life depended on it why she kept so many secrets from us or why all of this was happening to our family, but I can say that I knew my mother, and I knew everything she did had a meaning to it, just like when she asked me to get hold of Markese's phone so I could install a tracking device on it in case she ever needed to track him down. When I met up with him the other day, I acted as if I wanted to use his phone to check my Snapchat account, but in all reality, I was scheming for my mother, because neither one of my brothers would pick up any of her calls, I thought to myself as she released me from her hold.

"How have you been?" she asked with a smile.

"I've been good. Just keeping a low profile. You never know who's out lurking," I said as she took a look around my condo.

"Well, you don't have to worry about that," she said, looking back at me before taking the blunt out my hand.

"Really, Mariah?" she asked while holding the blunt up in the air.

"Come on, Ma. I'm grown now. Besides, with all this stuff going on, I need to smoke a blunt," I said, hoping she would believe my excuse.

"Well, fire it back up so we both can smoke it," she said as we walked over toward the couch while I lit the blunt from earlier and then hit it a few times before she began to speak.

"I know you have a lot of questions, baby girl, but first I want to tell you again how sorry I am that I lied to you all these years about Big Malik and for putting you in danger. I thought I was doing the right thing, but I see all I've done was cause a bigger mess, as well as cause both my sons to hate me," she said as I passed her the blunt. "Not to mention I'm to blame for my first grandchild not being born into the world," she went on to say as she hit the blunt a few times and then released the smoke she'd just inhaled. "So what do you want to know?" she asked, catching me off guard because I wasn't expecting her to ask me that, I thought to myself.

"I don't know. I guess I just want to know what really happened between you and my father and why he hates you so much," I said, causing her to smirk before she passed me the blunt.

"Your father is the true definition of bitch-ass nigga," she said strongly and boldly. "When I met Big Malik, I had no intention on really being with him. You see, I have a past of my own, one that I'm still running from. And in order for me to obtain the life that I have now, I needed someone who was easy to manipulate and control—you know, like a puppet. He was the man for the job. My whole life as a kid, teenager, and young adult, I was trained to learn the drug game and to manipulate men who were in high power, like kingpins and drug lords, but when that life came to an end, I didn't know what else to do because that all I had ever known," she went on to say. "Let's just say your father was my way out. I used him like a pimp uses a hoe. It wasn't until I got pregnant with Malik that I began to really love him. It wasn't really love; more like I loved that he gave me children and the life I had always wanted.

"I could never truly love a nigga who was easy to manipulate and control, especially by pussy. Later down the road, things between me and Big Malik took a left. I never cared that Big Malik had a mistress—side bitch, whatever you want to call it—or that he was doing deals behind my back not knowing that I've always been ten steps ahead of him. Where he had me fucked up was when he tried to set me up and take everything I had built. You see, baby girl, I'm the reason why your father was sentenced to prison. I gave the feds everything they needed to put him away. I knew eventually he would put it together and find out it was me, but one thing I've come to cope with and understand is no matter what you do in life, whether it's good or bad, it has to come back around. And as much as you don't want to reap what you sow, you have to.

"I just never thought that my karma would be coming back on my kids, and that's the part that's fucking me up the most." she said while taking a deep breath, leaving me to feel a bit sad for my father because I'd be mad too if somebody played me the way she did him. "I know what you're thinking," she went on to say, causing me to snap out my thoughts. "I'm wrong for what I did," she said, looking over at me. But before I could answer, she began talking again. "Believe me, if you only knew," she said, letting out a slight laugh. "You would have done the same thing too. But look, I can't stay long. I have a business meeting that I'm already running late for. Did you do what I asked you to do?" she asked in regard to Markese.

"Yeah, I did it," I said, making her smile.

"Thank you. Since neither one of my sons will answer my calls, at least if I need to find one of them, I'll know where he's at," she said as she stood up.

"I have to go," she said, reaching into her coat pocket and pulling out a gun. "It's a .380. Just what you need if you feel like you're in danger. Don't hesitate to pull the trigger, and if some shit does go wrong and you have to use it, don't call the police. Clear the scene, and call me at this number only if something goes wrong," she said, handing me the gun while pulling out a phone. And moments later, my phone rang with a number that looked like it was out of the country, I thought to myself before she reached out and hugged me. "I'll be in touch. Be safe, and I love you," she went on to say before walking toward the front door and walking out, leaving me standing there with the .380 in my hands and hoping like hell I would never have to use it.

YVETTE

You'd think that the saying "blood is thicker than water" or "turn the other cheek and let vengeance be the Lord" would be enough for me to overlook all the blood that has been shed, but it won't. It wasn't until I was ten years old that I realized everything my mother taught me about forgiveness would soon be tainted by my grandparents, who quickly taught me to never put shit past anyone and to never turn the other check only for them to smack you again.

I soon learned the hard way that my grandparents were right—you couldn't put shit past anyone, including them. I'd be the first to say what took place a few weeks ago was unexpected and low, even for Big Malik, I thought to myself as I flashed back on the way my son Malik looked as he held Cinnamon in his arms right before I lied and told him I was going to get more towels to put on her wounds. But in all reality, I was making a run for it. With the kind of past I had, if the feds had any idea me or Porsha was involved in the shooting, we would have had every cop and detective in America out to get us, which was why I couldn't stay at the crime scene. The last thing I ever wanted my kids to think was that I up and left them in mess, which was why I made sure Dominique gave Malik that envelope with everything he needed to play his cards right. You would think he would at least want to reach out to me for questions and answers. But after finding out Cinnamon lost my first grandchild, I knew it would be a cold day in hell before he ever spoke to me again, but the last thing I was going to do was sit around and cry about a decision I chose to make that was beneficial for all of us, whether he saw it now or later. My only real concern now was finishing what I should have done over twenty plus years ago.

It's one thing to come after me, but to come after my kids would only put a muthafucka at the top of my hit list. Little did Big Malik know he just had woken up a beast I had tamed to stay asleep all these years, I said to myself as I replayed his last words in my head: "Till death do us part." Then smiled because he was right. And it would be death, but on his part, I said to myself as I pulled up to the address my daughter had sent me. Although Malik and Markese hated my guts right now, my daughter understood me and wanted the same thing I did, and that was for everything to come to an end, I thought to myself as I rang the doorbell and waited for her to answer the door. And moments later, I was walking inside and taking a look around her new place.

I'd be lying if I said her living on her own didn't make me feel some type of way because up until the incident, she had lived with me. I wasn't ready for her to leave me just yet, but I didn't want her to feel like she had her whole life, and that was caged in, I thought to myself as I released her from my embrace before walking over toward the couch, where we took a seat. I knew she had questions of her own to ask me, and I knew I didn't have much time, so I didn't beat around the bush. I flat out asked her what she wanted to know and then let out a slight laugh as I hit the blunt when she asked why Big Malik hated me so much. I should have told her the whole truth, but I didn't. I only told her what she needed to know and hoped that one day I wouldn't have to keep as many secrets as I was keeping now.

After I had told her everything she needed to know, she informed me that she had installed the device I needed to track Markese's whereabouts. I knew the chances of Mariah getting a hold of Malik's phone were slim to none. He was too smart for that. Not saying Markese wasn't, but I knew my sons, and I knew Mariah could get to Markese before she could ever get to Malik. And since they were both ignoring me and wouldn't take any of my calls, this was the only option I had left. With all this shit going on, I'd be damned if I didn't have a location on at least one of my sons, and nine times out of ten, wherever Markese was, Malik would be, I said to myself right before pulling a .380 out and giving it to Mariah for protection, along with a number to reach me at if some shit where to go left before heading out.

I still had a meeting to attend, and I was already running late, I said to myself before hopping into an all-white Ford Focus and driving for about ten minutes, until I was pulling inside a parking garage. I pulled up next to an all-black tinted Audi and then hopped inside and pulled off while making sure I didn't see anything or anyone out of place, then continued to drive for about hour until I reached the warehouse my meeting was being held at. I parked my car next to an all-black tinted SUV and stepped out with a briefcase full of money in my hands at the same time as the three men I was meeting.

"Long time no see," one of the men said in a thick Colombian accent as we walked through the building before coming to a complete stop right in front of a round table, where he stood in an all-black fitted suit.

"It's good to see you too, Diego. Now, let's get down to business," I said, causing him to smile.

"Just like the old days," he said as he snapped his fingers for one of the men to bring over a duffel bag. And a moment later, he opened the bag, pulled out a brick, and set it on the table for me to test it. I grabbed the knife he held out for me and cut into the brick, and I instantly began smiling.

"See, I told you—just like the old days," he said as he stood there looking at me, waiting on my response.

"Yeah. Only thing different is, I'm legit now," I said, causing him to laugh out loud.

"You and I both know you'll never be legit," he said in reference to my past, but I didn't pay that comment any mind.

"Everything's all there," I said, sliding him the briefcase across the table that was in front of me. Then waited on him to throw me the bag full of bricks.

"It's eight bricks total," he said, causing my face to turn up, because I had only asked for six. But before I could reply, he began to speak again.

"Carlos said the other two is on him," he said, causing my heart to drop at the sound of his name.

"Really, Diego? I thought I asked you not to tell him about this," I said as I began to rub my forehead while pacing back and forth before the door opened and Carlos walked into the warehouse with four men following behind him. And for the first time in a long time, I was caught off guard, because if he was here it could only mean one thing, I said to myself as I continued to watch him walk in with a three-piece navy-blue suit on with a collar shirt underneath, standing at five foot seven with thick, black, short hair; a mustache that sat perfectly on his face; and a cigar in his hand that he hit a few times as he continued to walk until he was close enough to me.

"Danos un momento," he said, turning toward all the men in the room, which means "Give us a moment" in Spanish. And moments later they were all walking out of the building, leaving both of us alone.

"What do you want, Carlos? And why are you here?" I asked, getting straight to point as I watched him sit on the edge of the table smoking his cigar while blowing smoke my way.

"What I want?" he asked with a smile and his deep accent. "First, I want you to show me some respect you out of all people should know what happens to those who don't," he said, causing me to laugh out loud at that response. "Next, where's my hija?" he asked, causing my smile to fade away quickly. When he asked where his daughter was at, and I could tell by the way he said it and the way he was looking that he wasn't here to play any games. He could have easily called or sent a message. But for him to fly to the States himself and risk his freedom only meant he had either heard what had been going on or he's here to make a statement.

"I'm sure with all your connections and eyes you have lurking around, you know that she's safe."

"Then you should know I've heard what's been going on, and I'm here to give you a fair warning, Yvette. If something happens to my hija because of the games you chose to play," he said while getting up and walking closer to me as he reached out to grab the back of my neck, causing me to look him directly in his eyes, "just know i won't spare you this time, and I won't allow you to buy your way out again," he said before giving me a kiss and letting me go. "I'm giving you a week to have my daughter contact me," he said, causing my face to turn up. "And I'm going to give you another week to handle this situation you've gotten yourself into. Had you not run off with the help, we wouldn't be here today. I gave you strict orders to kill him when you had the chance, but what did you do?" he asked while raising his voice louder. "You sent him to prison, like that was going to solve anything! Dead people don't cause problems!" he yelled again as I stood there with a mean mug that could kill.

"Had you loved me the way i needed you to, then I wouldn't have done half the shit I did," I said, reminding him of the past.

"Mi amada," he said, which means "my beloved." "If I didn't love you the way that I do, then you and I both know I would've killed you a long time ago. If that's not love, then I don't know what is, mi alma," which means "my soul." And hearing him still referring to me as his soul after all these years made my heart do something it hadn't done in a long time, and that was smile.

"I'm getting older, Yvette, and I will not spend another day of my life letting my only daughter think another man is her padre!" he yelled. "I've stayed away only because of who I am and our past. I never wanted to bring exposure to her, especially after all you've been through to try to live a legit life. But your time is up, Yvette. I know how manipulative and sneaky you can be, so let me make myself clear. If I don't hear from her or you've failed to take care of this situation by the time I'm giving you, not only will I send someone to do the job I know for a fact you're capable of doing, I'm gonna take my daughter. And because I know you won't let that happen without a fight, I'm going to come for you too. Do you understand me, Ma'ma?" he asked, calling me by the nickname he had given me years ago. "Now that we have an understanding, I must be going. You know I can't be in the States too long without the feds tryna pick up on my signal. Consider this one on me," he said, referring to all the bricks that were in the bag. "I don't know how far you plan to get with that little bit of nothing, but when you're ready to really do business, then you know where to find me," he said as he fixed his suit up a bit then leaned in and gave me a kiss on the forehead. "Te amo, mi alma," he said before walking out and leaving me standing there in my own thoughts, wondering how the fuck I was going to get out of this situation, I said to myself before grabbing the duffel bag with bricks in them and the briefcase full of money then began walking outside, where I spotted only my car.

Once I was inside the car, I wasted no time pulling off. The whole ride back toward the inner city of Chicago, I plotted on a way to end all this shit. If it wasn't Big Malik, it was Carlos and my kids. It was like my past was fucking me up every chance it got, and there was nothing I could do about it, I said to myself as I pulled back into the garage where I had parked the all-white Focus then got out, but before I got inside the Focus, I bent down and look underneath the Audi and began to laugh. "Really, Carlos?" I said out loud, as if he could hear me. Did he really think I was that dumb? I asked myself as I kept looking at the tracking device he had placed underneath the car before I grabbed the briefcase and duffel bag.

Once I was inside the Focus, I headed to my next destination. The ride there was about hour and half away. When I pulled up, I reached inside my coat pocket and turned off all the motion sensors as I continued to drive through the field that had only two big barns sitting on two hundred–plus acres, I thought to myself as I pulled inside one of the barns and then shut the doors after making sure everything was locked down. I moved a stack of hay from over a latch that led to an underground tunnel and then stepped down the ladder. Once I was completely underground, I made a right and walked until I reached the room I needed. When I walked inside, I spotted Porsha sitting at a table with a layout of the city in front of her, and from the looks of things, she was marking off all the police stations, fire departments, and every way in and out of Chicago.

"Look who decided to pop up," she said as she looked up at me.

"I had some business to handle," I said as I took a seat across from her.

"Yeah, I know," she said, turning her chair around to face the three computers she had sitting by the wall, then pulled up a picture of Carlos and his entire team stepping off his private jet, I thought to myself as I began rubbing my forehead because I knew shit was about to hit the fan.

"Really, Yvette? Why the fuck is Carlos in the States?" she asked, turning back around to face me.

"I didn't know he was coming here. He popped up on me out of nowhere," I said, causing her to let out a deep breath.

"I don't think I need to remind you that we can't afford to be exposed, and this muthafucka right here!" she said, pointing to the computer screen. "He is going to be the one who fucks it up for us. What do you think? He's invisible? I know for a fact, if I can pick him up on my radar, the feds can too. What do you think they're going to think when they see the most dangerous Colombian drug lord here in the States? And the last time he was here was because of a woman who helped him bring in over 350 bricks—not to mention that woman is supposed to be deceased. Have you forgot that?" she went on to say, "This is not like old times, when we could move the way we wanted to. You of all people know if anyone finds out who you really are, we gonna we be wanted in and out of the county. I don't know about you, but it's already hard enough as it is to keep up with the life I got. I don't have time to be on the run again," she went on to say. "I know you, Yvette, and I know you'll do anything to help Malik out. But if you want to help him, I suggest you get a new plug, because this one is gonna be your downfall," she said as I sat there taking in everything that she had just said before clearing my throat to speak.

"I understand where you're coming from, Porsha, but you should know by now that I'm smart enough to handle anything that comes my way, especially Carlos. You and I both know if he's here in the States, it's for a legit reason. And as far as Malik goes, I'm doing what any mother would do for her child. You of all people should take that into consideration," I said, referring to the reason why both of us, as well as my sister Candace, had to fake our deaths when we were in Brazil, I thought to myself as I continued to speak. "And must I remind you this is chess, not checkers. That's rule number three," I said, reminding her of all the laws and vows our grandparents made us take as I watched her sit there staring at me while shaking her head back and forth before taking a deep breath.

"I'm trusting you on this one, Yvette. No matter how this shit plays out, I'm going to do everything on my end to make sure we come out on top. I can't risk losing another sister. My heart won't survive it this time," she said, making me smile a bit because if it was one thing our grandparents taught us, it was that we were stronger together than apart, I thought to myself. But I snapped out my thoughts when she began talking again.

"Did Carlos say what his reasons were for coming here today?" she asked, and if time could stand still, I wished like hell it would at this moment.

"Mariah," I said out loud. And if looks could speak, well, let's just say Porsha's look was telling me there was no end to the road we were on.

4

ONE MONTH AND THREE DAYS LATER

Big Malik, a.k.a. Grim Reaper
Breaking news. Early this morning, the Cook County Homicide Unit received a call from a woman who reported a dead body on her doorstep. When police arrived at the crime scene, there was a box with a dead man's head inside it, with a dozen red roses. About an hour after that incident, the police department received another call from a man who found his brother the exact same way as the first victim who was found dead earlier this morning. As of this time, we know that prior to this incident, one of the men who was found murdered this morning was involved in a shooting that took place a little over a month ago on the North Side of Chicago, leaving six dead and three in critical condition. As of right now, we do not know if this could be related to what happened a month ago. One of the detectives on the scene gave a statement and said they were investigating these homicides to the fullest. Also, one of the family members was offering a reward for any information or leads that would help find the person responsible for these murders. If you have any information, please call this number—" the news reporter was about to say until I turned the TV off.

"Shit shit!" I yelled as I stood up and placed my hands on top of my head while letting everything the news reporter just said register in my head as I began to wonder how the fuck Malik had found the only person who had gotten away in the van that night, and what the fuck did he tell him?

"Why would he bring this much heat on himself?" I asked myself out loud, because I knew for a fact that was who had killed them. Why else would he let them walk away without pressing charges? And who else would have posted a $50,000 bond? I asked myself as I bent down and began snorting the dope that was laid out on the table. For the last month, I had been lying low, waiting on Malik or Yvette to make their move. But they hadn't until today. Malik killing both them niggas and cutting their heads off was to get my attention, but I could care less about him killing them. At the end of the day, my real issue was with Yvette. Me sending them shooters to shoot up Yvette's house wasn't part of the plan, but when I came face to face with my son, he let me know in so many ways that he thought I was a joke. So I showed him who'd get the last laugh.

You see, most would think I was just some tender dick-ass nigga who couldn't accept the fact that his bitch had moved on, but that wasn't the case. This shit was much deeper than Yvette leaving me to rot in prison. She had played me like a violin. I shoulda known from the first time we met that a bitch like Yvette would never want a nigga like me. I didn't have much and wasn't standing on shit. I was a regular-ass nigga selling dime bags of weed just to make ends meet until she came along and made a nigga feel like a king. She gave me that boost I needed and made me feel like I couldn't be touched, like I was the most powerful nigga alive. Well, at least that was what I thought. It wasn't until we were about three years in that I started to realize shit about Yvette wasn't about the right. We didn't take pictures together. She barely left the house unless she was meeting with the connect.

She never went to the doctor, not even when she got pregnant. No bank accounts, nothing. Everything was in my name. It was like she didn't exist. But she did; she was the one behind the scene masterminding everything. It was like she was too smart for her own good. It wasn't until we had Mariah that I got an unexpected letter in the mail with photos of her and this Colombian nigga. There were pictures of them on yachts, at restaurants, all the way down to them fucking. So you can only imagine how that made me feel. While I was at home with the kids, she was out fucking and sucking the next nigga. She really had me thinking that she loved me, but in all reality, she was just using me, I thought to myself as I lit a cigarette while taking a seat at the table as I continued to reminisce.

I never planned on asking Yvette about the pictures that were sent to me. Instead, I opened up a shop down in Miami and had my mistress help me move in bricks of cocaine. I had plans on killing Yvette, but I still needed to find out who her connect was so I could cop them bricks myself. I could have gone out and gotten my own connect, but the cocaine she had was the purest to come. Thinking back on that shit now, I wish I would have killed her when I had the chance. Until this day, I still don't know how she found out I knew about her and the Colombian or that I opened a shop up down in Miami. But she did, and the next thing I knew, I was doing fed time for trafficking, smuggling, and murder that I didn't commit, but somehow they found a gun with my prints on it and gave me twenty-five to life.

It wasn't until I sent word for Yvette that I knew something was up, so I sent Susie to collect all the money I'd hidden from Yvette over the years. When Susie arrived at the spot where I hid all the money, Yvette had already cleared it out and left a letter that read, "This will always be a queen's board." Not only did she fuck me over and set me up to go to prison, she took all the money I'd been saving. And even then I was still trying to do right by my kids until they turned against me. Even in prison, when I got served the divorce papers, come to find out we were never married. Just locked into a financial agreement.

Had it not been for Susie fighting for my freedom and finding out the detectives who had been working my case were dirty, I'd still be locked down. So as you can see, a nigga got a lot to be pissed about. I lost a lot behind a bitch, but if it's one thing Yvette taught me, it was to always go about things the way you would go about chess. So you can only imagine how I mastered the art of chess over the past twenty years. And this time around, I would have the last laugh, I said to myself as I watched my daughter Rose walk in the kitchen and over to where I was sitting.

"What you got for me?" I asked, and I snorted the last line of dope that was on the table as she stood there and watched.

"Nothing, really. Malik hasn't made any real moves. I've checked all the cameras in the restaurant. He hasn't brought in any new shipments or placed any. And before you ask, no, I haven't seen any sign of Yvette," she said as I leaned back in the chair a bit.

"Are you sure he hasn't caught on to you?" I asked, eyeballing her.

"Yes, I'm sure. I don't think he would have made me the new manager if he thought something was up," she said, causing me to think a little deeper.

"What was the reason he moved your position again?" I asked with a bit of concern.

"Because Kim went to the other restaurant to help manage it and to train Malik's friend. Um, I think his name is Choppa," she said as I nodded my head up and down.

"You don't think he's using that restaurant to bring in a shipment, do you?"

"I don't know. I can't see him doing that. The restaurant isn't that big, and both of the systems are linked together. So I would know if he was," she went on to say. "That's all I have for now. I have to get going. I can't be late opening the restaurant, or Malik will know something's wrong," she said right before Susie walked in the kitchen.

"Hey, Ma," Rose said as Susie walked up and handed me the phone.

"Hey, baby," she went on to say before I placed the phone to my ear and listened to the person on the other end going off.

"Have you looked at the fucking news?" They yelled through the phone.

Detective Brown

"I knew I should have never gotten involved in this shit," I said out loud to myself as I paced back and forth while listening to what the news reporter was saying, right before the chief of police bust into my office.

"Have you taken a look at the got-damn news?" he asked as he threw a thick file on my desk.

"Not only do we have a missing detective, but now our only main suspect who was involved in an incident where six men were killed a month ago has turned up dead after bonding out of jail less than a week and a half ago, not to mention now we have a double homicide where we have to figure out how the second victim plays a part in all of this shit," he went on to say as he rubbed his forehead out of frustration. "I don't give a fuck what you have to do. I want everyone who was involved in that shooting down here for questioning now! I got the major so far up my ass for information on Brian that if I move wrong, my damn gall bladder may fall out. It's been over a week since you told me you had a team looking into his personal files and computers. I want some type of report on my desk by tomorrow morning with a lead on Brian's whereabouts.

"You've had this case long enough to give me something!" he yelled. "In the meantime, gather up a team and go grab everyone in that file, including the woman who paid the bond for the two men who were brutally murdered. Let me know when you have them all here," he said right before he walked out of the room, leaving me with no other choice but to bring in Malik and his whole team, I thought to myself as I snatched my coat off the back of my chair and headed out to my car. I speed-dialed the number I needed, and a moment later, he was answering the phone.

"Hello," he answered.

"What the fuck is taking you so long with the information on Brian?" I yelled into the phone. "I gave you his laptop a week ago for you to hack into, and you still haven't got back with me yet! I have my chief of police down my back for answers, and you're sitting up here taking your sweet-ass time," I said and waited on his response.

"I'm taking care of it right now. I'll have the information you need within the next few hours."

"You better, or else I'll be to find your ass next,'". I said right before I hung the phone up then took a deep breath. "Come on. You got this. Think about Jasmine and the baby," I said out loud to myself as I leaned my head back a bit on the headrest while I continued to think of a plan that could save not only my wife's and unborn child's lives but mine as well, I thought to myself right before I heard a tap on my window, causing me to snap out my thoughts as I jumped a bit before looking over at Derick standing there staring at me.

"What the fuck does he want now?" I asked myself before lowering the window.

"You all right?" he asked as he stuck his head through the window.

"Yeah, I'm good. Just a little stressed out. This Brian situation got me all over the place," I lied.

"Yeah, I know what you mean. But the good news is, his wife found a hard drive in his office safe. She's supposed to bring it by later on today so I can take a look at what's on it," he said, causing my heart to drop at the sound of that because I had no idea what could be on it.

"Are you sure you're all right?" he asked again, causing me to look his way.

"Yeah, I'm good. I'm about to go pick up some suspects that may have been involved in those killings that have everyone talking."

"Yeah. That was some fucked-up shit. But hey, think about it on the bright side. Two less criminals we have to worry about," he said as he hit the side of my car door before telling me he had to go and finish up some paperwork, leaving me to head over to Brian's home to catch his wife before she made it down to the station.

"If it isn't one thing, it's another," I said out loud to myself as I pulled away from Cook County, and twenty-five minutes later, I was pulling up to Brian's house and stepping out of the car as the garage opened and his wife pulled out, but she stopped at the sight of me standing there.

"Oh, shit. You scared me," she said as she rolled down the window. "I was just heading down to the station to speak with Detective Derick Thomason," she said.

"Yeah. He asked me to stop by and grab the hard drive from you. He said something about his daughter getting sick and taking the rest of the day off."

"Oh, I'm sorry to hear that. Well, here's the hard drive. I tried taking a look to see what was all on there, but I got locked out," she said while letting out a deep breath. "I feel so hopeless. I don't know what to do. I'm running out of things to tell our kids about their father. I can't eat or sleep knowing that he's still missing. A part of me feels like something bad has happened to him," she went on to say right before I promised her I'd do whatever it took to find him or anyone who had anything to do with his disappearance. Then I headed back toward the car, where I called in a team to meet me at Malik's restaurant, strip clubs, and any other places we had on file for him. Then I pulled off to bring him and everyone affiliated with him in.

MALIK

You have to know, with every action you take, a reaction will soon follow, I thought to myself as I sat at the end of the bed smoking a blunt while watching the news before pulling my phone out and calling Markese.

"Yo," he answered on the third ring.

"You watching this shit, fam?" I asked as I hit the blunt.

"Hell yeah. You already know what time it is," he said as I ashed the blunt and watched Cinnamon walk around the room in her Fendi robe, still ignoring a nigga because of the last conversation we'd had a week ago, I said to myself as I continued to wrap shit up with Markese.

"Yeah, I already know. But look. Hit Choppa and Zilla up and tell them niggas to be at work on time, and don't forget to leave their bitches at the crib," I said, referring to Choppa's chopper that stayed glued to him and whatever pistol Zilla planned on having on him today, because I knew it would only be a matter of time before the feds came knocking, I said to myself before ending the call and heading toward Cinnamon's walk-in closet, where I spotted her struggling to get the rest of her leggings up. Seeing Cinnamon going through this shit made me feel even more shittier that I hadn't offed that bitch-ass nigga yet, I thought to myself as I continue to watch her try to get dressed. That was, until she looked up and caught me staring.

"What are you looking at?" she asked me with a mug, causing me to let out a slight laugh as I walked closer to her, invading her personal space while throwing the end of my blunt in the small trash can that sat off to the side.

"I was coming to let you know I was about to head out, but then I saw you struggling to get dressed and thought you might need some help," I said, causing her to take a step back while still holding on to her leggings.

"Thank you, but I'm fine. I don't need your help, so you can leave," she said, causing me to smirk at that comment.

"I wasn't asking for your permission. You must have forgotten I don't need it, shorty. And it's obvious you can't do it yourself. You'd rather struggle than allow me to help you, but we both know Ima do whatever the fuck I want to do anyway. So you might as well save all that extra shit you got for a nigga," I said, causing her to roll her eyes as I began pulling up the rest of her leggings before reaching out and grabbing the bra she had sitting off to the side. After getting her fully dressed, I pulled her into my embrace and wrapped my arms around her waist while forcing her to look at me, because when Cinnamon is mad, she does this thing where she looks everywhere else but at the person she's mad at, I thought to myself before speaking.

"I know shit's fucked up right now, and I know I ain't been here for you like I should. And I apologize for that. But I promise, when all this shit is over with, Ima do whatever I gotta do to make you happy again. I ain't trying to lose you, and I damn sure ain't trying to have beef in the streets and at the home front," I went on to say, but I could tell by her facial expression she wasn't feeling shit a nigga was saying.

"Malik, at this point I'm too emotionally drained to put up a debt with you. How are you going to apologize but at the same time tell me nothing is going to change until all this shit is over with? That doesn't make any sense. I guess because you weren't the one who almost lost their life or had to endure a miscarriage, you couldn't possibly understand what I'm going through or how it feels to have a fiancé who's gone when you wake up and comes home when you're asleep. Especially at a time like this, when you need him the most. And not to mention I can't call the one person who understands me the most just to vent, because I don't want my mother judging you or our relationship. I've yet to tell her the real reason why I was shot in the first place. So please do me a favor and save that apology for when it really matters, because we both know it's doesn't mean shit as of right now. And if you haven't already realized, it isn't shit you can do to change what happened to me or the baby. I thought I'd tell you that since all you seem to care about lately is revenge," she said before walking out of the closet and leaving a nigga feeling worse than I already was.

 With all this shit going on, I couldn't even stay and try to make her reason with me, I thought to myself as I walked out of the closet and down the stairs, where I grabbed the keys to my pickup truck and pulled off toward the restaurant, where I thought about everything Cinnamon had just said to a nigga. Then I began tryna put myself in her shoes. She didn't have to say it, but I could tell she blamed a nigga for everything that had happened to her and the baby. I can't say I blame her, because I blame myself for everything that had happened to them, I said to myself as I pulled up on the street my restaurant was on and spotted two police cars parked out front and all-black car that looked to be a detective car, I thought to myself as I pulled up and parked. Then watched a five-nine bald-headed nigga with a goatee walk up to my truck and tap on the window. Instead of rolling it down, I opened the door.

 "Malik Green, I'm Detective Brown. We're going to need you to come down to the station for questioning," he said as the other two officers moved in slowly while clutching their pistols.

 "For what?" I asked, still sitting in my truck.

 "I'll explain everything when we get down to the station, but as of right now, Ima need you to step out of the car, please," he went on to say, and moments later, I was out of my truck and placed in handcuffs. Where I was taken to Cook County for question. Once I arrived at the police station and was inside. I spotted Choppa and Zilla being brought in as well, so I knew it was only a matter of time before they caught up with Markese, I said to myself as the detective walked me to a room where I sat for an hour before the door swung open, and the same detective who had picked me up came walking in with a file and a tape recorder in his hands, I thought to myself as I watched him take a seat across from me before turning the tape recorder on and opening this thin-ass file that sat in front of him and began flipping through the few pages that were inside.

 "Malik Green, age twenty-eight, no felonies, never been arrested except for the incident that took place a little over a month ago. You own a nightclub, two restaurants, and a strip joint," he said as he shook his head in disapproval of my strip club. "Very impressive," he went on to say as he leaned back in his seat a little before speaking again. "Malik, I don't know if you're aware that the man involved in the shooting that took place a month ago turned up dead this morning. His remains were sent to his family. I would say it's a coincidence that the same man who's responsible for shooting up you and your family home ends up dead exactly one week after bonding out from jail. What makes it even more suspicious is that you didn't press any charges. Why would an innocent man with no criminal record not want to press charges? Especially when it states here that your girlfriend, Ms. Cinnamon Jones," he said, looking back up at me, "was shot multiple times and in that process lost a child, which I'm assuming was yours. I don't know; maybe it's just me, but I would want to see that man go to prison, unless I had my own plans for him," he said, looking directly at me while waiting on my response. But I didn't have one for him. I knew better than to talk to the pigs without a lawyer—or at all, for that matter, I said to myself as I leaned back in the chair a bit to get comfortable and wait to either be released or for my lawyer to walk through the door.

"Look, Malik. I know you wanna get out of here and get back to whatever it is you were about to do before I picked you up, but the longer you sit here not answering any of my questions, the longer you will sit. So I suggest you cooperate," he said, causing me to smirk at his response.

"Detective Brown, is it?" I ask while clearing my throat. "You and I both know if I'm not being booked, then you can only hold me here for seventy-two hours. And as far as that other shit you're talking about, last time I checked, it wasn't my job to figure out what happened to him. Anything else, you can take up with my lawyer. You know, the one I asked for right before you put me in the back of your car. Other than that, I ain't got shit else to say to you," I said, causing him to smile like the Grinch as he leaned forward a bit.

"See, I knew you were a smart guy, Malik. I mean, you have to be seeing that you run a multimillion-dollar business with no paper trail of where your investment came from. You don't have any records of inheritance, and hell, you're twenty-eight years old and have never punched a clock a day of your life," he said, causing me to smirk. "And you're right about one thing: I can only hold you here for seventy-two hours. And since that's my job," he said, shrugging his shoulders in a sarcastic way, "I don't mind being here the whole seventy-two hours. But I know that you do. So let's start over. Where were you this morning between six a.m. and nine a.m.?" he asked. But just like earlier, I ignored his bitch ass. The last thing I was about to do was let this square-ass bitch-ass detective try to play mind games with me, I thought to myself as I continued sitting there watching his every move.

"No? You don't want to answer that question? OK, how about this. Why didn't you report your company truck being stolen a day prior to the shooting? You didn't think that was something you should have mentioned?" he asked right before the door swung open. But I never took my eyes off that nigga as he sat across from me, still smiling. Little did he know he had just given me everything I needed.

"I'm sorry it took me so long," my lawyer said, causing me to snap out my thoughts right before she looked up at Detective Brown.

"Please uncuff my client," she said, causing Detective Brown to stand up.

"Says who?"

"Me," a fat white man with grayish hair said as he walked in. "Mr. Green is free to go. His alibi checks out," the man said as he stood in the doorway, and my lawyer began to speak.

"Not only does my client's alibi clear him as a suspect in these murders, he's also been cleared from the case that was pending against him and the rest of my clients. The judge just ruled it as self-defense," she said while throwing a thick-ass file down on the table in front him, causing me to smile at the same time. "My client has many businesses to run and a name that doesn't need to be tainted or tarnished with false allegations. And because I know you don't like to lose or follow the rules, anything after today will be considered harassment. And with the kind of background you have, Detective Brown, by the time I'm done with you, you'll be back as a rent-a-cop with a flashlight patrolling schools for children. Now uncuff my client from this chair!" she said while staring him down.

"Uncuff him," the fat white man said, and moments later, he was walking around the table and uncuffing me from the chair.

"Enjoy your freedom while you still have it," he said, causing me to smirk before walking out of the room with my lawyer and right out of Cook County's doors.

"Markese, Choppa, and Zilla are waiting for you in that black SUV," she said, pointing to the SUV parked down the street as she handed me my wallet and phone, which had been taken from me when I was brought in, I thought to myself right before thanking her and telling her I'd be sending her some extra cash for getting this case thrown out as fast as she did. Then I jogged down the street where the SUV was parked and got inside, but before I could even shut the door all the way, shit hit the fan.

"Aye, fam, I don't know how long you're planning on letting this shit play out, but we're gonna have to off that nigga Detective Brown," Choppa said, causing Zilla to agree. But before I could even voice my opinion, my phone began to ring. It was Martha, telling me a man was at the house to see Cinnamon, and she wasn't sure if I knew about it. Ever since the shooting, I'd been having Martha keeping a close eye on Cinnamon. So when she hit me up saying that shit, I immediately got pissed off and headed to the house to see who the fuck this nigga was.

5

CINNAMON (TRUE COLORS)

Waking up this morning and seeing that Malik was still at the house was a surprise to me. He was usually gone by the time I woke up and didn't come home until I was in a deep sleep, I thought to myself as I stepped out of the shower while reaching for my Fendi robe before walking out of the bathroom and right past Malik, who was sitting at the end of the bed smoking a blunt while talking on the phone, I thought to myself as I kept walking toward my walk-in closet, not paying him any attention.

Ever since the last conversation we'd had, I'd been trying my best to avoid any real conversation with him, mainly because I was still pissed at the fact that he cared more about revenge than he did our relationship, not to mention that he still had yet to ask me how I felt or if I was OK. It was like the loss of our baby was only affecting me. Don't get me wrong; I'm not saying I don't believe Malik doesn't feel some type away about everything that had happened, but damn, it was either that he was really good at not showing his emotions or that it was not bothering him as much as it was bothering me, I said to myself as I began looking through the rack of clothes and finally decided on some Nike workout leggings and a Nike purple fleece, along with a matching bra-and-panty set, and threw everything I planned to wear on a table that sat in the middle of the closet then began trying to get dressed. But every time I tried to pull my leggings up, all I ended up doing was hurting myself, gotdamn I said right before looking up and catching Malik standing in the middle of the closet, just staring at me, I thought to myself before asking him what the fuck he was looking at.

I don't even know why I bothered telling him that I didn't need his help getting dressed and to carry on with his day, because that shit just went right out the window, I thought to myself as I listened to him tell me he was gonna do whatever he wanted to anyway, so it was pointless for me to even put up a fight with him. I began to think as I watch him pull the rest of my leggings all the way up while making me horny at the same damn time, and to make matter worse, he was looking good as hell in that Balmain outfit he was rocking with some matching Margiela shoes, his bust-down Rolex with a matching ring that sat on his left pinky, his Cuban-link GFM chain that would blind you if you stared at it for too long, that fade I loved so much, and he was smelling good as hell, I said to myself as I continued to stand there while he helped me get dressed.

Once I was fully dressed, he pulled me into his embrace and began trying to apologize for the way he'd been acting and putting everything before our relationship. But I wasn't tryna hear that shit, especially when I knew he was contradicting himself and that the apology was bullshit. After telling him how I felt, I walked out of the closet and over toward the dresser, where my phone was sitting, ringing nonstop, I thought to myself as I picked it up.

"Hello," I answered while walking out of the room and downstairs toward the kitchen.

"I'm surprised you're up this early," Stonie said into the phone as I walked into the kitchen, where I started the coffeepot.

"I should be saying the same to you," I said while grabbing a coffee cup. "You must have an appointment at the mall, because your ass is never up this early unless you have hair to do," I said as I listened to her laugh a bit before telling me her plans for the day, which included me. At first I was going to tell her I didn't want to leave the house, but I knew deep down if I wanted to get back to the old Cinnamon, I would have to take the steps in order to do so. And besides, I hadn't left the house since the shooting unless it was a doctor's appointment, I thought to myself before telling her I would go, but after my physical therapist came. That should give her slow ass enough time to get ready, and knowing Stonie, she wouldn't even start getting dressed for another hour, I said to myself as I sipped my coffee and waited for my therapist to come. And right on cue, exactly an hour later, the doorbell was ringing, and I was headed toward the door, where I heard Martha telling the man to wait outside until she spoke with me or Malik.

"He's fine, Martha. He's my new physical therapist," I said as she tried to close the door in his face.

"Oh, I'm sorry, Cinnamon. Malik didn't tell me to look out for anyone," she said as she opened the door all the way and apologized to the man as he walked inside carrying a bag.

"No problem. I completely understand," the five-ten, dark-haired, brown-eyed white man said as he smiled, showing off his deep dimples that reminded me of the white guy who played in *The Best Man Holiday*, I thought to myself as he held his hand out for me to shake it.

"You must be Cinnamon. I'm Dr. Fisher. I'll be your new physical therapist," he said as I shook his hand. "I have a table I need to bring in. Is there a place I'll be able to set up at?" he asked before following me down the hall. Once he had brought everything he need in and was set up, we began the therapy. I was about hour and half into the process when Malik walked in the room, causing both of us to jump at the sound of his voice.

"What the fuck is going on?" Malik asked, causing both of us to look his way and for me to get off the table.

"Malik, this is my new physical therapist. I hired him to help me regain my strength. He's one of the best and specializes in helping patients who have suffered from gunshot wounds," I said as I watched the man reach out to shake Malik's hand, but he just left it there hanging, I thought to myself as I stood there looking at Malik mean mug both of us. I didn't need a psychic to tell me that Malik was beyond pissed off, but for what? I began to ask myself, but I snapped out of my thoughts when Malik began speaking again.

"No disrespect, but Ima need you to pack up all this shit and get the fuck out," he said while reaching into his pocket and taking out a stack of money. "This should cover whatever services you have done for today," he went on to say while putting the money on the table not far from us and leaving both me and the physical therapist standing there like, What the fuck just happened? I thought to myself as I continued looking at Malik, who obviously didn't give a fuck that he was being so rude. At this point I was beyond embarrassed and pissed off, I thought to myself as I brushed past him and went down the hall, where I walked past Markese, Choppa, and Zilla, ignoring them as they all asked how I was doing. As far as I was concerned, I didn't have shit to say to them or Malik, I said to myself as I walked into my closet and began finding something to wear for the day while wondering where the fuck Stonie's ass was at, because at this point, I was more than ready to get the fuck out this house.

"When were you going to tell me you hired a therapist?" Malik asked, causing me to jump a bit at the sound of his voice. "And where the fuck do you think you're going?" he asked as I turned around to face him.

"I didn't feel the need to check in with you about shit, especially when it comes to my health," I said, looking him dead in his eyes while ignoring his second question.

"And why the fuck don't you?" he yelled. "Have you forgot what the fuck is going on, Cinnamon? You're bringing muthafuckas all up and through the house not knowing if this nigga is who he says he is or not. How could you be so careless and dumb?" he asked, stopping me in my tracks.

"Careless and dumb?" I asked with a little laugh as I turned back around so that I'd be facing him. "No. Careless and dumb would be me choosing to fall in love with a muthafucking kingpin who nearly got me killed and caused me to lose my fucking unborn child!" I said, but before I could get another word out, Malik had hemmed me up by my Nike fleece with so much force.

"Have you lost your muthafucking mind?" he yelled directly in my face as he pushed me into the wall while knocking some clothes off their hangers. "Don't ever in your muthafuck life disrespect me like that again or mention the fact my seed is gone because of me. You must have forgot who the fuck you're talking to!" he said as a few tears began to fall down my face. "You got me and life fucked up," he yelled again as he gave me another hard push before letting me go and walking out of the closet, leaving me to ball up in a fetal position on the floor as I began to cry out loud because I felt like I had lost everything within a blink of an eye. And now I felt like I had just lost the only man I ever truly loved.

Mariah
The last conversation me and my mother had shined some light on why my father hated her the way that he does and why she had told us so many lies, I said to myself as I looked over at the .380 she'd given me and hoped like hell I wouldn't have to use it. But just in case I did, I'd been at the gun range every day since I'd gotten it, practicing my aim and getting used to the feeling of shooting a gun, because it would be a cold day in hell before I ended up dead because of someone else's mistakes, I said to myself as I reached over for my phone, which was now vibrating with a text message from Stonie asking if I wanted to link up today.

It was crazy that she texted me, because I was thinking about calling her or Chyna to check on Cinnamon, since she never answer the phone these days. After replying to the text message, I got up and headed toward the bathroom, where I started the shower and got in while letting the hot water hit my body as I reached out for my toothbrush and toothpaste that sat off to the side and then began brushing my teeth before handling my business. And fifteen minutes later, I was out of the shower and rolling a blunt.

Once I had my blunt rolled and lit, I walked toward my closet and began finding me something to put on for the day as I smoked my blunt and blasted Kodak Black's *Project Baby 2* from the speakers I had inside my closet. After settling on a Fendi fit with some Fendi heels to match, I began getting dressed for the day. Once I was fully dressed, I wet my naturally curly thick hair with a spray bottle and then placed it in bun at the top before adding a Chanel clip to my shirt, along with a Rolex watch and an iced-out chain that had the letter *M* on it. After giving myself one last look in the mirror, I grabbed my Fendi bag, Channel frames, and the .380 and then headed out to the garage, where my all-black Audi was parked, and got inside while dialing Stonie.

"Hello," she answered as I pulled out of the garage.

"Where we meeting at?" I asked, and to my surprise, she said Malik's house. After telling her I would be there, I hung up the phone and then headed that way. The ride from my house to Malik's house was a good fifty minutes to an hour long, due to the fact I lived farther out of the city than they did, I thought to myself as I continued to drive. And an hour later, I was pulling up to their gates and punching in the code. Once the gates opened, I pulled in and parked next to Stonie's all-black Range Rover and headed for the door, where I was greeted by Martha once the doors opened. After I had talked with her for a few minutes, she let me know Cinnamon and Stonie were upstairs. When I finally made it to the room they were in, I spotted Cinnamon sitting in a chair not far from me, and from what I could see, she looked very sad and in her own world, I thought to myself as I continued to walk into the room.

"I was just about to call you," Stonie said while walking out of the bathroom and causing Cinnamon to snap out her thoughts before looking over at me.

"My bad. My condo is almost an hour away from here," I said while walking toward Cinnamon, who was now standing up and grabbing her purse so that we could leave.

"Hey, Mariah, how you been?" Cinnamon asked in a low whisper.

"I've been great. I should be the one asking you that," I said as I watched her take a deep breath before talking.

"I'm as good as I'm going to be for now," she said while throwing her shades on.

"Y'all ready?" she asked. And moments later, we were heading out of the house and getting inside Stonie's Range Rover.

"Where are we going first?" I asked as Cinnamon lit an already-rolled blunt.

"We gotta grab Chyna. After that we can start off by eating. Anything else, we can figure out later," Stonie said as Cinnamon passed the blunt to me as I rapped along with Key Glock's "My Momma Told Me" while hitting the blunt a few times, and twenty minutes later, we were getting Chyna and on our way to brunch, where each of us had at least five mimosas—well, all of us except Stonie, who kept running to the bathroom every five minutes, I thought to myself as I finished the rest of my drink. And for the rest of the day, we all got massages and caught each other up on the bullshit we had been dealing with.

I was surprised at the reaction Cinnamon gave me when I asked about Malik. She didn't have to say it, but I could tell shit between them wasn't good. And knowing my brother, when it came to dealing with pain or hurt, he would shut everyone out unknowingly. And at a time like this, that was the last thing he needed to be doing. But I wasn't going to get in the middle of their shit, especially when neither one of them had put me in it, I said to myself as I walked out of the spa. And a few hours later, Stonie was dropping all of us back off, and I was heading home to roll a blunt and watch *Power*.

Stonie

Waking up with morning sickness and sleeping from yesterday evening until this morning made me realize it was only so long that I could pretend that I was not pregnant, I thought to myself as I looked at my phone and peeped that Markese hadn't called or responded to my text message. I would be lying if I said that it didn't hurt my feelings a little bit, because it did. But overall, it gave me the answer I needed. I just hoped that later down the road, I wouldn't regret aborting this baby, because every day I was getting more and more attached to him or her. But no matter how I felt, I knew this was the best decision for me, I said to myself right before dialing Cinnamon. And on the fourth ring, she answered, and to my surprise, she was up, after telling her I'd be by to pick her up and that I wasn't taking no for an answer. I called Chyna.

"Hello," she answered, and from the sounds of things, she was still asleep.

"Get the fuck up. I'm about to grab Cinnamon and come get you," I said as I listened to her clear her throat before speaking.

"Why the fuck are you yelling in my ear? And where we going?" she asked.

"Does it matter, bitch? Get up and get dressed," I said as I hung the phone up before she could say no or get another word out. Then I sent Mariah a text message asking if she wanted to link up. I hadn't seen her since the incident first happened, and I didn't want her to feel like because shit went left, she couldn't come around. Hell, if Cinnamon was still fucking with the nigga responsible for all this shit, then we might as well keep shit coo with Mariah too. Besides, I thought all of us together would definitely brighten Cinnamon up a bit, I thought to myself as I lay in bed for another thirty minutes before getting in the shower, where I felt like I was either about to pass out or fall back to sleep.

Once I was out of the shower, I threw some fitted jeans on the bed with a long-sleeve brown and peanut butter shirt to match my Louis scarf and my Louis Vuitton booted heels, then I took a seat on the bed and began to lotion down.

"I don't see how bitches do this pregnancy shit," I said out loud to myself as I sat there trying not to fall back asleep. Once I got the energy to fully get dressed, it was almost an hour later. After getting dressed and doing my makeup, I placed the Louis Vuitton scarf over my Addikted The Collection twenty-inch weave that stopped right before it hit my ass. Then I curled the ends to give it a better look. After giving myself one last look, I put on a few white gold bracelets that a friend of mine bought me as a birthday gift last year, along with a matching necklace, and then headed out with my Louis bag and coat in my hands.

"Got damn it. Cold as hell," I said out loud as I got inside my car and then waited for about ten minutes before pulling off. "Hello," I answered while pulling away from Cinnamon's condo as I listened to Mariah ask me where we were meeting up at. After telling her to meet me at her brother's house, I continued to drive until I reached Cinnamon and Malik's gates, where I waited until the gates opened. Once they opened, I pulled in and parked next to an SUV and then got out and headed toward the door. But before I could even knock, the door opened, and I came face to face with Malik. And if looks could kill, his looks were saying he was either about to kill a muthafucka or he already had, I said to myself.

"Wassup," he said right before brushing past me toward the SUV. Where Choppa and his brother followed, leaving me and Markese standing in the doorway staring at each other. And if there was ever a time when I thought I couldn't be nervous or have butterflies, well, let's just say I stand corrected today, I thought to myself as I watched Markese close the door before turning toward me.

"How you been, shorty? Long time no see," he said, causing me to look away because his smile was so damn contagious.

"I've been good. And you?" I asked as he stood there, still looking at me while licking his lips.

"I been straight. I can't complain. I got yo text the other day, but every time I tried to call you, something came up," he said, causing me to let out a slight laugh.

"Still running the streets, I see," I went on to say, making him smirk a bit.

"Still can't accept the fact that I'm a street nigga. What else hasn't changed? But anyways, you told me to hit you up, so what's up?" he asked, causing my heart to start racing and for me to start contemplating on what to say, because at this point, my mind was already made up.

"I just felt like I needed to talk to you and make sure you were good. That's all," I lied.

"Aw, yeah," he said right before someone started blowing the horn for him to come outside. "Well, as you can see, a nigga straight. But look, Ima hit you up later," he said as he reached for the door and opened it. But before he walked out, he turned back around to face me. "Answer the phone when a nigga call," he went on to say before walking out and leaving me to wonder if not telling him about the pregnancy was the right thing to do, I thought to myself as I began calling out for Cinnamon. And moments later, Martha was walking up telling me she was upstairs.

Once I got upstairs, I still didn't see any sings of Cinnamon. That was, until I walked toward the closet and spotted her on the floor crying. "What's wrong, and why are you on the floor?" I asked as I knelt down to help her up. But instead, she just sat there with tears running down her face. After sitting there for about ten minutes, she finally told me what had happened, and that definitely explained why Malik had looked the way he did when he opened the door, I thought to myself, although I still felt some type of way about him ever since my cousin almost lost her life behind him and his family. I still felt like the shit Cinnamon said to him was dead-ass wrong and very hurtful. No matter if he showed his feelings or not, he was still human, and the baby was just as much a part of him as it was a part of her. "How could he not care?" I said as I expressed that to Cinnamon, because right is right and wrong will always be wrong, I said to myself right before helping Cinnamon get dressed in the outfit she had just picked out.

Once she was dressed and I was done with her hair, we waited on Mariah so we could leave. I was just about to call her when I came out of the bathroom, but she was already walking into the room looking like a black Barbie. Mariah was definitely one of the most beautiful black women I'd ever seen, with smooth chocolate skin and pretty curly hair that made her look like she could be mixed with some shit, I thought to myself as I watched her and Cinnamon have a few words before heading out to get Chyna.

Once we picked up Chyna, the rest of the day, we got massages, ate, smoked, and chilled until I had to take everyone back home. After dropping Chyna and Cinnamon off, I headed back to the condo, where I lay in bed and a began rethinking my decision. And before I knew it, I was falling asleep. When I woke, it was 1:30 a.m., and my phone was ringing nonstop. I reached over to answer it without looking. "Hello," I said into the phone as I reached for another pillow.

"You sleep, shorty?" Markese asked, causing my eyes to shoot open and my heart to start racing.

"I just woke up. Why? Wassup?" I asked as I listened to him take a deep breath then release it.

"Nothing much. A nigga just got a lot on his mind right now, but that ain't what call for. I called to see if you were ready to tell me what you really wanted. Because I know it was more than just seeing if I was OK," he said, and I sat all the way up in bed before responding.

"You said you had a lot on your mind. You want to talk about it?" I asked, ignoring his question as I listened to him let out a slight laugh before asking where I was at.

"I'm at Cinnamon's condo."

"Condo?" he asked, causing me to shake my head back and forth because I'd just run my mouth that damn fast. Maybe he wouldn't catch on or say anything, I thought to myself before he told me to send him my location. After thinking about it for a few minutes, I went ahead and sent my location and then began packing a bag. And thirty minutes later, he was calling, saying he was outside.

"I see you brought a bag," he said as I jumped into his truck while throwing my bag in the back seat.

"Boy, please. It's not what you think. You know I don't do that staying-the-night shit," I went on to say, causing him to start laughing.

"Yeah, we'll see," he said, and for the next forty-five minutes, we talked until we were pulling up to his gated mansion and walking inside. "Let me get that bag," I said as we walked upstairs to his room, where I walked toward the bathroom, but before shutting the door, I turned to face him. "I'll call you in when I'm ready for you," I said right before shutting the door and taking everything out of the bag that I needed. Then ran a hot bubble bath in a tub that looked like five people could fit in it, lit some candles, and threw some rose petals from some flowers I'd bought earlier for myself inside the tub. Then I rolled three blunts inside Backwoods and placed them on the edge of the tub.

Once I was done, I hooked my iPhone up to the speakers and put my playlist on before grabbing a robe that was hanging not too far away and laid it out for him to put on once he got out of the tub, although I had no real plans on having sex with Markese. I cared about him enough to try to ease his mind, and I was hoping this would work. Besides, this might be the first and only time I would ever get to do something nice like this for him, I said to myself right before hitting the lights and opening the door. Where I spotted him sitting on the bed smoking a blunt. That was, until I waved for him to come inside, and moments later he was getting up and walking toward the bathroom. I could tell by his facial expression and his big-ass smile that he hadn't been expecting me to do no shit like this for him, I thought to myself as I listened to him say I didn't have to do this for him.

"I know I didn't," I said, taking the blunt out of his hand and hitting it a few times as I took off his chains before going underneath his shirt and taking it off as well. "When I get back, I expect you to be inside the tub," I said as I sat his chains on the counter before leaving to get dressed in my robe and to get the wine glasses, the Dom P, and a bucketful of ice. Once I returned, he was sitting in the tub smoking the rest of his blunt while listening to Usher's "Can U Handle It?"

6

MARKESE (A VISIT FROM THE PAST)

"Pussy-ass niggas," I said out loud as I hit my blunt and listened to the news report talk about them niggas we cut up a few days ago. That was, until my phone began to ring with Malik asking if I had seen the news and telling me to leave all our bitches at the crib. After hitting both Zilla and Choppa up, I headed out for the strip club. I had just pulled up and was about to hit Stonie up when two police cars and a detective pulled up behind me, causing me to put the phone down. I knew these muthafuckas would be coming, but got damn, not that quick, I said to myself as I watched this black Mr. Clean–looking–ass nigga walk up to my truck and ask me to step out.

After he told me i was being taken down for questioning, I was placed in handcuffs and taken down to Cook County. When I walked in, I spotted my nigga Zilla sitting off to the side ignoring the officer who was asking him for all his personal information. After I sat for almost two and a half hours telling the detective who was questioning me to eat a dick, me, Zilla, and Choppa were released and told by our lawyer to wait in the all-black SUV she had for us parked down the street while she got Malik released.

"Aye, fam, I don't know how long Malik plans on letting this shit play out, but I got a feeling we're going to have to dirt that hoe-ass nigga

Detective Brown sooner than later," Choppa said as we got inside the SUV.

"Ain't no feeling. Or maybe we are going to have to dirt that nigga," Zilla said as I shut the passenger-side door and began looking out the side mirror for any sign of Malik.

"Yeah, something going to have to shake, and fast," I said, still looking out the mirror. And twenty minutes later, I spotted Malik and our lawyer walking out of the building, I thought to myself as I watched Malik begin to jog toward the SUV before getting inside. I was just about to respond to the comment Choppa made to him about Detective Brown when his phone started to ring, and we had to head toward his spot. When we got there, I wasn't expecting to get caught up in the middle of his and Cinnamon's shit, but honestly, I felt where he was coming from. With all the muthafuckas out to get us, Cinnamon should have let him know that she had a therapist coming by so we could've at least checked this nigga out to see if he was who he said he was. I thought to myself as I sat in the living room watching Cinnamon walk past, ignoring me, Choppa, and Zilla when we asked how she was doing. I always thought Cinnamon was mean as shit, but got damn, shorty's something different when she's mad, I said to myself as I watched Malik walk the therapist out before heading upstairs. And a few minutes later, he came walking back downstairs with a look that I'd only seen a few times, and that was when he caught his first body and recently when Cinnamon lost the baby and the shipment got hit, I said to myself as I watched him walk right past us. And moments later we heard him breaking shit up in his office.

"Aye, fam, go holla at that nigga and make sure he's straight," Zilla said while looking over at me.

"Nah. Ima let that nigga cool off," I said as I leaned back on the couch a bit and waited on Malik. After waiting for about thirty minutes, I stood up to go check on him, but before I could make it out of the living room, he came walking down the hall.

"Let's go," he said, and I walked back to where I had been sitting and grabbed both of my phones and headed toward the door, where I came face to face with Stonie. I ain't going to stunt. Seeing shorty caught me by surprise. A nigga had to do a double take when I saw how good she was looking in that Louis Vuitton she was rocking, and her ice was hitting just as hard as mine, I thought to myself as I continued to stare her down, because something about her was different. Shorty had a glow about her that I hadn't seen before, I said to myself as I asked her what was up, because she had texted me the other day saying hit her up when I got time, I thought to myself as I listened to the bullshit-ass answer she was giving me. It wasn't that I didn't think Stonie cared about a nigga. I just knew deep down that wasn't what she wanted, and I could tell by the way she looked that it was something else. But I couldn't force her to tell me, and I damn sure wasn't about to beg her to, I said to myself as I listened to one of them niggas blow the horn for me to come out. After telling her I'd hit her up later, I walked out and hopped into the back of the SUV, and we took off for the strip club. Once we got to the strip club and in Malik's office, I took a seat and rolled a blunt as I thought about Stonie and the conversation we'd just had. But I snapped out of my thoughts when Malik's office door opened and Dominique came walking in.

"Wassup, fam," I said as I blew out some smoke from the blunt while giving him some dap.

"Same shit, different day," he said, turning toward Choppa and giving him some dap before Malik began talking.

"All right, y'all. Ain't shit changed. We still going to keep going along with the original plan until this shit's over with. The only thing different is the case that was pending against us was thrown out this morning," he said, causing everybody in the room to let out a breath of relief.

"About got-damn time," Choppa added as he threw his dreads back to get them out of his face.

"With this case out of the way, we can open the shop back up, but we're going to go about it a different way. Just because we don't have an open case doesn't mean we're not still being watched or that the feds won't try to fuck with us because of that nigga Detective Knight," he went on to say before Zilla butted in.

"Speaking of detectives, what are we going to do about that nigga Detective Brown? Something tells me we're about to have some problems with that nigga, fam."

"Shit, we already got problems. But we're going to do the same thing we been doing—letting shit unfold and play out. Everybody's days are numbered. Speaking of that, Dominique, I need you to take that trip to Miami tonight and pick that package up for me," he said, and Dominique gave him a head nod letting him know he got it. "Good looking on that other package," Malik said in reference to the bitch who paid the bond for them niggas we killed. I was sure Dominique offed her ass, I said to myself as I continued to listen. "Y'all already know I ain't stopping until everybody that was involved is body bagged, so expect the feds to keep picking us up every time a body pops up. Eventually they'll get tired of fucking with us, and by that time, we'll have them for harassment. In the meantime, we're still playing that role like we're legit businessmen. So show up to work every day. Markese, Ima run the strip club tonight. It's a birthday bash going down, and I need to be here he said as I ashed the blunt and then gave him a head nod. "I'll have us a new trap house by Monday and a new route to take. Until then, everybody already knows our main priority is that hoe-ass nigga that responsible for all this shit," he said, referring to our father. "We gonna keep taking everybody out until we reach him. I'm sure by now he knows about them niggas we body bagged, and once Dominique picks up that next package, shit's really going to hit the fan. I know I don't have to tell y'all niggas to stay on your p's and q's. Y'all already know what we're up against," he went on to say as he put the end of his blunt out before reaching for a bottle of Hennessey and downing it like it was water, I thought to myself as I shook my head back and forth.

I knew, whether Malik wanted to admit it or not, he was going through it. But knowing him, he would never show it or admit it, I said to myself as I watched him continue to drink from the bottle.

After going over the rest of the plans and talking for a few hours, I posted up at the strip club until it was about 1:00 a.m. I was just about to head downstairs and grab my favorite white bitch but decided not to. I had a lot on my mind, and it was only one muthafucka I wanted to be around, and that was Stonie, I said to myself as I sat in Malik's office and rolled a blunt before heading downstairs to let him know I was heading out. Once I got outside to my truck, I fired up my blunt and called Stonie. And to my surprise, she answered. After telling her I'd be there to get her, I headed toward the address she'd given me. When I pulled up, I noticed it was Cinnamon's old place. I thought shorty had gotten rid of her spot, I said to myself as I pulled up and parked and then waited on Stonie.

Once she was in the car, we headed to my spot. When we got there, I wasn't expecting her to go all out for me the way that she did, I thought to myself as I stood there looking around the bathroom at all the candles she had lit that sat around the tub and on the floor, the blunts she rolled that sat on the edge of the tub, the red rose petals that floated on top of the water, and the robe she had laid out for a nigga. I'd be lying if I said seeing all the shit she did for me didn't make me feel some type of way, especially when I never had a bitch go out of her way to do something like this for me, I thought to myself as I thanked her. But at the same time, I told her she didn't have to do all this shit for a nigga. But she stopped me in the middle of my sentence as she took the blunt that I had been smoking out of my hand and began hitting it a few times before blowing the smoke right in my face, causing me to let out a little laugh as I watched her hold the blunt with just her lips as she took off my chains as well as my shirt before handing me the blunt back and telling me to be inside the tub when she got back. Then she left me standing there in my thoughts, still smoking on my blunt.

Once I was fully undressed, I walked over toward the tub and got in. "Got damn, this shit is hot as hell," I said out loud as I slid down into the tub while laying my head back on the pillow that sat behind me, and moments later, Stonie was walking in with a short silk pearl robe on and a bottle of Dom P with two wine glasses. After pouring us each a glass, she sat behind me with just her feet inside the tub and began giving me a massage as I listened to her sing bits and pieces of the Usher song "Can U Handle It?," which was playing in the background, and I reached out for one of the blunts she had rolled and lit one before hitting it a few times.

"Here," I said as I tried to pass her the blunt, but she turned it down.

"Nah. That first blunt is all yours. You need it more than I do," she said as I continued smoking the blunt.

"Aye, for real though, Stonie, you know you ain't have to do all this shit for a nigga. I'm still shocked that you went out your way to do all of this for me, seeing that every time I look up, you disappear on me," I said as I listened to her take a deep breath before releasing it.

"I know I didn't have to do this, but I did. I'm not doing it because I want you to feel special or to make you feel some type of way. I did it because I actually consider you a friend, and I can look at you and tell that you're mentally and physically drained. But your pride is too strong to admit that," she said, causing me to smirk. "And for the record, you can't disappear on a nigga. That's not yours," she went on to say as I ashed the blunt and thought about the shit she just said before replying.

"You're right about most of that shit, shorty. I'll give you that. But that last part—you can miss me with that shit," I said as I leaned all the way up while looking back at her sitting on the edge of the tub with her robe cracked open, with no bra on, just a thong. And for a few moments, we just sat there staring at each other. I can't tell you what it was about Stonie, but she had that certain kind of vibe that would have you questioning every bum bitch you ever came in contact with. It wasn't about the sex or how fine she was. She actually gave a nigga peace of mind. And to me, that meant more than she would ever know, I said to myself as I put the end of the blunt out.

"Get in with me," I said, still looking at her, and for a minute I thought she was going to say no until she began taking her robe off. And moments later, I was helping her take off her thong. Shit, my dick was already hard, but seeing Stonie ass naked made my shit rock hard, I said to myself as I watched her get inside the tub as I grabbed the glass of Dom P while she lit another blunt.

"You know, Stonie, a nigga wasn't trying to go MIA on you. I just had a lot on my plate, and I would rather push you away than take all my frustration out on you," I said as she passed me the blunt while saying, "Ummhuh."

"I guess I can let this one slide, seeing that I'm always the one that's going MIA," she said right before busting out laughing.

"What's so funny?" I asked as I passed her the blunt and watched her inhale the smoke.

"This should be your theme song," she said, referring to the Tupac song "Run tha Streetz," which was now playing in the background, and I started laughing with her.

"When are you going to get over the fact that I'm thug-ass nigga that runs the streets," I said as she passed me the blunt back, and I began to hit it a few times.

"I'll never be OK with that shit," she said while looking up at me with a smile. "But even thugs need love too, right?" she asked, but instead of answering her question, I bent down and began kissing her, causing her to turn around to face me as she wrapped her arms around my neck while hitting the blunt I'd placed to her lips, and she sang along to this Rihanna song, "Yeah, I Said It," that had just come on.

"I want you to homicide it. Go in slow, boy. I want you to pop it," she said, looking me in the eyes as she continued to sing. "We don't need a title. Yeah, I said. Yeah, I said it. Fuck a title," she sang into my ear as I reached out for the bottle of Dom P and began pouring it down her body while sucking on her neck and titties and then wrapped my arms around her waist and placed her on the edge of the tub where the wall could hold her up and poured the rest of the Dom P down her pussy and thighs and watched her go wild as I licked and sucked all the Dom P off her pussy.

"Oh my God, Markese," was all I kept hearing as I bent her legs all the way back and continued to suck the life out of her until her legs began to shake and she was squirting on my face.

"Oh shit, oh, oh, oh, shit," she yelled as she ran her hands through my dreads and begged me for a break, but that shit went in one ear and out the other as I planted kisses on her clitoris and listened to her take deep breaths before I picked her up while making her wrap her arms around my neck and her legs around my waist. Then walked her over to the counter and sat her down with her arms and legs still wrapped around me, I thought to myself as I looked down at her before reaching underneath her chin and making her look up at me.

I could tell by the way she was looking at me that she hadn't been expecting shit to go like this, seeing that every time we fucked, it was just a fuck. But not tonight, I thought to myself as I gently grabbed the front of her neck and began kissing her while slowly working my dick inside of her.

"Umm, baby," she said, looking down at my dick going in and out of her pussy. Shit, I was looking too. I know I hadn't fucked Stonie in a few weeks, but got damn, I said to myself as I felt how wet she was, and I continued to slowly move in and out of her as she matched me stroke for stroke. And what had been light moans were now loud ones as she wrapped her legs around me tighter, and I hit her spot over and over again, causing her head to fall back and her legs to begin shaking.

"What you waiting for?" I asked as I picked her up and hit her with the Melvin squat—you know, off the movie *Baby Boy*.

"Oh my god, Markese, my stomach," she kept saying. Every time I squatted down, I went deeper and deeper in her guts until she started shaking, to the point where I had to put her back down.

"Turn around," I said as I bent her over the counter and spread her ass cheeks apart and began eating her ass. "Stop running," I said as I smacked her ass as hard as I could and watched her body jump as she screamed "Fuck," and I continued to lick all in her ass until she was coming.

"No, no, no," she said, trying to run again, but I held her tight by the waist, causing her to grab my forearm with so much force as she screamed my name over and over again as she came, I thought to myself as I smacked her on the ass once again before standing up and looking down at her lying on the countertop, out of breath, not moving.

"You want to keep going?" I asked her as I locked eyes with her through the mirror that was in front of us and watched her nod her head yes as I took the tip of my dick and slid in and out of her. "That's not good enough," I said, going deeper this time before pulling out.

"Oh, shit, yes," she said in a low whisper.

"Yes what?" I asked as I slid back in and slowly began stroking her before pulling back out again and slapping her ass hard, causing her to raise up a bit.

"Yes, I want to keep going," she moaned out as I slid back in and began slowly fucking her as she threw her ass back and made her ass cheeks jump at the same time, I thought to myself as I watched her through the mirror the whole time. "Look at me, Stonie," I said, and she tried to look back at me, but I dug deeper, causing her to let out a scream I'd never heard before as she tried to place her hand on my stomach, but I moved it out of the way as I leaned down and told her to look up and not to take her eyes off me as I hit her spot over and over again. I could feel her pussy muscles begin to tighten up as her eyes began to roll.

"What did I say?" I asked as I smacked her ass hard back to back, causing her to look at me before I told her she was mine forever in her ear, and moments later we both came together, and I was picking her up and carrying her to the bed, where she wasted no time falling asleep on my chest.

I'd be the first to say I never thought I would make love to no bitch. But Stonie wasn't just a bitch to me. Shorty was definitely more than that. I just didn't know what that was, I said to myself as I watched her lie there asleep, knowing that if I hadn't fucked her to sleep, she would be trying to up and leave a nigga, I said to myself before falling asleep feeling like I had everything I'd never thought I would want. That was, until a nigga woke up to a text message that read "I'm pregnant."

Amanda / restaurant manager

I'll be glad when all this shit is over with, I said to myself as I entered Malik's office in hopes of finding something to give to my father to keep him off my back and from beating my mother's ass, I said to myself as I sat behind his desk and began looking through his computer in hopes of finding his next shipment or something that would lead me to it, seeing that I was the one who had found out about his last shipment.

At first, I couldn't find anything thing that led me to believe that Malik was indeed a kingpin, but the more I began to put things together, the more information I began to find. And I will say this. Malik was far smarter than I ever thought he was. The average Joe wouldn't have been able to crack the riddle he set up in order to keep muthafucks from finding his shipment, I thought to myself as I let out a breath of frustration because this person that I was being forced to be wasn't me at all. And truthfully, I didn't understand why my father hated Malik's guts so much.

Ever since I started working for him to gain information to give to my father, he had been nothing but good to me and always treated me with the utmost respect. Come to think of it, I had never seen him mad or get out of character, which was why I felt bad for everything he was going through and wished I wasn't forced to make his life a living hell—especially since I didn't know the real reason behind his and my father's beef or how he even knew him, seeing that they were almost twenty-five years apart and my father been locked away for the past twenty years. And if I had to keep it real, I wished that he was still locked away. Before he was released from prison, my mother's life and mine weren't shit like this. I couldn't believe I used to cry as a child because all the other kids had fathers and mine was locked away, and now I was wishing that he would just up and disappear, I said to myself as I continued to look through all the files that were on the computer. That was, until I looked up at the screen that was in Malik's office and saw that he was pulling up, and I hurried up and shut the computer down. "Why is he here so damn early?" I said out loud to myself as I headed out of his office and toward the front to play like I was getting things ready for the restaurant to open. But I stopped in my tracks when I saw Malik being placed in handcuffs. "What the hell happened now?" I asked myself as I continued to peep out the blinds until they were gone, then pulled my phone out and dialed my father.

"Yeah," he answered on the third ring.

"Malik was just arrested," I said into the phone.

Malik

When I pulled up and spotted Cinnamon and some nigga she had hired as her therapist in my crib, I instantly got pissed off. Not at the fact that she wanted to get healthy—I understood that—but what I couldn't understand was why the fuck she ain't run that shit by me. Here I had just gotten released from questioning to come home to a muthafucka in the house that I'm not sure is who he says he is, not to mention I'd told her more than once about telling me shit before she did it. So when I pulled up and saw that shit, I made that nigga pack up all his shit and get the fuck out. I didn't give a fuck about how he felt, and I damn sure didn't give a fuck how she felt or the way she was looking at me before she stormed off.

When I finally made it to our room, I began questioning her about how careless she was being. I nearly spazzed out when she mentioned the fact that loving me was careless and I was the reason my seed was gone. I'd be lying if I said those words didn't hit a nigga's spirit hard. I had to remind myself that Cinnamon was a woman as I hemmed her ass up against the wall in the closet and reminded her just who the fuck I was before walking out, leaving her in tears. But at that point, I could give a fuck about those fake-ass tears or any hurt feelings that she had. I'd been putting up with Cinnamon's attitude and mood swings for the last month only because I knew what she been through. But shorty had another thing coming if she thought I was about to let that shit slide.

Had she been anybody else, I would have broken her fucking jaw for disrespecting me like that. I was beyond shitty to the point I where started breaking shit up in my office just to release all the anger I had built up inside me. After finally calming down a bit and getting to the strip club, I went over the next part of the plan with everyone and sent Dominique down to Miami to pick up a package that I'd been having him keep a close eye on for the past couple of weeks. After grabbing my truck from the restaurant and reassuring Amanda that everything was good in regard to me being taking into custody, I headed over to my other house no one knew about except for Markese and Dominique.

When I got there, I rolled a blunt and downed a fifth of Hennessey—like I wasn't already tipsy from the drinks I was having at the strip club, I thought to myself as I began replaying everything Detective Brown had said to me in the interrogation room. It was one thing that nigga said that stuck out to me the most. He mentioned something about my restaurant truck going missing the day before the shooting. How would he know that my shipment got hit or that it was my truck? I thought to myself as I hit the blunt a few times before exhaling the smoke. I wasn't a dumb nigga and would always be able to read between the lines. I knew for a fact that the truck that got hit couldn't be traced back to me or the restaurant. Any truck I used to bring in drugs was registered in someone else's name, and that truck was registered to a muthafucka who was no longer living. So I knew for a fact that was not how he had found out, I said to myself as I continued to smoke my blunt and plot on my next move, because it damn sure had to be one of my best moves.

After I sat and went over everything, it was going on 11:00 p.m., and I had to get ready to head back to the strip club. One of the local rappers had bought the club out for the night, and I had to be there to make sure shit ran right. Once I was dressed, I headed out to the club. To my surprise, Cinnamon never tried to call a nigga. Not once. I knew how I felt about her, but I also knew if shit didn't get better between us soon, I was going to have let shorty go, I said to myself as I continued to drive until I reached the club. When I pulled up, it was 1:00 a.m., and the line was wrapped around the building. I stepped out of the car and walked up to the door.

"Wassup," one of the security men working the door asked as he moved out my way and let me in.

"You already know. Same shit, different day."

"I already know," he went on to say as I walked inside and through the crowd of people, where I spotted Markese getting ready to leave. After talking with him, I headed upstairs to my office, where I rolled a blunt and placed a call down stairs for Honey to come to my office. When she made it there, she was ass naked with nothing on, I thought as I reached into a drawer for a stack of ones, and I lit an already-rolled blunt and then began walking toward the bar, where I grabbed another bottle of Hennessey before taking a seat so she could dance for me. Not even ten minutes into the dance, I was asked to come downstairs. When I got down there, the nigga who was renting the club out began bitching about security not letting the rest of his people in, due to capacity. After walking over toward security and reassuring them it was coo to let only those few people in, I headed back toward my office. But before I could make it all the way there, I ran right in to Tina. I had to do a double take to make sure that was her. I haven't seen shorty since I got with Cinnamon, I said to myself as I watched her walk closer to me.

"Well, if it isn't Malik," she said with a smile. "For a minute I didn't think you stayed in Chiraq anymore," she said over the loud music, causing me to smirk at the comment she'd made because she knew, like everyone else knew, that I ran this city, I said to myself before replying.

"Yeah, it's good to see you too," I said, ignoring her last comment.

"I doubt that, seeing that you cut me off without so much as a kiss my ass," she went on to say.

"We were never together for you to be cut off, shorty," I said reminding her that she was nothing but a fuck.

"Whatever, Malik," she started to say before Ebony's big-mouth ass came walking up.

"Girl, what are you doing, talking to this nigga after the way he did you?" she said, looking at Tina with a mug as she waited for her to respond, but I gave her one. Normally I wouldn't be so disrespectful to a woman, but this bitch was asking for it.

"Maybe because this is my club. But your bum ass already knew that, and since you got so much to say…" I said, looking over to my left as I waved for one of my security to come over. And when he did, I turned back to face her. "Aye, big Dew, throw this bitch out of my club and put her on the don't-enter list," I said right before she threw a drink in my face, causing the security to hem her ass up.

"Fuck you! And this piece-of-shit-ass club," she yelled as she was getting thrown out. But I didn't pay that shit no attention as I wiped my face with a napkin one of the bottle girls who was walking by gave me.

"Really, Malik. That was my ride home," Tina said as I continued to wipe my face.

"Well, I suggest you go catch your ride home, then, because that bitch won't ever step foot back in my club," I said, looking her dead in her eyes.

"I'm not ready to go home yet. Why can't you take me home? Aw, yeah. I forgot your bitch probably wouldn't like that, huh?" she said in a sarcastic tone.

"Look, shorty, I don't have no problem taking you home, but as far as my bitch, that ain't got shit to do with you," I said, and I could tell my response hurt her feelings. But I didn't give a fuck. No matter how I felt about Cinnamon at the moment, I wasn't about to let the next bitch know shit between us wasn't good, I said to myself.

"So are you taking me home or not?" she asked, bringing me out of my thoughts.

"Yeah, but it won't be until after the club closes and I count all my paper," I said, and for the next two hours, I waited for the club to end and then counted all the money I had made for the night before heading back downstairs, where Tina was waiting for me.

"All right, let's go," I said as I watched her stand up while pulling her dress down a bit before we headed to the car. I know Tina was the last bitch a nigga should be with, but truthfully, at this point, a nigga couldn't lose more than he already had, I said to myself as I jumped in the car and pulled off. The car ride to Tina's house wasn't that long. I was expecting her to ask me a million and one questions about why I had stopped fucking with her, but to my surprise, she didn't. Instead, she caught me up on what had been going on with her. I was surprised to hear that she finally had opened the nail solon she had always wanted, and I was proud of her for that. Tina had never been a lazy, bum-ass bitch. Shorty just didn't know her worth and was too easy to manipulate, which was why I could never fuck with her, I said to myself as I pulled up in front of her house.

"Thank you for taking me home, I really appreciate it."

"No problem," I said as I waited on her to get out of my car.

"You know you can come inside, right? You don't have to just leave," she said, causing me to smirk.

"You and I both know that's not a good idea. I got a bitch, and you know that," I went on to say, causing her to roll her eyes.

"Nigga, it ain't nothing like that. I just thought we could finish our conversation. Besides, I been there, done that," she said as I let out a little laugh before cutting the car off. And moments later, we were walking inside and she was pouring me a glass of Hennessey as we finished our conversation. After about the fourth glass, I was on another level. I was already drunk from the shots that I'd been taking all day, so these four glasses sent me over the edge.

"You know, Malik, I really do miss you, even though we were never anything serious," she said, bringing me out of my thoughts. "I actually did care about you," she said before downing the rest of her Hennessey and pouring herself another glass. "You want another one?" she asked, holding the bottle up in the air.

"Nah, I'm good," I said as I looked at the time, which now read 6:00 a.m., I thought to myself as I watched her stand up and walk toward me with the drink still in her hand, and she downed another glass before setting it on the table next to mine and pulling up her dress, exposing her ass and pussy. Tina never did wear panties, so it didn't surprise me that she didn't have any on, I thought to myself as I watched her begin unbuckling my Versace belt while pulling my dick out. But I knew better than to run up any bitch outside of mine without a condom, so when she tried to sit on my dick, I stopped her.

"Nah, shorty. You know I can't fuck you without a condom," I said, causing her let out a breath of frustration.

"You don't have one?" she asked, and I shook my head no. And I damn sure wasn't about to take one from her if she had one, I said, and moments later she was on her knees swallowing all of my seeds. "Shit," I said under my breath as I released my seeds down her throat. I had forgotten how good this bitch could suck dick. Outside of Cinnamon, I didn't know a bitch alive that make my dick spit up, I said to myself as I watched her stand up and then walk to the back of the house. Moments later, she was bringing me back a towel to wipe my dick off.

After cleaning myself off, I told shorty I'd hit her up later, then I headed back to my other spot to shower. When I got there, it was well past 8:00 a.m. And I knew if Cinnamon hadn't tried to call me before, she damn sure was about to blow a nigga's phone down after l allowed the sun to beat me home, I thought to myself as I ran upstairs and placed my phone on the charger before hopping into the shower. And ten minutes later, I was out, and my phone was blowing up nonstop with text messages and voice mails from Cinnamon. I was just about to call her back when my phone began to ring.

"Wassup," I said as I snatched a jump suit off the hanger and put it on. "What I yelled into the phone as I listened to Dominique on the other end tell me he just touched down in the city, but that my mother had the package I sent him to get last night. After telling him I'd meet up with him in an hour, I call Markese.

"Wassup, fam? Where you at?" I asked as I threw a pair of Timbs on.

"At the spot. Why? Wassup?"

"Meet me at my house. I'm on the way there. That package I sent fam to get—somehow it got delivered to mama," I said.

"What? How the fuck that happen?" he asked through the phone in a confused tone.

"I don't know, but we're about to find out," I said as I stuck the .45 in my waistband.

"All right. Give me about hour and some change. I got to take Stonie back to Cinnamon's old spot," he said, causing me stop in my tracks and to ask what spot he was talking about.

"You know, the condo I met you at a few times," he said, and I nodded my head up and down as if he could see me.

"All right," I said as I hung the phone up and headed out to see just what the fuck this nigga was talking about, because last time I checked, Cinnamon had gotten rid of her condo when she moved in with me, I said to myself as I continued to drive until I reach our house. Once I pulled up and parked, I headed inside and straight for our room. When I didn't see any sign of her, I began yelling her name to see if she was somewhere else in the house, but I stopped when I spotted her engagement ring sitting on the dresser not too far from where I was standing. "What the fuck," I said out loud as I picked up the ring and then began calling her cell phone to see where the fuck she was at. But I got no answer, and that shit pissed me off even more than I already was, I thought to myself as I walked to her side of the closet to see if any of her shit was missing. Once I saw everything looked the same, I called her again, and this time she answered.

"What?" she answered with an attitude.

"What the fuck you mean what? And where the fuck you at? You don't see me calling you. And why the fuck is your engagement ring off your finger?" I asked and listened to her laugh out loud.

"You're a real fucking joke, Malik. Why the fuck would I wear a ring for a nigga that can't even come home or answer the phone when I call?" she yelled before hanging up in my ear and leaving me to wonder if our relationship was at an end.

7

YVETTE (TABLES TURN)

It had been a week since the unexpected visit from Carlos, and I knew it was only a matter of time before he came for me or Mariah, I thought to myself right before shooting this old Puerto Rican man in the neck with a Royal Blackheart tranquilizer gun and watching his body fall to the ground before dragging it off to the side.

You see, I had every intention of telling Mariah about who her real father was, but it would be on my time. And as far as Big Malik went, let's just say every day was a step closer to killing his bitch ass, which was why I took this trip to Miami. Big Malik was expecting me to hit his warehouse where he kept all his drugs and money, but I knew better than to play the same game that he was playing, which was why I went and picked up a valuable key player in his operation. You would think that he would have at least learned something in all those years of me fucking him over, but I guess not. Not only was I using this muthafucka to get Big Malik's attention, but my son's attention as well.

Once I saw that he had killed the two men involved in the shooting, I knew he would be coming for this muthafucka next, seeing that he was one of the people I'd listed in the file that I gave him after the shooting. I knew my son well enough to know he would take the bait whether we spoke or not. It's all a part of my plan, I said to myself as I took a seat in one of the chairs that sat not too far from the door and listened to Porsha tell me through the earpiece I had in that Dominique was approaching the house, I thought to myself as I sat and waited for him to walk in. And moments later, he was entering the house wearing all black, with a Glock that had a silencer on it, I said to myself as I watched his facial expression change at the sight of me sitting off to the side not too far from the body he had been sent to get.

"Come in and take a seat," I said right before Porsha walked in, causing him to turn around to see who was coming through the door before turning back to face me with a smirk.

"I should have known one of y'all was around. Getting in here was just too easy," he said, walking closer as he stepped over the old man's body before taking a seat across from me while asking, "What were we doing here?"

"I think you already know the answer to that question," Porsha said. "But the real question is, Why do you feel the need to be looking into shit that has nothing to do with you?" I asked in regard to me and Porsha's past.

"Same reason y'all felt the need not to tell us what we were really up against," he said boldly, causing me to smile a bit because his attitude was just like my sister Candace—ruthless and blunt, I said to myself as I listened to Porsha tell him our past didn't concern him or anyone else before I added my two cents, changing the conversation.

"Look, I'm going to make this real short and quick because I have a flight to catch, and I'm sure you do too, seeing that you won't be returning with him," I said, looking over at the man who was still lying out cold on floor. "Tell Malik to stop interfering with what I got going on. I gave him that information so that he would know what he was up against," I said, lying, knowing that once Malik heard that, I would be one phone call away, I thought to myself as I stood up. "In the meantime, stop digging for shit that has nothing to do with you. I'm sure by now you know how deep this shit can get, and before you tell my son what's going on, leave that for me to do. Last thing I need is for any of my kids to find more out about me from someone else in between that time. Stay out my way, and I'll do the same," I said before walking over toward the old man and grabbing him by his legs as Porsha grabbed his arms, and then we headed out to the car and drove to the private jet and got inside to head back to Chicago.

"You think it's going to work?" Porsha asked, causing me to snap out of my thoughts as I plotted on my next move.

"What you think?" I asked as I watched her lean back a bit.

"I guess only time will tell," she said as the jet took off, and a few hours later, we were landing in Chicago and stepping off the jet.

"I'll meet back up with you in a few hours," I said to Porsha as I helped her get the old man's body in her car to be taken back to the underground shop we had.

"All right. Be safe," she said before hopping into the all-black Dodge and pulling off as I got inside the all-gray tinted BMW I had parked on the side and pulled off toward the inner city. But before I could reach the tolls, my phone began to ring, and it was Malik, I thought to myself as I cracked a smile. "Right on, Q," I said out loud, as if he could hear me, before answering the phone and listening to him calmly ask me where the fuck his package was at. After I told him I'd meet him at his restaurant, I hung up and headed there while plotting my next move the whole ride there. When I pulled up, I noticed that they were kind of busy, I thought to myself as I popped the trunk, grabbed an all-black duffel bag out, and then walked inside, where I was greeted by a young lady at the door. After telling her I was there to see my son, I continued to walk toward the back, where his office was. On the way there, I ran into another young lady, and if looks tell a story, hers were saying she had just seen a ghost, I said to myself as I cracked a smile and continued to walk until I reached Malik's office. Then I knocked on the door and waited. And moments later, my son Markese was answering the door.

"Well, hello to you too," I said, pushing my way past him.

"'Sup, Ma," he went to say as he shut the door behind me. I'd be lying if I said seeing both my sons didn't warm my heart, but this wasn't a personal visit. It was a business meeting, one that neither of them would or could afford to turn down, I said to myself as I watched my son Malik get up from behind his desk.

"Out of all place we could have met, you chose to meet here," he said as I placed the bag on his desk.

"Hello to you too, and we both know if I chose to meet here, it's a reason behind it. Must I remind you I've been doing this shit way before you were even thought of," I said while never breaking eye contact with him.

"All right, you here now. So where's he at?"

"Safe and hidden until I say different," I said, causing him to rub his hands across his face out of frustration.

"So why the fuck are you here, then? I don't have shit to say to you," he said, causing me to walk up on him.

"Just because things between us went left doesn't mean i still won't bust your ass, so I advise you to choose your next words wisely, son," I said before changing the conversation. "I know you're not slow, so read between the lines. If or when you do plan on opening the shop back up—because I know you're planning on it—I have a place that will work for you. It's out of the way and off the radar," I said while walking over to the bag, pulling out a brick, and sitting it on the table. "When you're ready, give me a call. I won't wait forever, and as far as that package, he's all yours when the time is right. I can't have you running around fucking up my plans thinking it will mean something, because it won't. In the meantime, I trust that you have this shit under control," I said before looking over at Markese, who seemed to be in his own world. That was, until I called out his name. "I know I don't have to tell you this, but I will anyways. Take care of your brother," I said, looking back over at Malik. "He's hurting right now, and a hurt man isn't good for nobody," I said, never breaking eye contact with him because I knew my son, and I also knew that everything he'd been through was changing him for the worse, I said to myself before telling both of them that I loved them. Whether they said it back or not, I meant it and always would. "Oh, and Malik, take care of Cinnamon. You don't want to lose a good woman, and if I know you like think I do, you've probably been spending more time plotting than you have with her. And after everything she's been through, she needs you the most right now," I said before walking out and right past the young lady, who seemed to be starstruck when she saw me earlier, I thought to myself before walking out of the restaurant.

"One down, one to go," I said as I got inside my car and headed to the hotel I'd been staying in for the past two days just to keep everything on my end straight, I thought myself as I stepped off the elevator toward my suite, where I used my room key to open the door and then walked inside.

"Time's up," I heard a voice say as I cut the lights on and came face to face with Carlos. I had known it was only a matter of time before he popped up on me again, which was why I had gotten this room, I said to myself as I walked around the suite and over to the bar, where I poured a shot of Patron before walking over to where he was sitting, smoking a cigar without a care in the world.

"What did you think, Yvette? I wouldn't come back?" he asked in his thick accent.

"I knew you would be here, just like you knew I wasn't about to have Mariah contact you. You and I both know right now is not the time to tell her the truth. At least allow me to see my plan all the way through," I said as he blew smoke my way.

"Which is?" he asked as he moved his hand a bit for me to explain the plan.

"Big Malik only cares about one thing. Well, two," I said as I shrugged my shoulders. "His main focus right now is me, and after the move I just made, he will have no choice but to act on it. And when he does, I'll kill him. After that we can discuss Mariah. Until then, I have a proposition for you," I said, causing him to laugh.

"You have a proposition for me?" he asked, still laughing. "I'd love to hear that," he said in a sarcastic tone.

"I want you to plug my son in. He's going to need a shitload of product at a fair price," I said as I poured a shot of Patron.

"And what makes you think I would want to do that?" he asked as he ashed his cigar.

"Because if you don't, I'll kill the muthafucka who started all of this shit, and you and I both know I could give a fuck about how you feel or the consequences that are going to come with it. I think we both know by now that I'm good at what I do, and my sister is even better. So that security you have protecting that bitch won't mean shit if we have to go that route," I said as he leaned up a bit to put his cigar out.

"You know where I'm from, we don't do well with threats," he said, looking back up at me.

"And you know where I'm from, we don't make threats. We make examples," I went on to say. And for a minute, I just stared at him, hoping like hell he wouldn't make me dirt his ass in this suite—that was, until he got up and moved closer to me.

"You know, Yvette, I never understood why I love you so much, especially after all the hell you've put me through," he said, causing me to look away. But he just ended up turning my head back around to face him. "But now I know why we're one and the same. No matter how much you try to deny it, you know like I do when this is all over and done with where you're going to be at," he said as he rubbed the side of my face with the back of his hand, sending chills down my body. And before I knew it, we were making love in more ways than I could imagine. And if there ever was a time when I felt like my heart was homeless, let's just say I felt at home today.

Stonie
Waking up this morning next to Markese only confused me and made me reconsider my decision on getting an abortion. When I came over last night, I wasn't expecting him to make love to me the way he had or for me to fall asleep in his arms, considering that was one of my main rules, I thought to myself as I paced back and forth in the bathroom as I contemplated whether or not if I was going to tell Markese about the pregnancy. "I should have never fucked that nigga," I said under my breath, because before he hit me with that dope dick, I was good. My mind was made up. And now I was right back at square one, confused, I said to myself before walking over toward the sink and brushing my teeth.

Once I was done, I headed toward the room, where I spotted Markese sitting in a chair smoking a blunt while watching *The First 48*, I thought to myself as I watched him wave for me to come over. Once I was close enough to him, I sat on his lap and began rubbing my hands through his dreads.

"You need a touch-up," I said, causing him to let out a light laugh as he passed me the blunt.

"What you think I got you here for, shorty?" he asked with a smile.

"I'm here because you need a friend, not because you need a hairstylist," I said In-between hitting the blunt.

"When you going to stop fronting like you don't fuck with a nigga when I know you do, ma? You could be anywhere else, but look where you at," he said while looking around as if someone else were in the room. "You're here with me. I know you got some type of feeling for a nigga because despite all that disappearing shit you be on, every time I call, you was always there for a nigga. I'm not asking you to be my bitch. I'm just asking you to stop acting like you ain't got feeling for a nigga, because I can tell by the way we fucked last night that you do," he said, causing me to flash back on the night before and to get horny all over again, I thought to myself. But I snapped out my thoughts when he said, "Pass the blunt." I passed him the blunt in between my laughs before responding to what he said.

"Markese, I never said that I didn't feel some type of way about you, but me telling you how I feel won't change shit. You're still going to be the same nigga that has a thousand and one hoes. You're still going to run the streets, and you're still going to place your pride in front of everything. So it's pointless," I said as he nodded his head up and down. "I enjoy when I'm with you, whether it's an hour or a whole day, because when we're together, we're in our own world. But I'd be playing myself if I tried to make us anything more than what we are. And truthfully, I don't need no title to understand what we have. I don't want to fuck up a good thing to try to get something better. I love us the way that we are, and let's not talk about disappearing when you just did the shit to me," I said while turning around so that I'd be facing him, and then I wrapped my arms around his neck as he finished smoking the blunt.

"More than half of that shit makes sense, so I can understand where you're coming from," he said as I bent down to suck the smoke out his mouth. "But the least you can do is spend my birthday with a nigga," he went on to say as I released the smoke. After he told me his birthday was a few days away, I agreed to spend the whole day with him.

I was just about to suck the skin off his dick when his phone started to ring, and I could tell by the conversation he was having that it was Malik. I damn near froze up when he mentioned Cinnamon's condo. Hearing him telling Malik that was where he had to take me had me regretting having him pick me up from there. Last thing I wanted Cinnamon to think was that I had run my mouth, because I hadn't. I just knew I had to hurry up and tell her before Malik could, I thought to myself as I raised up off him and headed toward the bathroom, where I started the shower. "Markese," I yelled out, but when I turned around, he was standing right behind me, ass naked, dick hanging, I thought to myself as I began smiling. "I was just about to ask you for something to wear home," I said as he walked up on me and began taking my robe off while opening the shower door, where I began riding his dick like I was auditioning for a cowgirl role.

After I fucked him and got dressed, he dropped me back off at Cinnamon's place and told me he would be back to get me later, I thought to myself as I walked inside the condo and up the stairs, where I spotted Cinnamon smoking a blunt, looking like her old self before she went into depression. Fine and sharp-ass shit, I said to myself before she asked me where I'd been.

Cinnamon

I'd be lying If I said I didn't feel bad or regret the last words I said to Malik yesterday or that I didn't want to fix things and make it right between us, but when he didn't come home last night or answer any my calls or text, that shit quickly went out the window. I don't give a fuck what happens between us; I'd never stay gone all night no matter how mad I was at him. I spent most of my night worried sick and praying to God that he was OK because I would never be able to forgive myself if something did happen to him and my last words were "You're the reason for our unborn child not being here and for me almost losing my life."

At the time, I wasn't thinking straight. And truthfully, I just wished that I could take those words back, but I couldn't. No matter how shit played out between me and Malik, I vowed to never say anything hurtful to someone I loved again, because you never know—those might be your last words. But I can say this little stunt Malik pulled not coming home last night gave me the boost I needed and reminded me who the fuck I was, because for the last month, all I'd been doing was moping around crying, not giving a fuck about how I looked or nothing. But today, all that was going to change, I thought to myself as I stood in my condo looking in the mirror with a smile on my face. For the first time in a month, I actually looked nice. I was Dolce and Gabbana down with an iced-out Rolex that Malik had bought me for a Christmas gift, my Cuban-link chain that was hitting harder than the sun, and I was loving the quick weave Stonie had done for me last week. Speaking of Stonie, where the fuck is that bitch at? I asked myself as I walked back toward the living room, where my phone was now ringing.

Once I was close enough to see who was calling, I let out a slight laugh. "Now this nigga wants to call me back," I said out loud to myself as I let Malik's phone call ring all the way through before taking a seat on the couch and turning the TV on. I didn't have shit to say to Malik and wasn't about to play these games with him. I learned a long time ago to never be a tit-for-tat type of bitch, I said to myself as I began to look for something to watch on TV but stopped once I noticed I didn't have cable or internet—that was, until my phone began ringing again, and this time, I answered it. "What?" I said into the phone, and I listened to Malik on the other end ask me a million and one questions. His last question made me laugh, I thought to myself before telling him he was a joke and hanging up the phone. I wasn't about to let Malik reverse psychology on me or make me feel bad for taking off my engagement ring.

What the fuck do I look like, wearing a ring for a nigga that can't even come home? Most bitches would have taken their ring off when they almost lost their life, I said to myself as I reached into my Chanel bag and pulled out a sack of weed along with some Backwoods and began rolling a blunt. I was half way done rolling my blunt when Chyna called asking where I was at. After telling her to meet me at my condo, I lit my blunt and sent Stonie a text message asking where she was at as I hit blunt a few times. "Got damn," I said in between my coughs, because the blunt was hitting hard—a little too hard, I said to myself before I heard the front door open. And moments later, Stonie was walking up the steps with a glow about her that I hadn't seen before, I thought to myself as I hit the blunt and asked her where she had been, because her car was parked out front. I could tell by the way she looked that something was wrong, I thought to myself as I watched her walk over toward me and take a seat next to me.

"You look fly as shit," she said, causing me to smile.

"Thank you, and you look like you just got hit with some dope dick," I said, causing her to bust out laughing.

"Only you would be so blunt," she said as I passed her the blunt and watched her facial expression change.

"Don't be mad at me, Cinnamon," she said as she hit the blunt, and I sat up a bit to hear what the fuck I shouldn't be mad about.

"I let Markese pick me up from here last night, and this morning I heard him telling Malik he would meet up with him after he took me back to your condo. I know you said Malik doesn't know you kept this place. I just don't want you to think I ran my mouth, because I didn't, and I don't want you to be caught off guard if he asks you about it," she said while passing me the blunt.

"Girl, I'm not worried about Malik. I can handle him, and I knew the moment you walked in where you had been. Besides, who the hell do you know in Chicago well enough that you would bring them to the place you lay your head?" I asked, and I continued to hit the blunt.

"Yeah, you're right. I just wanted to tell you before shit hit the fan. And where the hell is your car at? I didn't see it parked out front."

"I parked it in the garage down the street," I went on to say before Chyna called saying she was on her way.

After I smoked the rest of the blunt with Stonie, she headed to the back to get dressed so that we could go and check out Mariah's new place.

Little did she know we were about to have a housewarming party. On my way to my condo, I stopped and got alcohol, food to cook, some house gifts for her, and, of course, a strip pole to break it in, I said to myself as I headed downstairs to open the door for Chyna, and her expression was the same as Stonie's when she saw me all dressed up.

"OK, BITCH," she yelled as she walked inside.

"What? What y'all yelling for?" Stonie asked, standing at the top of the stairs with nothing but a towel wrapped around her.

"What you mean?" Chyna asked as she walked up the steps. "I know you see my bitch standing here looking flyer than a pilot," she said, causing me to laugh and Stonie to roll her eyes.

"I thought something really happened."

"It did, bitch. You're last to get dress per-usal," Chyna went on to say, but Stonie just stuck her middle finger up as she walked toward the back to finish getting dressed. I could honestly say that I missed being around these crazy-ass bitches.

Once Stonie was fully dressed, we headed out toward Mariah's house. The ride there was longer than I expected. I don't know why she chose to live outside the city, but if she liked it, I loved it, I said to myself as I continued to drive. And a few minutes later, we were pulling up to her condo and walking inside.

"This muthafucka is nice," Stonie said while taking a look around the condo.

"Thank you," Mariah said with a smile. "What's all this?" she asked, pointing to the bags we had in our hands.

"What? You thought we were just coming to see the condo? This is a housewarming party," I said, and her smile grew bigger.

"I'm glad to see that you're in a better mood, and you look sharp ass. Fuck," she went on to say as she hugged me, and for the rest of the day, we turned up, played games, cooked, and ate, and Chyna showed us how to dance on the pole. Well, she showed them because I couldn't do much with my fucked-up arm and shoulder. By the time I left Mariah's house, it was going on two in the morning, and I was beyond drunk. Luckily, Chyna caught an Uber home, and Stonie got sick and passed out at Mariah house. When I finally made it home, it was close to three o'clock, and Malik was nowhere to be found. After undressing and taking a shower, I fell asleep, not giving a fuck if Malik didn't come home, because he was digging his own grave, one that I didn't mind throwing the dirt over.

8

DOMINIQUE (UPPER HAND)

Pulling up in Mami only to bump right into my auntie Porsha and Yvette didn't surprise me one bit, seeing that my auntie Yvette was the one who had put us onto this nigga in the first place. But what did surprise me was that they never once denied or hid the fact that they faked their deaths. My auntie Yvette's only concern was me not telling Malik before she could. I had plans on meeting with Malik so that I could hear what she had to say, but once I got word that she wanted to meet at the restaurant, that shit went right out the window.

With the feds lurking somewhere, I couldn't afford to be spotted in the same place as any of them. The last thing I needed was for them to identify me as an accomplice, I thought to myself as I sat and began putting two and two together, because once again shit wasn't adding up to me. Out of all the places my auntie could have met Malik at, she chose the restaurant, knowing that the feds had just picked him up there less than twenty-four hours ago. Not to mention that was where we were bringing in all of our drugs before that nigga the Grim Reaper hit the shipment. And if he was a smart nigga like he betray himself to be, then I was sure he was out somewhere lurking as well, I said to myself but snapped out of my thoughts when my phone began to ring.

"Wassup," I said while answering the phone.

"Meet me at the chop shop. I just got some cake mix, and this shit tastes different," Malik said into the phone, causing me to sit up a bit.

"All right. I'm on my way," I went on to say as I stood up while grabbing the keys off the table before letting Chyna know I was heading out. But she just kept doing her hair and makeup like she didn't hear me talking.

Ever since the day Chyna "called herself" trying to leave a nigga, she had been real distant and giving me the cold shoulder, even after I fucked her and ate her pussy the other day. Shorty still wasn't fucking with me. Her excuse for having sex with me was because she didn't want to get it from anybody else. Hearing that shit pissed me off to the max, especially since I knew Chyna's attitude toward a nigga was because she thought I was out here fucking off when I wasn't. Shorty damn near got me contemplating on telling her about my double life, but that was easier said than done, I said to myself as I walked out the door toward my run-down whoopie and popped the trunk.

And I came face to face with the white bitch I paid to pay the bond for that nigga we offed last week. I could tell by the way she was looking at me that she was scared for her life, but I had made a vow to myself to never off another woman after what I did to my pop's side bitch, I said to myself before shutting the trunk. She could sit there until this shit was over with. If she was still breathing at the end, then she would be free to go, I said to myself as I jumped in my Benz and headed toward the chop shop. When I pulled up, I notice Choppa, Markese, and Malik were already there, I said to myself as I walked inside and down the hall, where I spotted Zilla and Markese shooting dice.

"Wassup, fam?" Choppa asked as he gave me some dap.

"You already know, fam," I said as I looked over at Malik, who was smoking a blunt while sitting on the edge of the pool table, I thought to myself as I gave him some dap.

"Shake them dice before you roll 'em, nigga," Markese yelled out with a mean mug.

"Nigga, you just shitty. I'm getting in yo ass," Zilla said as he rolled the dice and snapped his fingers before jumping up with a smile as he picked up all the money he had just won.

"How you let this nigga beat you out ten bands?" Choppa asked while shaking his head back and forth.

"Ten bands ain't shit to me, Markese," went on to say as he stuffed the rest of his money back into his pocket before giving me some dap.

"Y'all niggas done yet?" Malik asked as he stood and unzipped an all-black duffel bag that was sitting on top of the pool table, and he pulled out a brick.

"Got damn," Choppa said as he walked closer to the pool table. "I can look at that shit and tell it's pure," he went on to say while cutting into the brick so he could taste the product, and moments later, his eyes were lit up like a Christmas tree. "Aye, fam, where you get this shit from?" he asked, still rubbing his finger across his gums.

"My mother," he said, causing Choppa, Zilla, and me to look his way.

"Yo moms?" Zilla asked with a confused look.

"Yeah, my mother. But look. Before I make any real decisions, I need to know if y'all niggas are ready to open the shop back up."

"Nigga, are we ready? I never wanted to close down in the first place," Choppa said.

"Fo sho," Markese added as he leaned up against the wall a bit as Malik put the end of his blunt out.

"All right, then. That's it. But before we get started, I got to say this," he said. "I got a bad vibe from that nigga Detective Brown."

"I been saying that shit," Zilla said.

"Yeah, I know, but this vibe is different. When I was in the interrogation room, he mentioned something about my truck going missing the day before the shooting," he said, causing everybody's face to turn up with confusion. "Y'all know like I know that shit can't be traced back to none of us, and I for damn sure know none of us ain't been talking," he said while sitting back on the edge of the pool table.

"Hell nah," Choppa said with a mean mug. "It's fed or dead this way! You already know that shit," he went on to say.

"I'm with you when you right, fam," Zilla added as he gave Choppa some dap.

"Well, that only leaves one other way. Y'all niggas ain't slow, so I know y'all can read in between the lines. Before we make any real moves, we going to continue to play with these pussies like we been doing, and when it's time to make the drop, that's going to tell us everything we already know. In the meantime, I'm getting with my moms to see if we can get a shipment in this week coming up. Choppa, Markese, and Zilla, hit y'all people up and tell them shit back up and running. And as for Detective Brown," he said while looking over at me, "Dominique, I want to know that nigga's every move, as well as that third package," he went on to say, and for the next two hours, we went over the plan as well as how we were going to bring in all the drugs. After coming up with a plot that would work, I headed back home to see if I could work some shit out with Chyna. But shorty never came back home, and by that time, I was dressed in all black and ready to grab my next victim, I thought to myself as I stood next to the door and waited for them to walk in. And seconds later, the door opened, and I was placing a towel covered in desflurane around their face, knocking them clean the fuck out.

Big Malik, a.k.a. Grim Reaper
"What the fuck you mean you don't know where he's at?" I yelled as I stood over Susie with my fists balled up.

"I don't know," she said in between her cries as she held her face in fear that I would hit her again. "I've been trying to call him all morning, but I can't get in touch with him. Something has gone wrong," she said, causing me to kneel down so that I'd be on her level as I reached out and snatched her by her hair so that she'd be looking at me.

"If I find out you trying to play me, not only am I going to kill you, but I'm going to kill his ass too, because I don't play about my fucking money. And right now, your father is missing, and he has a shitload of my money," I said while looking her dead in the eyes, because one thing about them muthafucks is, they don't lie. "Now, I suggest you book a flight and get down to Miami and find out where the fuck my money is at. I'll handle Rose from here on out. And don't think for one minute that I won't kill her ass, because I will," I said while letting go of her hair. "And before you leave, take care of our guest," I said as I headed to the front of the house.

Where I began to question if Yvette had anything to do with Susie's father going missing. Why else would he just up and disappear after all these years of us doing business together? But I couldn't see her making that kind of move. If she was down in Mami, why not just hit my warehouse? But then again, we were talking about Yvette, and that bitch was capable of doing anything. So I couldn't put this shit past her, I said to myself as I took a deep breath. At this point, all I could do was wait until Susie touched down in Miami to see what the fuck was really going on, I said to myself as I reached out for the phone that sat on the table not too far from me and dialed the only contact I had saved. And on the third ring, he answered.

"Yeah," he said into the phone.

"When the fuck was you going to tell me that Malik got arrested? And why the fuck do I got to hear this shit from another muthafucka?" I said, referring to my daughter Rose, who had called me yesterday morning saying Malik had been arrested outside his restaurant. "Must I remind you, you're in no predicament to be leaving that type of information out," I said into the phone, and I listened to him tell me he had run into a jam-up, and things were becoming more difficult on his end. "Does it sound like I give a fuck about what's difficult for you?" I yelled into the phone before telling him that if I had to hear some more shit through a third party again, his third party would be cut out. And he knew exactly what the fuck I meant when I said that shit. "Now, do I make myself clear?" I asked as I took a seat at the table and waited on his respond while sparking a cigarette as I listened to him say we had an understanding.

"All right. Now, this is what I need you to do next."

Chyna

As I got dressed for the day to meet up with Cinnamon and Stonie, I smoked a blunt and listened to the Cardi B song "Be Careful," because that's how i was feeling. "Teach me to be like you so I cannot give a fuck," I rapped along with Cardi as I continued to hit the blunt.

After the last conversation Dominique and I had, had, I'd been keeping my distance from him. Well, except for a few days ago when we fucked, but that was only because I was horny and I wasn't about to pass up that God-given head that he had. But as soon as we were done fucking, things went right back to the way they had been. I'm not the one to stunt, and I would hate to lie to myself—I do miss my man, but until he can prove to me that he's not fucking off and can explain to me why he's so fucking weird, then we don't have shit to talk about, I said to myself as I hit the blunt while ignoring him as he told me he was leaving out.

Once I was fully dressed, I headed out to meet Cinnamon at her condo. When I got there, she was fully dressed and looking like her old self. And of course I had to hype her up. Not because of everything she had been through, but because she was actually fly-ass a muthafucka today, I said to myself right before reminding Stonie that we were always waiting on her to get dressed. After waiting two lifetimes for Stonie to do her hair and makeup, we finally headed out to Mariah's house, where we got lit and fucked up all night. Well, all of us except for Stonie. She kept complaining about feeling sick, something about drinking the night before, but I knew better than that. Plus, she stopped smoking once that first blunt went around, and that wasn't like Stonie at all. If anything, she was going to be the last one up smoking.

After taking shot after shot and teaching Mariah some pole moves, I noticed that it was 2:00 a.m., and I needed to get home. And since Cinnamon was just as fucked up as I was and we were already far as hell away from home, I called a Uber to come get me and take me home. So that she wouldn't have to make any extra stops, of course, Mariah offered me to stay at her house. But I knew better than to not come home, especially when I knew I was dealing with a psycho like Dominique. I could just have Stonie or Cinnamon come get me tomorrow and take me to get my car. Once the Uber pulled up, it was damn near 3:00 a.m., and I was beyond tired. Not to mention I lived an hour away from Mariah, so the car ride there was long and slow. When we finally reached my house, I told the Uber driver let me out at the gates, and I began walking up the long driveway until I reached the door and was walking inside. But before I could shut the door all the way, I felt someone grab me from the back, and moments later I blacked out.

And now I was blindfolded and tied down, with the worst headache ever, I thought to myself as I listened to the door open and shut before feeling someone touch me. And I immediately began to panic as I cried out for help and begged whoever was in the room to let me go. And moments later, the blindfold was coming off, and I was blinking my eyes to clear out all the blurriness I was having. When I was finally able to see where I was and who was in the room, I began going the fuck off.

"What the fuck are you doing, Dominique?" I started to yell. But I stopped when he pressed a button, sending a sensation to my pussy.

"I'm in charge now," he said, turning it up another notch, causing me to let out light moans before he cut it off and took a seat in a chair next to the sex table he had me tied down to, ass naked, I thought to myself as I looked down at the sex toy he had covering my clitoris.

"Now that I have your attention, let's talk," he said with a smile. "Why do you insist on playing with me Chyna?" he asked. But I just lay there and ignored him. And moments later, the toy that was covering my clitoris came on again, but this time it was turned up higher than before.

"Oh my God," I moaned as he stood up and grabbed some clamps and clamped them on my nipples. Then he sent shocks through them, causing me to jump. "Please, baby, please," I moaned out in pleasure as he stood over me with a smirk and watched me go crazy at the feeling that the toys were giving me. "Oh shit, umm shit," I yelled out loud as I began squirting and trying to break free. But I couldn't. All I could do was lie there and let him torture me, I thought to myself as I tried to catch my breath and few seconds later, he stopped both the toys and sat back down.

"Every time I have to get up, you're going to feel something different. You may like it, or you may not," he said as I lay there, still trying to catch my breath while thinking of all the ways I was going to fuck him up once I was free.

"Now answer my question," he went on to say, bringing me out of my thoughts.

"How the fuck am I playing with you, Dominique? Look at the shit you're doing to me after you told me you wouldn't drug me again, but here I am, tied down once again. I should be the one doing this shit to you after all the shit you've been doing," I yelled as I watched him sit there staring me down with a blank expression on his face.

"So you really think I'm out here fucking off on you, huh?" he asked, causing me to look away because deep down I felt like he would never hurt me. But then again, what real nigga does the shit that he does? I thought to myself as i watched him get up.

"No, no wait! What are you doing?" I asked as I watched him grab a bucket full of ice.

"You took too long to answer my question, shorty," he said as he placed an ice cube in my pussy before turning both the nipple shockers up as well as the toy that was still on my clitoris.

"Oh, oh, oh, shit," I moaned out loud as my eyes began to roll to the back of my head. I was feeling like I was having an out-of-body experience. The nipple shockers were shocking me back to back, and the toy mixed with the ice was driving crazy. "No, no, no, baby. No," I yelled once I felt an ice cube go in my ass, and my toes began to curl. For a minute I thought I was having a seizure as I yelled louder than I ever had in my life as I let lose an orgasm, hoping like hell he would stop it, but he wouldn't. "Dom…Dom…Dominique," I stuttered as I felt myself get hit with another orgasm. "Oh, oh, shit, oh God, no," I yelled with tears in my eyes. And a few seconds later, everything came to a stop, and he was sitting back down. "Pl-ple-please," I said in a low whisper. "Please, baby, please. I can't take no more," I said with the last bit of breath I had left in me.

"Really? Because I'm convinced you like when I do this shit to you. Why else you would be walking in the house at damn near five in the morning?" he asked. "I keep telling you, Chyna, but you don't listen. A nigga don't need no other bitch, shorty. I can admit that I was wrong for the days I stayed gone too long, but before you, I didn't have nobody that I had to answer to. So when I'm out in the streets doing me, I lose track of time. But I can't have you out here thinking that you can do whatever the fuck you want, because that shit's not about to happen. And as far as me drugging you, I gave you a fair warning. You of all people should know by now that I hate repeating myself. I shouldn't have to do all this shit just to get your attention, but that's the only way I can seem to get you to listen," he said as I lay there with my legs still shaking while taking in everything he was saying. "And before you ask, don't. Because it doesn't take a rocket scientist to tell what type of nigga I am. I know you already have some type of idea in mind of what else I may be doing out there in the streets, and you're right, ma. But I'm not going to flat out tell you what you want to know. I don't need you to look at me like the weird-ass nigga you already think I am because of the lifestyle I live. All I can say is that I'm not trying to lose you, Chyna, for real. I can't promise you anything because of the way shit is set up in my life right now, but I'm going try my best to make it back home to you every night. But all this extra shit you've been on lately, you're going to have to dead that shit, shorty, for real, because I'm not that nigga that's gonna put up with that shit. Period! Now, before I let you loose, do we have an understanding, or do I need to stick them balls up your ass? And believe me," he said, looking over at the balls that were sitting on a table not too far from us, "them muthafuckas will shock you worse than them nipple clampers," he said, looking back at me. I nodded my head to let him know that I understood him clearly. Last thing I was about to do was argue with this nigga and get my soul snatched from me again, I thought to myself as I watched him remove all the toys before untying me from the sex table and picking me up.

Where he carried me to our room and started the shower while I lay on the bed and thought about everything he had just said and began taking it into consideration, although I still had questions of my own to ask. I knew my man enough to know that he was telling me the truth. Besides, I was tired of being at odds with him, especially when I didn't have any real facts to prove he was really fucking off. But I would say this: the moment I got my energy back, I was fucking him up for what he had done to me, I said to myself right before he came back into the room to get me. And moments later we were in the shower making love, on some straight Mimi-and-Nikko shit. Only thing different was I hung off one of the shower heads and not the shower pole.

9

MALIK (A CHANGE OF HEART)

I should have known when my mother went and grab my package that she had a hidden agenda of her own, I thought to myself as I sat in my pickup truck and waited on her to pull up so that we could talk. Shortly after meeting up with Dominique, Choppa, Zilla, and Markese, I hit her up so that we could discuss this new product and to see if we could get a new shipment in this week coming up. I knew with all this bullshit going on that my mother was the last person I wanted to do business with, but I'd be a fool to pass up this opportunity. After all, she was the reason why I was playing this game of chess in the first place, I said to myself as I watched an all-gray BMW pull up next to my truck. And seconds later the window rolled down, and she was waving for me to get in with her. Once I was inside the car, she wasted no time pulling off.

"Where we going?" I asked as we pulled out of the parking garage.

"Does it matter?" she asked, causing me to smirk at the comment that she just made but that quickly faded when my phone began to ring non-stop, I thought to myself as I hit the ignore button on Tina's call. Shorty had been blowing me up ever since I let her polish my dick.

"I know you can't be that dumb," my mother said, bringing me out of my thoughts and leaving me to wonder what the fuck she was talking about. "Come on, now. I am your mother. I know you like the back of my hand," she said while jumping on the interstate. "I suggest you dead that shit with whoever you call your self fucking around with before I have to do it for you," she went on to say, but I let that shit go in one ear and out the other. I wasn't here for no damn therapy session, and I damn sure wasn't about to admit to shit that she was talking about. And as far as I was concerned, whatever had happened between me and Tina was already dead, I said to myself as I leaned my seat back a bit. And for the next fifty minutes, we drove in silence—that was, until I noticed we were in the middle of nowhere. My mother must have felt the vibe I was giving off, because she spoke on it.

"We're almost there," she said as she continued to drive, and five minute later, we were pulling up to a barn that sat on acres of land, I thought to myself as I watched my mother hit a button before diving closer.

Once we were close enough to the barn, the doors opened, and we were driving in and getting out of the car. "You just going to stand there? Help me out," my mother said as I watched her move a stack of hay before reaching down and pulling on a latch that led to an underground tunnel. "Let's go," she said as she stepped down the ladder, and few second later, I was following her down the ladder.

I was expecting it to be nasty as hell when we got underground, but it was actually clean, with cameras set up everywhere, I thought to myself as we passed by a few rooms until we hit a room full of guns, knives, bombs, cameras, and computers.

"Took you long enough," my auntie Porsha said while looking over at my mother, who was taking off her trench coat as well as the two .40 Glocks she had on her.

"I got tied up, as you can see," she said, looking over at me before looking back at my auntie. "Did you grab that package?" my mother asked Porsha.

"What you think?" she asked while standing up and walking over to a door, where she opened it and exposed the old man I had sent Dominique to get and a woman who looked like she been getting her ass beat.

"Damn. What did you do to her?" my mother asked as she walked toward the closet and then knelt down so she could get a closer look at her.

"She was like that when I got to her," my auntie Porsha went on to say before my mother asked for her phone, and Porsha handed it to her.

"Before I take this tape off your mouth, I want you to listen to me very closely. You are to do exactly what I tell you to do, or I'm going to make sure that your death is one to remember. Do I make myself clear?" she asked, and moments later the woman was nodding her head yes. "All right," my mother said as she snatched the tape off her mouth. "Call Big Malik and tell him that you found your father. He's going to ask you what happened, and when he does, you're going to tell him that he's in the hospital recovering from a stroke. Hell, his old ass is older than dust anyway, so that won't be too hard to believe. He's going to ask you about his money. Reassure him that you have all the money and will be back as soon as your father is released. Make it sound believable," she went on to say as she looked through the woman's phone until she came across his name, and then she pressed the call button and placed it on speaker.

"Where the fuck you at?" he yelled through the phone, and she cleared her throat and told him exactly what my mother had told her to say. But he wasn't trying to hear none of that shit. That nigga wanted his bread, and i could feel him on that because I wanted mine too, I said to myself as I continued to listen.

"If I find out you're lying to me you, will regret it, and so will your father," he said before hanging up the phone.

"Please," she tried to say, but my mother placed the duct tape back over her mouth before she could get another word out and then stood up and shut the door back, leaving the old man and the woman in the dark.

"All right. We got less than seventy-two hours before Big Malik catches on to what's going on. Once he realizes both these muthafucks are missing, shit is really going to hit the fan," she said, looking over at me. "Now, within those seventy-two hours, we need to get this place ready for your shipment. Follow me," she said, and we walked down a hall and into another room. "This room is fully ready to go. You can cook whatever you need as well as stash anything here," she said, moving a couch out of the way and exposing a safe that would drop underground if someone tried to break into it. "I know you don't have a place to work out of, so this is yours if you want it. It's off the radar and has three main exits that lead to a getaway place if you need it. All the cameras work, and there are motion sensors all around this place. There are certain parts of the building as well as the land that are wired with explosives, so be very careful. No one will ever think twice about this place, seeing that it was never listed as a main underground tunnel. I had this place built twenty years ago, just in case I would ever need it," she said while walking over to a table. "This is a full layout of the underground tunnel. I suggest you get familiar with it. In the meantime, you have a shipment coming in next week. My plug doesn't deal with any costumers that are not looking to cop a hundred bricks or more, so that should give you an idea of what you're looking to get yourself into. Now, I know you're your own man, but if there was ever a time I thought you should listen to me, it would be now. One hundred plus keys is well over enough to keep you good for a lifetime. I can't tell you what to do or how to do it; I'm just telling you what I see best for you. My grandmother used to always tell me to pay attention to the signs and that there is always a warning before destruction. This is your warning," she said before taking a seat while letting out a deep breath.

"Last but not least, I know you don't what to hear this, but I have to tell you anyway. I never meant to lie to you or misguide you. I only did what I saw best for our family. As I told you before, my grandparents raised us to be ruthless as well as the best drug dealers and hit men alive. In the midst of all that, someone ratted us out, causing me and both my sisters to fake our deaths and become different people. In the mist of that, all my money, my bank account, and my stash spots were frozen and hit, leaving me with nothing. When I met your father, I never had real intentions of being with him. I saw him for what he was, and that was my puppet. I'm not going to say I didn't eventually fall in love with your father or love him, because I did. He gave me something that I couldn't give myself, and that was you and new life, one that would allow me to live behind the scenes. But overall, my heart has always belonged to one man and still does to this day. But because of our run-in with the law, I had to choose freedom or love, and I chose freedom. But that has never stopped me from finding ways to be with him," she said while letting out another deep breath.

"So you can only imagine how your father felt once he realized I was using him to do the things I couldn't do on my own because of who I am," she went on to say. "Once your father found out I was using him, he began plotting against me," she said and let out a little laugh. "Once I realized what he was doing, I set him up to go to prison. When he went away, I hit all the places where he hid money from me. If I had not done that, I would either be dead or in jail. And with three kids to raise, neither of them was an option for me. It was either us or him, and I chose us. You see, son, when you're tied in like I am, you don't have as many options. And the ones that you do have, you must weigh them bitches until you can't weight them anymore, even if that means losing everything and going completely broke just to buy your freedom so that you can be around to raise your kids," she said while trying to hold back a few tears. "I know what I've done was wrong, but I will never apologize for doing what was best for me or my kids. I gave your father a life that he would never have had if it wasn't for me. I can't change the past, and even if I could, I wouldn't because it made me who I am today. My life was confused and fucked up way before I gave birth to you. Had I not faked my death, I would have told you the truth a long time ago. I never wanted you to take the same road as everyone else in the family. I wanted better for you, but I see now it's in your DNA to hustle. And if I never told you this before, son, I'm telling you now.

"You've made me so proud over the years. Watching you become a kingpin wasn't what I wanted, but you've done it better than anyone I know. I guess it's safe to say you are a re-creation of your great-grandmother," she said, causing me to swallow the lump that was in my throat, because although I was still pissed off at my mother, I now know why she had to take the road she did. Did that make it right? Hell nah, but it made sense.

"So as you can see, son, I'm not perfect, and I never will be. All I can do is right my wrongs. I don't want you to be like your father, a man that's hurt, because, as you can see, a hurt man ain't good for nobody, and a man that doesn't have control over his emotions will always fail at anything he does. I can't blame your father for being pissed off at everything I've done to him, but the moment he came after you, that shit was dead. And I could never respect a man that would cross out his own seed just to prove a point. We've played with him long enough. It's time for this road that we're on to come to an end. So whatever you got planned, I advise you to put it in motion, because in the next few days, shit's about to get ugly. But the good news is, we've been playing chess while he's been playing checkers," she said. And for the next couple of hours, we went over everything, from the plans I already had to the new ones we were making together.

After talking things out with my mother and listening to her talk about Cinnamon and the loss of our baby, she dropped me back off at my truck, and I headed home. When I finally made it there, it was damn near five in the morning, and Cinnamon was asleep. For a minute, I just stood there looking at her while letting everything my mother had said replay in my mind about not losing a good woman. I knew she was right, but it was only so much a nigga could do when he had already don so much.

Markese
The last thing a nigga was trying to hear this morning when I woke up was that I might have a seed on the way by a bitch I don't give two fucks about, so you can only image how a nigga was feeling right now. Not to mention my feelings for Stonie were now getting deeper, and getting her to admit this morning that she did have feelings for me made me look at shit a lot differently. But now that I might have a seed on the way, I knew any thought I did have of us being more than what we were was about to go right out the window. I knew Stonie well enough to know she wasn't about to put up with no bitch, especially a pregnant one. I also knew better than to take the word of any bitch, so after meeting with my moms and the team at the chop shop, I headed over to the first CVS I could find and grabbed three pregnancy tests. This bitch was about to piss on every last one of these muthafuckas, I said to myself right before dialing shorty up, and on the third ring, she answered.

"Hello," she said into the phone.

"Yeah. Where you at?" I asked. After she told me she was at the crib, I headed her way as I dialed Stonie to let her know I would be there to grab her in an hour or so. But I got no answer, I thought to myself as I continued to drive until I was pulling up to shorty's spot, where I knocked on the door and waited for her to answer. And moments later she was opening the door, and I was walking inside.

"Wassup," she asked.

"What you mean wassup? You sent me a text this morning of a pregnancy test. That's what's up," I said with a mean mug as she stood there with her arms crossed.

"Yeah, I did."

"All right. Well, here," I said, reaching into the bag and pulling out one of the pregnancy tests for her to piss on.

"Really, Markese? A pregnancy test?" she asked with her face twisted up a bit.

"Yeah, really. I didn't see you piss on no stick, just like I didn't see you take that Plan B pill," I went on to say, and I could tell that comment pissed her off. But I could give two flying fucks about how she felt. It was the truth, whether she liked it or not.

"How many times I have to tell you I don't need to trap you. What the fuck can you do for me that I can't do for myself?"

"That's something you need to ask yourself. I'm not here for all that. You can either piss on the stick or not. Either way, I'm still not claiming shit till I get a DNA test," I said bluntly and boldly so that she understood exactly where the fuck we stood. I didn't trust no bitch that wasn't mine, and even if she was, I still felt like every man should have a DNA test done, I said to myself as she snatched the test out of my hands.

"After I take this test, I don't want to hear from you until it's time for a DNA test, because I ain't aborting shit," she said, walking off toward the bathroom. Where I followed and watched her open the box before pissing on the stick. "Here, let me know what it says," she said, handing me the stick before walking off toward the living room, leaving me standing there praying to God this test would come back negative. A nigga damn near had to do a double blink when the test read pregnant. For a minute, I just stood there in my thoughts. I knew deep down no matter what, if this seed was mine, I was going to do whatever I had to do to make sure he or she was good. I didn't have to be with Erica to make sure that shit happened, and I damn sure wasn't going to let this bitch play with me or my seed, I said to myself as I walked back toward the front, where she was sitting on the couch.

"If you want a DNA test, we can do one as soon as I'm ten weeks. That way, you will know sooner rather than waiting for me to have the baby. And no, I don't need your money to pay for it. As you already know, I'm well off," she said.

"All right. Well, in the meantime, if you need anything, just let me know," I said as she stood up.

"Nah. I'm good. I don't need shit from you until this baby gets here," she went on to say, causing me smirk.

"Let me make some shit real clear for you, shorty. I'm not the type of nigga that's going to let you play mind games with me or my seed, if it is mine. I know you know what type of nigga I am, so I don't mind body bagging yo ass if I need to go that route. So I suggest you let that shit sink in," I said right before opening the door and walking out, where I sat in my car for a few minutes while asking myself, How the fuck did I get caught up with this bitch? If God was going to hit me with a baby, I'd rather it be by Stonie. At least I gave a fuck about her, I said to myself as I headed to the strip club and waited for Stonie to call me back. But she never did, and when I did talk to her, it was the next morning, and shorty was speaking out the side of her neck.

Cinnamon
"Hello." I answered the phone while holding my head because of the hangover I had from all the drinking I had been doing the night before, I thought to myself as I listened to Chyna on the other end ask me could I give her a ride to her car and then looked over at the time. "Yeah. Give me a minute. I have to shower and get dressed," I said before hanging up the phone. "Oh my God. Why did I drink so much?" I said out loud to myself while rolling over and coming face to face with at least two dozen red roses.

I can't even stunt. Seeing them roses laid out next to me made my heart smile. But that still didn't change the fact that this nigga didn't come home, and that was one thing I wasn't about to overlook or forget, especially for no damn roses, I said to myself as I sat up in bed before walking toward the bathroom, where I started the shower and got inside. I allowed the hot water to hit my body as I stood under all the shower heads hoping like hell I wouldn't throw up all the alcohol that I'd drunk the night before. After showering and finding something to put on for the day, I settled on a Valentino lipstick-wave-printed dress with some thigh-high heels to match it and began getting dressed.

Once I was fully dressed, I ran the flat iron through my hair. I felt like I could have done a better job if I could raise my left arm and shoulder up higher, but fuck it, this would have to do, I said to myself as I walked out of the bathroom and over to my dresser full of jewelry and grabbed three bracelets full of diamonds and placed them on my left wrist along with a watch to match and my heart-shaped necklace that had a picture of me and Malik in the middle of it, only because it went along with the rest of my jewelry. Once I had everything on, I gave myself one last look in the mirror before grabbing my Valentino purse along with my long trench coat and headed downstairs, where I ran right into Malik. And I could tell by the way he was looking at me that he wasn't expecting me to be all dressed up, I thought to myself as I tried to brush past him like he wasn't there. But that shit didn't work, because he gently grabbed me by my arm, stopping me from walking any farther.

"So you gonna act like you don't see me standing here?" he asked, turning me around so that I was facing him. "And where the fuck you think you're going?" he asked with a slight mug, causing me to roll my eyes.

"Wassup?" Malik I asked in a voice that said, "You're irritating the fuck out of me."

"That's what i'm trying to figure out. You're all dressed up. Shit, I know we're going through some shit right now, and we got some small issues to address, but damn, can you at least tell me when you're about to leave the house? I don't know why I have to keep expressing this shit to you, Cinnamon. How am I supposed to protect you if you keep doing shit behind my back?" he asked. But I didn't answer his question. Instead, I just told him where I was going.

"Look, I'm running late, and I have to pick Chyna up. So now that you know where I'm going, I have to go," I said, but once again, when I tried to walk away, he stopped me.

"When were you going to tell me that you kept your condo? What you feel the need to lie to me for?" he asked boldly, as i thought about my response.

"Let me ask you a question, Malik, on some real shit," I said as I crossed my arms and looked him dead in his eyes. "When you didn't come home the other night, where were you?" I asked, and for the first since I'd been with Malik, he couldn't even look me in my face, I thought to myself as I watched him look away before looking back at me.

"Just answer my question," he said, causing me to smirk as well as give me the answer I needed

"I kept my condo for responses like the one you just gave me when I asked where you were at," I said before turning my back on him and walking away while trying my best to hold back the tears that were trying to come out. But I couldn't, and the moment I got to my Benz truck, I allowed them all to fall down as I laid my head on the steering wheel and cried out loud.

I didn't need a fucking psychic to tell me what my gut was saying. The moment he didn't answer my question, my women's intuition told me what was up. Up until this point, I never thought Malik was out fucking off on me. I just thought he was mad and didn't want to come home, I said to myself right before I felt my driver door open, and Malik's hands reached out and touched mine. I could tell by the way he looked at me when he saw me crying that he knew I was hurt. Besides the day I found out we had lost our baby, he had never seen me shed one tear, I thought to myself as I listened to him tell me I wasn't going anywhere until we talked. A part of me wanted to start my car and pull off, but the other part of me knew that If I didn't talk to him now, tomorrow might be too late. After wiping my tears away, I got out of the car and headed back inside the house, where I sat on the couch and watched him take a seat next to me. For a few minutes, we just sat there in silence, until he finally spoke.

"Ima keep it real with you, Cinnamon. I ain't feeling this shit at all," he said, causing my face to turn up a bit. "I know you been through a lot, being shot up and dealing with the loss of our unborn child," he went on to say as I tried to fight back the tears that were trying to fall once again. "And I know I haven't been here for you like I'm supposed to be, and I apologize for that. I also know, whether you meant what you said the other day or not, you blame me for everything that happened to y'all," he said, rubbing his hands across his face while letting out a deep breath. "Shit. Sometimes I blame myself, but being mad at each other is not going to change shit, ma. You think I'm OK with knowing that I couldn't protect my family like I should have or that my first seed is gone?" he asked while looking directly at me. "Well, I'm not. I can't wear my heart on my sleeve like you can. I can't be weak when I know you need me to be strong. You thought it was OK to throw what happened to y'all in my face like that shit was coo. Had you been anybody else, you wouldn't be sitting here right now," he stated boldly. "I told you when we first met that I wasn't the type of nigga that would try to control you, and I meant that shit. But If I ask you to do something or to tell me your whereabouts, then it's for a good reason. If only you knew half of the shit that's been going on, maybe you would understand where I'm coming from and why I don't want you in these streets alone. I'm in love with you, Cinnamon, and there ain't no stunting in that. But Ima be real with you, shorty. I can't keep putting up with this shit. We live in the same damn house, but every day we walked past each other like we're strangers," he said, causing a few more tears to drop because I knew deep down that everything he was saying was true. "I'm not trying to lose you, Ma. I told you when we first met, you would be mine for forever, and I meant that shit. But a nigga can't force you to stay in this relationship if you're unhappy. So Ima ask you one time and one time only: What is it that you want? If you wanna leave, you know Ima make sure you're straight no matter what, but if we're gonna work this shit out, then I need you to tell me now," he said as he reached out to wipe the tears that were falling nonstop.

As I tried to come up with the right words to say, but I just ended up breaking down. Here it was. I had a man who understood me better than I understood myself at times, and I'd been pushing him away when I needed him the most, I thought to myself as he reached out and began hugging me as I sobbed the words "I'm sorry" over and over again as he held me in his arms and told me everything was going to be all right.

10

STONIE (NO SECRETS, NO LIES)

Waking up this morning at Mariah's house with morning sickness left me bent over on the toilet. "I can't take this shit no more. This baby is killing me," I said out loud to myself right before the bathroom door burst open.

"I knew it," Mariah yelled as she stood in the doorway with her hands on her hips. "I knew something was up with you when you stopped smoking last night. Bitch, you're pregnant," she went on to say with a smile as I stood there trying to come up with something to say. But fuck it. There was no sense in lying about the shit.

"Yeah, I'm pregnant. But please, Mariah, I'm begging you not to say anything to Cinnamon or Chyna. Nobody knows about the pregnancy, and with Cinnamon just having a miscarriage, the last thing I want to do is bring this up to her," I said as I leaned up against the bathroom wall and held on to my stomach.

"I'm sure Cinnamon would be happy for you despite everything she's been through, but I understand where you're coming from. I won't say anything," she said before asking the million-dollar question. "So who's your boyfriend, and when do I get to meet him?" she asked with a smile, and all I could do was shake my head.

"Markese, and he's not my boyfriend. Just the nigga I got pregnant by."

"Markese who?" she asked as her facial expression began to change.

"Your brother Markese."

"What? Wait—how? When? I didn't even know you two fucked around," she said, still confused by the answer I'd given her.

"Nobody knew we were fucking around. And before you ask, no, he doesn't know. And I would like to keep it that way until I can figure out what the fuck Ima do."

"What do you mean, figure out what you're going to do? You're going to keep the baby, right?" she asked. But before I could answer the question, my silence answered it for me. "Really, Stonie?" she yelled. "You can't possibly be thinking about getting rid of it," she asked, and by that time, she sounded pissed off.

"I don't know what I'm going to do," I said while running my hands across my face. "I just can't see myself having a baby by Markese. I just can't. I mean, look at everything that happened to Cinnamon. You know just like I do, Mariah, that Markese will never leave the streets. I'm not trying to end up a single mother or have to worry about him every night and day, hoping that he's OK. And on top of that, we're not even together or in love," I said as I continued to watch her looking at me like she didn't give a fuck about the excuse I was trying to make.

"First of all, you can't compare what happened to Cinnamon to your situation, because it's different. Had my mother not lied to us, Cinnamon would have never been shot or lost her baby. All three of my brothers are more than capable of protecting their families, so you can miss me with that shit. And people who aren't together have babies every day. And how you going to say y'all not in love, but neither one of y'all took the steps to prevent this from happening? Hell, my brother must care about you, because he didn't use a condom with you, and that's his number-one rule," she said with a bit of frustration in her voice. "I don't know, Stonie, but one thing I do know is no matter what decision you make, that's something you're going to have to live with. Just make sure it's one that you can deal with. I'm not going to get involved in y'all's shit because it's not my place, but if you're not going to keep the baby, the least you can do is tell him. He does have the right to know," she went on to say before walking out and making me feel worse than I already did, I thought to myself as I took in everything she had just said as well as the conversation Markese and I had had yesterday morning.

I'd be lying if I said that after the talk we had that I didn't feel like I wanted to keep our baby, but right now I was just confused and wanted God to give me a sign, I thought to myself as I began brushing my teeth and washing my face. Once I was done, I headed toward the living room, where I picked up my phone and noticed I had missed calls and a voice mail from Markese. When I saw the voice mail he left, I decided to listen to that first before calling him back. When I pressed Play, I damn near dropped my phone as I listened to Markese and some random-ass bitch talking. The more I listened, the more pissed-off I started to get. My heart damn near broke when I heard them mention that she was pregnant, I thought to myself as I continued to listen until the end. "I can't believe this shit," I said underneath my breath as I paced back and forth, still in disbelief at the shit I had just heard. Here I was feeling bad about getting an abortion, and this nigga got a whole other bitch pregnant, I said to myself as I took a seat on the couch and let my mind wander for a few minutes before calling him.

"Wassup," he said into the phone, and it took everything in me not to mention the voice mail he had left on my phone.

"Not much," I said while taking a deep breath before finishing what I had to say. "Look, I've been doing some thinking, and I feel like Ima take a step back from you. I mean, shit between us is getting too serious—well, on my end anyways—and I don't want to just up and hit ghost on you right before your birthday," I lied. "I feel like I owe you that much. Besides, you got your hands full with enough shit," I went to say before Mariah walked into the living room.

"All right, Stonie. I'm ready to go. I had to roll a blunt after the bullshit I just heard," Mariah said, but I just ignored her as I told Markese to take care and be safe and then hung up the phone up while turning it off at the same time before he could get a word out.

"All right, I'm ready," I said as I stood up and faced Mariah.

"What's wrong?" she asked as she stood there smoking a blunt.

"Nothing at all. Just thanking God for saving me from the biggest mistake of my life," I said as I grabbed my Louis bag and coat off the couch and headed out the door with Mariah right behind me.

Once we got in the car, she drove me back to Cinnamon's place, where I rolled the fattest blunt ever and then sat in a hot bubble bath and smoked the whole thing while asking myself, How could I be so damn dumb? How could I fall for a nigga like Markese? I must have asked myself that question a million times in hopes for an answer, but I didn't have one. Just when I was about to let my guard down, God had showed me just why I needed to leave it up. But I couldn't stop feeling like no matter whether it was up or not, I couldn't change the fact that I had somehow ended up falling in love with him. And that was something only time could heal or change. I guess Cinnamon was right when she said there was no such thing as a friend with benefits, that one of us, if not both, would fall for the other. I just wish I hadn't been the one who had fallen, I said to myself as I hit the blunt and continued to try to make some sense of all this shit. But the more I thought about everything, the more my heart ached, and the more it turned colder than it already was.

Malik

The conversation me and Cinnamon had, had a nigga feeling like shit. Seeing her break down the way she did hurt a nigga's soul. I knew Cinnamon was hurting, but actually seeing it made me feel some type of way, especially since I hadn't been there for her like she needed me to. Not to mention the fact that I went and fucked off with Tina's hoe ass. All I could do was shake my head and hope like hell she would never find out, I thought to myself as I watched her get off the couch as she wiped the crust out her eyes from the nap she had taken. She had cried so much after we talked that she cried herself to sleep, I thought to myself, but I snapped out my thoughts when she said she was going upstairs to change. After sitting there in my thoughts for a few minutes, I headed upstairs, where I spotted her trying to get out of the dress she was in without hurting herself.

Once I was close enough to her, I reached out and pulled the drees down, ripping it a bit, but I didn't give a fuck. I'd rather rip the dress than to hurt her by trying to get it off, I said to myself as I stood there staring at her in that lime-green bra-and-panty set. Standing there looking at her made my dick hard, I thought to myself as I watched her reach out and begin unbuckling my belt while I took my shirt and chains off. Once I was fully underdressed, I led her toward the bed, where I removed her panties. The whole time I was taking her panties off, she never took her eyes off me—not once. I could tell by the way she looked at me and the way her body was shaking that she was nervous, I thought to myself as I watched her reach down and grab my dick and place the tip of my head inside, making me feel how wet she was.

"Shit," I said under my breath as I slowly worked the rest of my dick inside her as she dug her nails into my back while letting out light moans as I began kissing her.

"I missed you so much," she moaned out as I went deeper and deeper, trying to hit her spot without busting a nut too fast. Cinnamon had some of the best pussy I ever had, not to mention I ain't been knee deep in no pussy in almost two months, I said to myself as I went deeper and deeper. "Ummm, baby, right there. Yes, right there," she said as she wrapped her legs around my waist while working her pussy muscles at the same time.

"Shit," I said out loud before turning her around and laying her flat on her stomach, and I entered from the back and began hitting her spot over and over again as I whispered "I love you" while planting kisses on her back and neck.

"Oh my God! I love you too, baby," she moaned out as I went as deep as I could go. "Oh shit, baby. Oh shit," she screamed.

"Let that shit go," I said into her ear as she grabbed the sheets, and moments later she was coming all over my dick.

"Oh my God, Malik," she said, out of breath, as I pulled out and then turned her on her side before going back In as I grabbed her thighs to keep her from running and then bent down and began sucking on her titties as she moved her hips back and forth, trying to match my rhythm as I dug deep into her guts. "Shit," she yelled out as I hit her spot, causing her to place her hand on my stomach.

"You love me?" I asked her as I held her in place and gave her everything I had.

"Yes, baby. Yes."

"Yes what?" I asked, smacking her ass while grabbing it at the same time.

"Yes, I love you. Shit, baby, I love you so much," she screamed, and moments later we both were coming together, and she was lying on my chest trying to catch her breath. For about five minutes, we just lay there in silence as I held her in my arms while still rubbing on her ass.

"I love you, Malik, and I'm sorry for the way I've been acting this past month and a half. I was in a really bad place at the time. I've never had to deal with this kind pain before. I guess I wasn't handling my emotions the right way, and I apologize for that," she said while letting out a deep breath.

"It's cool, baby. You don't have to apologize for shit. I already knew that shit was affecting you, and I also know we can't replace the baby we lost. But whenever you're ready, we can try again. You know I got enough power to keep going," I said, causing her to laugh a bit. But I was deadass serious. "I'm for real, Cinnamon. I'll wait until you're ready to have another baby, but I'm not going to wait forever, shorty." And for a few minutes, things got quiet again—until she sat up a bit so that she would be looking at me.

"I'm sorry about the comment I made about the baby," she tried to say, but I stopped her before she could get another word out. Last thing I wanted to do was relive that shit again, I thought to myself.

"We gonna let that one go. I don't ever want to talk about that shit again," I went on to say as she sat all the way up in bed while placing the cover over her body before staring me down.

"What you looking at me like that for?" I asked, but I could tell by the way she was looking at a nigga where this conversation was about to go.

"The day we got into an argument about the baby, why didn't you come home?" she asked, leaving me with a dilemma to tell the truth or to lie. But I didn't feel the need to tell her about that night because I didn't fuck shorty. She just sucked my dick, I said to myself before looking over at her.

"I couldn't come back here after the shit you said to me," I tried to say, but she cut me off.

"All these damn rooms in this house, and you couldn't come home?" she asked with a mug as she crossed her arms. "I don't know, Malik. I saw the way you looked this morning when I asked you about it. You couldn't even look me in my face," she said while letting out another deep breath. "Baby, if there's something you need to tell me, just let me know now, so we can try to fix it," she said, but I knew better than that. And I damn sure wasn't about to tell on myself or lose my bitch over some head and a bitch that didn't mean shit to me, I thought to myself as I reached over for the drawer next to me and pulled out her engagement ring.

"You going to put your ring back on, or what?" I asked, ignoring her question.

"I don't know. Are you sure you don't have anything to tell me?" she asked, as if I was going to change my answer. And when I didn't, moments later she was holding her left hand out for me to put her ring back on.

"You know if you take this ring off again, you won't get it back," I told her, and I was dead-ass serious.

"If I take it off again, I won't need it back," she stated boldly as she looked me dead in eyes. And for some reason, I felt that shit in my soul, I said to myself. And for the next few hours, we fucked and made love. That was, until it was time for me to meet with the team and go over the plan for Detective Brown's bitch ass.

Detective Brown

Ever since Malik and his team were cleared from the case, I'd been walking on eggshells, trying to hold my part of the deal up in the hope of saving my wife and unborn child. But every time I looked up, I was getting deeper and deeper into this shit, I said to myself but snapped out of my thoughts when I heard a knock on my office door. "Come in," I said out loud to whoever was on the other side of the door. Once the door opened and I saw who it was, I immediately got irritated. "What's up, Derrick? What can I help you with?" I asked while pushing some paperwork out of the way.

"I don't know. You tell me. I just got off the phone with Brian's wife, and she told me you stopped by a few days ago and picked up the hard drive she had for me. I'm just wondering why you didn't tell me about this," he said, shrugging his shoulders a bit as I reached inside my office drawer and pulled out the hard drive, which I had already wiped clean a few days ago, and tossed it to him.

"Here," I said as I leaned back in my chair a bit while I watch his every move.

"This is it?" he said while reaching down to pick it up.

"Yeah, that's it. Now, if you don't mind, I have shit to do. As you can see, my desk is full of paperwork," I said while never taking my eyes off him.

"You know you have been acting really different lately. You sure you good?" he asked while looking at me with a funny look.

"I don't think they pay you to worry about me," I said right before my phone began to ring. "Do you mind?" I said, giving him a head nod letting him know to get the fuck out as I picked up the phone to see who was calling. Once he was out of the room, I answered the call. "Yeah," I said, and listened to the sick muthafuck on the other end begin to question me about Malik. After telling him that I had been kicked off his case and had no control over it anymore, he began threating me with my unborn child, leaving me with no option but to do what he asked me to do. After he told me what he needed me to do next, I headed out and over toward Malik's restaurant. Once I pulled up, I was greeted by a familiar face.

"Hello. How many?" she asked as she grabbed a menu.

"I'm here to see Malik Green," I said while flashing my badge.

"OK. Give me one moment. Wait right here," she said before walking away, and moments later the two of them were walking back toward me.

"At this point, you're just harassing the fuck out of me," Malik said as he came to a stop right in front of me.

"Calm down. I'm not here for that. I was just stopping by to apologize and let you know we got the men involved in the killings that took place a few weeks ago. I just want you to be the first to know and to make sure we don't have any misunderstanding," I went on to say as I lied.

"Aw, yeah," he said, nodding his head up and down. "Well, send that information over to my lawyer. Anything else, you can discuss with her," he said before walking away and leaving me to walk out to my patrol car, where I placed a call. On the third ring, he answered.

"Yeah," he said through the phone.

"It's done," I said before getting in the car and pulling off.

11

MARKESE (PLAN IN EFFECT)

After finding out Erica was really pregnant, the last thing a nigga was trying to hear this morning was that bullshit Stonie was talking, I said to myself as I tried calling her back a few times. But her phone was going straight to voice mail. How the fuck did shit go left that fast? I asked myself as I shook my head back and forth while replaying her words in my head. "what the fuck does she mean i got my hands full?" I asked myself, trying to read between the lines, but I snapped out of my thoughts when my phone began to ring.

"Wassup," I asked while leaning back in the chair a bit.

"You already know. Same shit, different day," Malik said into the phone. "But look. I need you to go grab Choppa from his condo. Brittany's crazy ass done put all this nigga's cars on flats," he said, causing me to shake my head because I knew Choppa, and I knew that nigga must have got caught up with some bitch again because that was the only time she spazzed out like that, I said to myself as I listened to Malik tell me he was going to send me his location so we could meet up before hanging the phone up and leaving me to roll a blunt.

Once I had my blunt rolled, I headed out to grab Choppa. On the way there, I tried to call Stonie again, but her phone was still going straight to voice mail. That was when it dawned on me that I had heard Mariah's voice in the background, and I began calling her. On the third ring, she answered.

"What am I owe this phone call seeing that you never answer my calls these days," she said, causing me to let out a slight laugh.

"Yeah, yeah, yeah. I miss you too. I'm just checking on you. I haven't talked to you in a while," I said as I busted a left for Choppa's spot.

"Yeah, whatever. I'm not doing anything. Just cleaning my condo," she said as I pulled up to Choppa's condo.

"Condo?" I asked with a slight mug.

"Markese, don't start with me. Yes, I have my own place, and I don't need your or Malik's approval," she went on to say as I parked my car before blowing the horn.

"Aw yeah," I said.

"Yeah" she said in asassy tone.

"All right. Well, when I'm done taking care of business, I'll stop by and see you. You know, bring you a housewarming gift. Just send me the address," I said. And I could tell by the excitement in her voice that she was happy that I didn't get on her ass about her new condo, but truthfully, I already knew about her having her own spot. Dominique had already filled us in on that. Besides, we had somebody watching Mariah's every move, just in case that hoe-ass nigga the Grim Reaper was somewhere lurking, I said to myself as I stepped out of the car and began walking toward Choppa's condo. But before I could get to the door, two bad bitches that looked like twins were walking out. "Got damn," I said out loud as they walked past me before turning back around and spotting Choppa at the door wearing a Versace robe while smoking a blunt, I thought to myself as I continued to walk until I reached the door.

"Wassup, fam?" I asked while giving him some dap.

"You already know, fam. Dealing with crazy-ass bitches and dropping dick in new ones," he said while shutting the door, and I let out a laugh because I understood exactly where he was coming from, I thought to myself.

"Aye, give me like thirty minutes. I need to wash my nuts," he said while passing me the blunt before taking off upstairs. And for the next hour, I waited until he got dressed. Luckily, Malik hadn't sent over the location to meet up yet, I said to myself.

"All right, fam. I'm ready," Choppa said, coming down the stairs dressed in a sweat outfit.

"Nigga, it took you that long to throw on some sweats and some Timbs?" I asked while I lit the blunt I'd rolled earlier as he took a seat across from me.

"I ain't going to lie, fam. I had a wild night," he went on to say as he reached out for the jar of weed that sat on the table in front of him and began breaking down a blunt.

"See? That's the reason why your cars are on flats now," I said, passing him the blunt.

"I'm not worried about that shit, fam. After what happened last night, Brittany's ass is canceled on my grandmother," he said as I gave him the look that said "Yeah, right." "I'm for real, fam. I'm done fucking with shorty. Once the feds get involved, I got no choice but to drop her ass," he went on to say as he passed me the blunt and then started to roll the other one.

"Damn. I didn't take Brittany to be a police type of bitch," I said as I hit the blunt.

"Shit. Me neither. She knows what we're up against and still didn't give a fuck, so fuck her," he went on to say right before I received a text message from Malik with his location. After telling him we were on the way, we headed out the door to meet up with him.

"You sure we're going the right way? I don't see shit out here but fields," Choppa asked as I looked at the GPS.

"Shit, this is what he sent me," I said, pulling up to a field that had nothing but two barns sitting on it. "Yeah, this got to be it, fam, and them cars right there," I said as I turned the car off and moments later. Malik, Dominique, and Zilla stepped out of their cars. "Where the fuck you got us at, fam?" I asked Malik as I gave him some dap before doing the same thing with Dominique and Zilla.

"This is the new Brenda," he said, causing all us to laugh out loud.

"You can't be serious," Choppa said as we walked inside the barn and down a ladder that led to an underground tunnel. Once we were fully underground, we made a right toward a room that was set up like a trap would have been.

"Like I said, this is the new Brenda," Malik said as we all took a look around the room.

"I ain't going to lie. This shit's too hard. I know you said you was going to come up with some shit, but I wasn't expecting this," Zilla said as he walked over toward the stove.

"Yeah, well, you can thank my mother, because she found this place," he said, causing all of us to turn around and face him right before my mother walked in dressed in all black.

"Don't be so surprised," she said. "Y'all ain't the only ones that can make some shit shake," she went on to say as she looked over at me and Dominique. "Y'all not speaking today," she went on to say as Dominique gave her a head nod.

"Wassup, Ma," I said, keeping it short.

"You know, Markese, if you need to get something off your chest, this would be the perfect time," she said, causing me to smirk.

"I think we both know how I feel, so we can leave it at that," I said. She let out a lit laugh, but I didn't pay that shit no mind. Malik may have given in easy to the bullshit, but I wasn't entertaining it, I said to myself.

"All right. Let's get down to the real reason why we're here," Malik said, causing me to snap out of my thoughts. "In a few days, we will be bringing in one of the biggest shipments ever. The plug we're dealing with is not fucking with us if we're not copping a hundred bricks or more," he said as we all looked at each other. "That should give y'all niggas some type of motivation."

"Hell yeah," Zilla said as he rubbed his hands together like Birdman does after we finished listening to everything Malik had to say.

"Now, I got two shipments coming in the same day. One of them will be the real one shipment, and the other one is a decoy. This is where you and Zilla come in at," Malik said, looking over at me. "The truck that will be used as a distraction y'all will be driving, while me and Choppa are on the other side of town bringing in the real shipment. I would send Zilla and Choppa, but I know with the kind of past you got, you can't afford to get caught up in no bullshit. Besides, I know you're not going nowhere without the chopper."

"Damn straight," Choppa said while throwing his dreads back.

"Now, the truck y'all will be driving is only going to have supplies for the restaurant on it. I set the route up the same way as before. Not only will that keep muthafuckas away while we cop these bricks, but it's also going to expose that hoe-ass nigga Detective Brown. And speaking of that pussy, he stopped by the restaurant before I came here, claiming that he got the niggas that was involve in the killing," he said, causing me to mean mug.

"How we standing right here?" I asked.

"What the fuck this nigga on?" Choppa asked with a slight mug.

"What y'all think? He's doing the same thing we doing. He trying to play us like we playing him," my mother said.

"Yeah, well, we're playing chess, not checkers," Malik went on to say before finishing what he was saying. "After the drop, we're going to meet up at the chop shop so we can handle that nigga the Grim Reaper. We gave him enough time to breathe. His time is up."

"Fasha," Zilla added.

"All right. Now, the room we're standing in is me and Markese's room. Choppa and Zilla, y'all shit down the hall," he said as he pulled out a layout of the building and sat it on the table as we all moved in closer to see. "This place is fully loaded and is off the radar, so it can't be traced. It has cameras and motion sensors all round this place, and on the other side, it's wired up with explosives just in case some shit goes left," he said while pointing to the spots where the bombs were wired. "This building has three main exits that lead out of here if we need to make a getaway, but I doubt that we will ever need to use them. But just in case, y'all niggas need to get familiar with the building," he said, looking up at Dominique. "What's the deal with the other package?" he asked.

"I'm already on it. A nigga had to tie up some loose ends," he said, and Malik gave him a head nod.

"All right," he went on to say, and for the next couple of hours, we went over the whole plan on how we were going to move these bricks and handle that hoe-ass nigga the Grim Reaper—that was, until my mother's phone began going off, causing her to leave, but not before she told me she wanted to talk and she would hit me up later. After going over everything and looking around the underground building, me and Choppa left.

"Aye, fam, I know you don't want to hear this shit, but we should have been teamed up with yo moms. I like the way she does business, but on a more serious note, whatever type of grudge you're holding against her, you need to let that shit go. I lost my moms at young age, and I'd give anything to see her again. Shit, just a month and half ago, I almost lost Zilla to the streets," he said, referring to the shoot-out that had taken place. "All I'm saying is, tomorrow's not promised, fam, and the way we're living… shit, I'm thankful for every minute," he said as I pulled up in front of his condo. "I'm just saying, fam, when it's a feud in the family, it isn't good for nobody," he said as he grabbed his chopper from the back seat.

"I feel that," I said as I gave him some dap. "Aye, you know if you need a car, you can come grab one of mine," I said as he opened the car door.

"Nigga, I'm going to cash out on something new in the morning. That bitch ain't stopping shit," he went to say, and we both let out a laugh.

"All right, fam. Hit me up later," I said as I pulled off while dialing Mariah to let her know I was on the way. After telling me she was home, I headed her way. I was happy that Mariah was smart enough to get a spot outside the city, but got damn, this was a long-ass drive, I said to myself as I continued to drive. And almost an hour later, I was pulling up and walking inside. "This is nice," I said once I was all the way inside.

"Thank you. I'm glad you like it. And where the hell is my housewarming gift?" she asked as I took a seat on the couch while laughing out loud and dug into my pocket and counted out five thousand dollars.

"What?" I asked as she rolled her eyes.

"I would have preferred you to actually get me a gift and not just money," she said as I stuffed the rest of the money back in my pocket.

"You either want it or don't. I didn't have time to grab you a gift. On top of that, you live all the way out in never-never land," I said, causing her to laugh out loud before snatching the money out of my hands. "Yeah, that's what I thought," I went on to say as she took a seat not too far from me and lit the blunt that she had sitting on the table.

"I know you're not here just to see my place, so what's up? And why haven't you talked to mama yet? Everybody else has," she said in between hitting the blunt.

"I'm not everybody else, now, am I?" I asked while grabbing the blunt, that she was passing me.

"Yeah, that's obvious," she went to say in a sarcastic way. "But for real, what's going on with you? I can look at you and tell something's wrong," she said as I leaned up and ashed the blunt before hitting it again, and I contemplated whether I should tell her about Erica and the baby, seeing that nobody knew, I said to myself as I passed her the blunt. "I just found out I might have a seed on the way," I said as I took a deep breath before releasing it as I watched Mariah's reaction to the news I'd just told her. But to my surprise, she didn't have one.

"Well, I'm glad she finally told you. I was just sitting here thinking, How am I going to get through this conversation without telling you? Now that you know, that must mean she's not going through with the abortion, right?" she said as I sat there confused as to what the fuck she was talking about, because I knew for a fact that Mariah didn't know Erica. Well, at least I thought she didn't, I said to myself right before asking her what she was talking about.

"You're talking about Stonie, right?" she asked, causing my heart to drop. "Who else would you be talking about? I don't know any of them hoes you've been having sex with," she said, but I was still stuck on the fact that she said Stonie was pregnant with my seed, I thought to myself as I listened to her continue to talk about how happy she was to be an auntie and how she hoped it was a girl. That was, until I cut her off.

"Hold the fuck up. What the fuck you mean Stonie's pregnant?" I asked as I stood up. And at that moment, I could tell by the way Mariah looked when I asked that question that she knew she'd fucked up.

Stonie

Bang bang bang! I heard what sounded like someone trying to kick the door in, and I sat up in bed before looking at the clock, which read 12:00 a.m. Bang, bang, bang. "Who the fuck is banging on the door like that?" I asked out loud as I jumped up while grabbing the Glock from underneath the pillow before heading downstairs to see who was beating on the door like the damn police. "Who the fuck is it?" I asked through the door as I held the Glock in my hand and waited on the person on the other side of the door to respond.

"Open the muthafucking door," Markese yelled, and seconds later I was opening the door. And if looks could kill, well, let's just say I was a dead bitch, I thought to myself as he walked in and slammed the door.

"What the fuck is your problem, and why the fuck are you banging on the door like you lost your fucking mind?" I started to say but stopped when he grabbed the Glock out of my hands while pinning me up against the wall.

"Why the fuck you ain't tell me you were pregnant with my seed?" he yelled directly in my face, and for the first time in my life, I was scared, I thought to myself as I stood there looking at him while trying not to cry, knowing that the only way he could have found out was Mariah because no one outside of her knew about the pregnancy, I said to myself but snapped out my thoughts when he began yelling, "Answer my muthafucking question, Stonie. So, what, you wasn't going to tell a nigga? You was just going to up and kill my seed?" he asked while closing the little space we had between each other. "That's how you really feel, shorty? Then, on top of that shit, you around this bitch drinking and smoking like you ain't pregnant. What type of shit you on?" he asked as a few tears began to fall down my face.

"Why do you even care?" I asked as I began to wipe away the tears that were still falling. "You already have a bitch that's willing to have your baby," I said, causing his facial expression to change as I let out a slight laugh. "Oh, you didn't know?" I asked, still laughing a bit. "You left a voice mail on my phone last night. I heard everything y'all were talking about, so you can miss me with that shit," I yelled. "When I wanted to tell you about the baby, you went MIA on me. And besides, I had my mind made up the day I found out I was pregnant that didn't want to have a baby by a nigga that I'm not with, let alone one that's knee deep in the streets and has more hoes than a pimp does," I said while looking him dead in his eyes. "I thought getting an abortion was the right thing to do until we spent the night together. And for the first time, I didn't see you as the nigga who ran the streets or the nigga whose heart is just as cold as mine. For a minute, you really had me thinking that keeping this baby was the right thing to do and maybe we could work on us later down the road," I said as I swallowed the lump in my throat to keep from breaking down even more. "I really feel dumb as fuck for falling for a nigga like you," I said as more tears began to fall down my face. "I don't even know how I let that shit happen," I went on to say as I let out another slight laugh to keep from crying more than I already was. "I mean, let's be honest. We were never shit to begin with. Just two muthafucks who got caught up in the moment. I'm not justifying shit that I've done or making it seem like not telling you about the baby was the right thing to do, because it wasn't. And I know no matter what, you're going to hate me anyways. But you have another thing coming if you think I'm going to keep a baby when I already know you have another one on the way. I'd be a bigger fool than I already am. What real woman would want to share her first pregnancy with another bitch?" I asked. "Not this bitch. So you can hate me till the end of time, Markese, but it's going to take God himself to come down here and tell me to keep this baby, and you and I both know that shit is not going to happen," I said as I stood there looking at him, hoping like hell he wouldn't spaz out more than he already had, I thought to myself as I watched him stare me down with a look of disgust.

"You know, Stonie, I used to hold you up on a pedestal, shorty," he said with a smirk. "But now I see you're just like them other bitches. You're basic," he went on to say with a mean mug, causing my heart to break more than it already had. "If you kill my seed, you're dead to me, shorty. Either way, I'm not fucking with you. If you do decide to keep it, Ima do whatever I got to do on my part, but any feelings or love I had for you are gone," he said while placing the Glock on the step before turning toward the door and walking out, leaving me standing there with tears falling down my face for a few minutes until I realized how long I'd been standing there and headed back upstairs.

Where I lay in bed and cried more than I had in my whole life, not because of the baby or the hurtful, mean things Markese had just said to me, but because deep down in my heart, I knew I loved him. Although he was never my man, he was the best friend I'd never asked for but always needed, and that was something I could never replace but would always miss.

Yvette
After the last conversation me and my son Malik had, I was feeling a lot better knowing I'd mended things with at least one of my sons, I thought to myself as I looked at the phone, which wouldn't stop ringing, before I opened the door where I had Big Malik's bitch and her father tied up. And then I bent down a bit so I'd be on her level, I thought to myself as I placed the FNM to her father's head before speaking. "When he calls back—because I know he will—you need to tell him exactly what I told you to say earlier. If you don't, I'm going to kill this old muthafucka. Now, do we have an understanding?" I asked, and she nodded her head. Moments later, the phone began to ring again. "Showtime," I said with a smile as I ripped the tape off her lips before placing the phone to her ear.

"Where the fuck you at, and where the fuck is my money?" he yelled through the phone, and I listened to her tell him she would be back the day after tomorrow and that her father would be clear to leave the hospital.

"You better hope like hell you're not lying to me, Susie, because we both know I'm not going to spare you or Rose. And make sure you have that nigga with you when you come back," he said before hanging up the phone.

"Please, just hear me out. He's going to kill my daughter if I don't return with the money," she said with tears running down her face.

"You know, if y'all hadn't tried to kill my kids, I would feel sorry for your daughter. But I don't, and I damn sure don't have any sympathy for a bitch that was trying to set me up twenty years ago," I said as I watched her eyes get big. "Yeah, I know all about the plot you and Big Malik had planned against me, but just like back then, I'm always gonna outsmart you bitches. But hey, thanks for taking him off my hands. Now you get to see how much of a bitch he really is," I said before taping her mouth closed while listening to Malik and the rest of his team talking in the next room. That was, until I walked down the hall and into the room that they were all in.

I had to remind them that they wasn't the only muthafucks who could put some shit together, I said to myself right before asking my son Markese if he needed to get some shit off his chest, because I could feel the tension between us, and the last thing I needed was to still be at odds with my son knowing that any day now Carlos could expose me. And then I would have an even bigger problem with my daughter. It was like I couldn't win for shit. One minute I made things right with one of my kids, and the next I was right back at odds with another one. I swear I'll be glad when all this shit comes to an end, I said to myself as I sat and listened to Malik go over the plans to kill big Malik and to bring in his next shipment.

I'll be the first to say I was proud of my son. Not only had he been playing chess, which was something I had never taught him, but he could have taken Big Malik out a long time ago. But now I saw what my son had been doing, and it made sense. I couldn't do anything but respect it and give him the title he had already earned, and that was kingpin, I thought to myself. But I snapped out my thoughts when I received a text from Carlos saying meet him ASAP at the address he'd just sent. After telling Markese we needed to talk later, I headed out. Once I was in the car, I pulled off and headed toward the location that was sent to me. I knew better than to stall or prolong this visit, seeing that the last time I had seen Carlos was a few days ago, and we had ended up fucking. I will admit that, that wasn't a part of the plan, but I'd spent the last twenty-plus years denying the love I had for this man. No matter how far we drifted apart, the universe always ended up bringing us back together, and it was about time for muthafucks to understand that, I said to myself as I continued to drive until I was pulling up to the building. Once I was parked, I was greeted by two men in suits holding guns.

"Can you please step out of the car," one of men asked in his thick accent, and I opened the car door and stepped out, where I was searched head to toe.

"Can you hurry the fuck up? It's cold out here," I said to the man, who had just taken both of my Glocks from me.

"All right. You can go inside," he said, and I smirked before walking off toward the building, where I walked inside and down the hall. Once I entered the room, I let out a slight laugh when I came face to face with Carlos's wife, Valentina.

"Don't look so disappointed to see me, Yvette," she said in her thick accent as she stood there in her two-piece cream fitted suit with diamonds dancing from her neck, wrists, and wedding ring. Her long jet-black hair was pushed back behind her ears with a perfect part down the middle, I thought to myself as I watched her reach out for a cigar, cut the end, and then light it.

"Why would I be disappointed? I think I know Carlos well enough to know he would never call or send a text before he comes," I said as I walked closer to the table she was standing behind. "I know you didn't come all the way here just to look at my fine ass, so what the fuck do you want?" I asked. Because as far as I was concerned, I didn't have shit to say to this bitch, I said to myself as I watched her take a seat while hitting the cigar like she was some type of queenpin.

"Have a seat," she said while extending her hand for me to take a seat in the chair across from her, I thought to myself as I let out a slight laugh because it was clear this bitch was feeling herself.

"I'd rather stand."

"Well, that's OK. I'll make this quick. I know Carlos been helping you, and I have no problem with that, seeing that it's beneficial for me and my family," she said while blowing smoke from the cigar out.

"You brought me here just to tell me this shit?" I asked with a mug.

"No. I brought you here to tell you like a woman not to be fucking my husband," she said, looking me dead in my eyes. "I put up with a lot of shit in the past that I will not tolerate this time around. I will protect my family by all means necessary, even if that means protecting my husband from a washed-up has-been," she said, causing me to laugh out loud at the "has-been" part as I reached out for a cigar and cut the bottom before lighting it. "I'm sure you understand where I'm coming from. I'm just trying to make sure everything stays in rotation and that everyone can make it home to their families in one piece," she said, and at that moment I knew by the subliminal threat she had made I was going to have to kill her ass sooner rather than later, I said to myself before exhaling the smoke.

"You know, Valentina, I never understood why bitches always felt the need to step to the next woman with that 'I'm coming to you like a woman' bullshit," I said as I laughed out loud, knowing that would get underneath her skin because she was a weak bitch. "You flew halfway across the country to remind a washed-up has-been not to fuck the man she willingly let you have because you and I both know even if you were my clone, you still couldn't measure up to me. Had I not chosen my ex-husband, we both know you would still be somewhere trying to suck and fuck your way to the position you're in now. You're so worried about me trying to take a spot that's mine whether I want it or not, but you already knew that. That's why you're here. You oughta tell Carlos to do a better job at grooming you, because it would be a cold day in hell before I ever let the next bitch know I give fuck about her. That just goes to show, no matter how much Carlos tries to mold you, you will never be me. Not even twenty-plus years later. Now, what I will do for you is walk out of here without breaking your fucking jaw," I said while ashing the cigar. "Seeing that you were the one who sent my ex-husband all the information about me, but you knew better than to expose who I am because exposing me would mean you would be exposing Carlos. And we both know he wouldn't hesitate to behead you," I said with a smirk as I watched her sit in the chair looking like she was ready to kill me. "Now, since you're the one who started all of this shit, I need you to pull all of your connections you have down in the Cook County Police Department. It's a Detective Brown I need taken care of ASAP. If you can do that for me, then maybe I'll think about not fucking your husband again," I said as I put the cigar out before turning for the door. I'd said all I had to say to this bitch, I said to myself as I continued to walk but stopped in my tracks when she began to speak.

"Every bitch has her day," she said, causing me to turn around and face her.

"Yeah, you're right. And if you keep making subliminal threats, you're going find your day coming sooner rather than later. And that security that Carlos pays to keep you comfortable the way that you are won't be enough to stop me whenever I do decide to come get you," I said before walking out of the room and back toward my car, where I grabbed my two .40 Glocks and sped off. But I stopped once I got a few miles ahead. "Are you close?" I asked Porsha as I stepped out of the car.

"Yeah. I'm pulling up now," she said through the phone, and moments later she was pulling up in an all-black tinted SUV.

"How did it go?" she asked as I got inside the car.

"You already know. Just another mad bitch I should have killed a long time ago," I said in a sarcastic way as Porsha shook her head.

"I told you, bitches like that have to be taken care of the first time around," Porsha said.

"You're right about that. But look, I need you to track Markese's phone so I can see exactly where he's at. It's time me and him had a talk."

12

DOMINIQUE (ONE STEP CLOSER)

"What the fuck!" I yelled as I jumped up and wiped all the water off my face that Chyna had just thrown on a nigga while I was sleep, I thought to myself as I watched her run up on me while giving me a clean two-piece to the face.

"You got me and life fucked up," she yelled as she continued to swing on me. "How many times have I told you to stop fucking drugging me," she yelled. By this time I had her ass pinned down to the bed, and all she could do was try to kick while I held her down. "Get the fuck off of me," she yelled as I stood over her with water still dripping off my body.

"Calm the fuck down, Chyna. For real, I'm not about to keep letting you put, your hands on me, shorty."

"And I'm not about to keep letting you kidnap and drug me up either," she said, causing me to laugh a bit at the "kidnap" part.

"I never kidnapped you, so let's get that shit straight. We never even left the house, and the drugging part—I told you from the jump what I was capable of doing. I'm not a dumb-ass nigga, Chyna. Anything I've ever done to you, I made sure it wouldn't harm you. I told you last night that that's the only way a nigga can get your attention," I said, causing her to roll her eyes.

"So drugging me is getting my attention? You don't have to drug me to fuck me," she said, causing me to smirk.

"You and I both know that I don't need to drug you just to fuck you shorty, so you can miss me with that shit," I said in a serious tone. "But for real, though, answer this question: Did you or did you not like it?" I asked, causing her to get quiet. "Answer my question, Chyna. Did you or didn't you?" I asked again, but just like before, she didn't say anything. "That's what the fuck I thought. You're more mad at the fact that you didn't have any control than you are at the fact that you got drugged. Stop acting like you didn't enjoy the shit, because your pussy was telling me something different, and make that the last time you put your hands on me, shorty. I don't do the domestic shit," I went on to say as I released my grip.

"Whatever, Dominique. You heard what the fuck I said. Stop fucking drugging me," she went on to say as I pulled her close to me and made her sit on my lap.

"You done yet?" I asked while taking her robe off, and for the next two hours we fucked and talked out our problems and came to a mutual agreement that would work for the both of us, I said to myself right before my phone began to ring. "Wassup," I said into the phone.

"You already know. Same shit, different day," Malik said before telling me we needed to meet up and that he would send the location.

After telling him I'll be there, I hopped in the shower and got dressed. Once I was fully dressed, I headed downstairs, where I spotted Chyna smoking a blunt while cooking breakfast, I thought to myself as I walked up behind her and pulled her close to me while planting kisses on her neck, causing her to turn around.

"Where you think you're going?" she asked with a slight mug.

"I got some business to handle," I tried to say, but she turned back around in the middle of my sentence, I thought to myself, right before I turned her ass right back around while picking her up and sitting her on the island we had in the kitchen. "Why you always playing with me, Chyna? Didn't we just come to an agreement about this shit?" I asked as she rolled her eyes while ignoring my question. "What? You don't hear me talking to you, ma?"

"Yeah, I do, but I didn't think you were going to just up and leave that fast, especially while I'm down here cooking you breakfast," she said as she sat there with a sad expression on her face, and I could tell by looking at her that all she wanted was for me to be at home with her, I said to myself.

"Look, bae, once this shit is over with in the street, we can go on a vacation. You know, hit a couple different countries. Just us. For however long you want," I said, making her smile a bit. "Is that coo?" I asked while looking down at her.

"Yeah, that's coo. We can do that," she said while wrapping her arms around my neck and giving me a kiss before getting off the island.

"Aw, yeah. And where's your car at?" I asked as she stood over the stove checking the food.

"It's at Cinnamon's place. Ima get it later," she said as she relit the blunt and hit it a few times.

"All right. I'll hit you up later," I said as I smacked her ass. "Aw, yeah. Before I forget, clean up that mess you made," I yelled on the way out the door.

Once I was in my Benz, I headed to the location Malik had sent me. When I pulled up, it was nothing but two barns sitting on hella of land. Well, at least that was what I thought it was. Come to find out it was an underground workshop. Malik didn't even have to tell me how he had come up with this shit. It had both my aunties' names written all over it, I thought to myself as I listened to Malik tell us all the plans he had to bring in a hundred bricks and to dirt that nigga the Grim Reaper. After chopping shit up with them, I went and bugged my first package car so that I would know their every move, I thought to myself as I pulled up to the parking lot the car was parked in. I hopped out while making sure no one saw me, as I walked up to the car and placed a tracking device underneath it before jogging back to my Benz.

Where I drove off to do the same to Detective Brown's car. After waiting outside Cook County for damn near five hours. He finally came out, I began to follow him. I made sure I stayed three cars behind him, and when he turned the corner, I didn't turn with him. I waited and watched from the stop light until I felt he wouldn't notice me. Luckily, this hoe-ass nigga decided to stop at a bar, I thought to myself as I watched from a parking lot across the street for about fifteen minutes before getting out of the car and jogging across the street. Once I was close enough to his car, I placed the tracking device underneath it and then jogged back toward my Benz and pulled off while dialing Malik.

"Yo," he said into the phone.

"You already know, fam. I just got the conformation for those two packages. You can go ahead and track them now."

"Aw, yeah. Good looking out, fam," he went on to say, and for the next couple of minutes, we rapped on the phone, just to throw the conversation off. After hanging up with Malik, I headed back home since I didn't have any hits to do, and besides, I was trying to pick up where we had left off this morning.

Malik

I can honestly say a nigga was starting to feel a lot better about the hand that I had been dealt. I had a new plug with some of the best cocaine I'd seen in a long time, I had a new trap house that was fully loaded and off the radar, me and Cinnamon were back on good terms, and the best news was that I was one step closer to dirting that bitch-ass nigga who was responsible for all this shit, I said to myself but snapped out my thoughts when my phone began to ring with Dominique telling me he had taken care of Detective Brown's bitch ass, as well as the other package. I was glad to hear that because I was ready to off his bitch ass, and him popping up at my restaurant earlier on some bullshit only made me want to roll the dice on his bitch ass sooner.

After wrapping up the phone call with Dominique, I began to put together a surprise birthday party for Markese. His birthday was a couple of days away, and I could tell by just looking at that nigga earlier something was wrong with him. I tried to hit him up after the meeting to see if he was good, but he didn't answer the phone or hit me back, I said to myself right before Cinnamon walked in the theater room and sat on my lap while lightin a fat-ass Backwood.

"Why did you start the movie without me?" she asked in between hitting the blunt.

"I just pressed Play. It ain't even started yet," I said while grabbing the blunt that she was passing to me, then I hit it a few times before telling her what was on my mind. "Tomorrow I got a wedding planner coming by so you can start planning our wedding. I wanna be married by our one-year anniversary," I said and hit the blunt a few more times as I watched her face turn up.

"Malik, it's January. There's no way in hell I can plan a wedding in less than five months, and you're talking about you found a wedding planner. How do you know I would even like her or him?" she asked while snatching the blunt out my hand.

"I don't know, but what I do know is that she's the best at what she does. I honestly don't give a fuck if we don't have a wedding as long as we get married in five months. I just know that a big wedding is something that you want. I don't care how much it costs or how much you spend, but that's the day I'm getting married, and ain't shit changing that," I said as we sat there staring at each other before she broke the silence.

"Let's make a deal. I'll give you a wedding if you can give me one thing," she said, never breaking eye contact with me. "You have to leave the street. I can't get married to you knowing that you're still waist deep in the streets. I can't chance getting shot up again or you getting killed. I know you, Malik, and I know you're going to want me to have another baby soon. What are we going to do if something happens to you, or worst all, of us? I love you to death; don't get me wrong. But if you can't get out of the streets before our one-year anniversary, then there won't be no wedding. So take it or leave it," she said as I sat there smoking the blunt while I let everything she had said register in my mind.

Truth be told, I was already planning on getting out of the streets once I sealed this deal with the new connect. I planned on turning everything over to Markese and Choppa. I wasn't a dumb-ass nigga, and I paid attention to the signs. Besides, you can't do this shit forever and expect the feds not pick you up or the ground not hold you. I made enough money to last me three lifetimes, and I still had all my businesses bringing in millions. So I'm good, and the talk me and my mother had only made me realize that leaving the streets was the right thing for me to do. Besides, almost losing Cinnamon as well as my seed opened my eyes up and showed me life is much more precious than I ever thought, and I couldn't afford to keep gambling with the only life I got, I thought to myself before looking back up at Cinnamon, who was sitting there with a look that read, "Nigga, what the fuck you going to do?" I said to myself as I let out a little laugh. "It's a deal," I said and then watched her smile harder than she ever had before.

Markese

When I pulled up to confront Stonie, I was expecting her to have some type of real reason for not telling me she was pregnant with my seed. I knew shorty could be coldhearted, but got damn, I said to myself as I replayed all her words in my head while hitting the blunt before taking a shot of Hennessey, the last thing I was expecting to hear when I got there was that I had left a voice mail on her phone with the whole conversation me and Erica were having. Here it is: I got a bitch I don't even want a baby by that I'm treating like shit, and now I got Stonie, who I don't mind having my seed, but shorty doesn't even want it. How the fuck does that work? I asked myself. Come to think of it, outside of us fucking a few days ago, I hadn't fucked her since the shooting. So she had been pregnant and ain't said shit. And the fact that Mariah knew the whole time and didn't say shit either pissed me off even more. Had she not thought I was talking about Stonie the whole time, a nigga probably would have never found out, I said to myself as I continued to hit the blunt and think about everything that had just gone down. That was, until I heard my doorbell began to ring. I knew for a fact it had to be family because nobody was that dumb to pop up on me, I thought to myself as I grabbed the Draco off the table that was in front of me and walked toward to the door to see who the fuck was popping up at my house unannounced.

"What the fuck does she want?" I asked myself out loud before opening the door and coming face to face with my mother.

"Well, are you going to let me in?" she asked as I hit the blunt before moving out of the way so she could come inside.

Once she was inside the house, I walked back toward the living room and took a seat while pouring another shot of Hennessey. "Wassup," I asked as I leaned back a bit on the couch and finished smoking my blunt as I watched her take a seat not too far from me.

"You tell me. You're the one who seems like you need to get some shit off your chest," she said while looking over at me as I leaned up to ash the blunt.

"Like I said earlier, I'm sure you already know how I feel. Me expressing myself still ain't going to change the shit that happened, Ma. Whatever your reason was for hiding all this shit from us, it's still not going justify how I feel. I mean, damn, you couldn't trust us enough to keep it real? After all the years we kept it real with you about the streets, all this shit could have been avoided or handled a different way, Ma, if you would have just told us what we were up against. After all the years of us being in the streets, we ain't never had to deal with no shit like this. As a matter of fact, this ain't even our beef. We're being held accountable for the mistakes you made. Then you want to be mad at us for feeling some type of way about the situation you put us in? Tuh," I said as I let out a little laugh to keep from being more pissed off than I already was. "At the end of the day, you're still my mother, and can't shit change that. But don't expect me not to feel some type of way or think that just because Malik and Mariah are over the shit that I'm supposed to be. I'm my own man at the end day, and I deal with shit on my time, not yours or anybody else's," I said while putting the end of my blunt out.

"I can respect that," she said while taking a deep breath. "I know I can't take back what I've done, Markese. And you're right—you are entitled to feel any way you want, but tomorrow's not promised, son, so being mad at me for making a decision I thought was best for me and my kids at the time is still not going to change shit. There's going to come a time when you become a father, and you may be hit with a difficult decision to make. You may think you're doing what's best for you and your children, but let me tell you something. Ain't nothing harder than being a parent and having to make decisions that may come back to haunt you later down the road, because sure enough, the universe will get back with you. Whether it's good or bad, you just have to know, deep down in your heart, that you did the best thing for you and yours regardless of the outcome. Nevertheless, you're right. I should have trusted y'all enough to hold my secrets, but I didn't, and that's something I'm dealing with," she said with a slight laugh. "That's the fucked-up part. People don't know that karma doesn't always come back just on you, and it doesn't always come back the way you dish it out. I'm strong enough to eat that shit when just dealing with me, but to see my karma fucking with my kids hurts me more than you'll ever know. I may look strong on the outside because I have no choice but to be, but never think for one minute that I'm not fucked up behind the choices I've made. Only thing is, I won't allow that shit to break or fold me. All I can say is that I'm sorry for not telling y'all a long time ago about my life. But I won't apologize for doing what I thought was best at the time for all of us. Now, what you do with that is on you," she said while reaching for the bottle of Hennessey and taking a shot straight from the bottle as I sat there listening to everything she was telling me and knowing that I might have two seeds on the way if Stonie didn't go through with the abortion. I could feel where she was coming from because I would do anything to protect mine, even if that meant they would hate me for it later, I said to myself as I ran my hands through my dreads to get them out my face.

"I can understand that, Ma, especially seeing that I got two seeds on the way," I said, causing her to spit out the Hennessey she was pouring in her mouth.

"Two babies, Markese? Are you fucking serious? I told you about fucking all these nothing-ass bitches," she yelled.

"I already know, Ma, but with one of them, the condom just up and broke. And the other one…" I said while shaking my head at the thought of Stonie.

"Let me guess. You really liked the other one, huh?" she asked, and I looked up at her while taking a deep breath.

"Yeah, I did. I can't even stunt, Ma. I was feeling shorty for a minute. I felt like she was the one. Well, shit, at least that was what I thought until I found out through a third party that she was pregnant with my seed. She wasn't even going to tell me she was pregnant. She was just going to up and get an abortion behind my back. And to make matters worse, when I went to speak with the other broad that claims her baby is mine, my phone accidentally called her. So now she knows about the other baby. And she ain't feeling that shit at all. It's like I got Erica, who I don't want a baby by, who's keeping it no matter how I feel. Then I got Stonie, who I don't mind keeping my seed, and shorty don't even want it," I said while taking another deep breath because I was beyond frustrated.

"Yeah, that's tough. Stonie is Cinnamon's cousin, right?" she asked, and I gave her a head nod that said yes. "Well, you may not want to hear this, son, but it serves you right. I mean, how many times have I told you to stop fucking all these hoes? Now here it is. You have two different women pregnant at the same time. I mean, I wouldn't want to be pregnant while another bitch is pregnant either, and if she's anything like Cinnamon, then I know she's not going for that shit. But that doesn't make it right that she didn't tell you. But even if she did tell you, you would still be mad at the fact that she doesn't want to keep it. So either way, the outcome would have been the same. I don't think that makes her less of a woman because she doesn't want the baby. Hell, she has to be something special to have you feeling this way about her. But at the end of the day, regardless of how shit goes, whether she keeps it or not, you still need to be there for her at a time like this. And with the way you're talking, it's like you know for a fact that baby is yours. I never heard you say y'all used condoms. Not once. And as for the other young lady, mama baby daddies maybe get your ass a DNA test," she said, making me laugh a bit. And for the next two hours, we sat and talked while she filled me in on how we'd gotten caught up in all this bullshit with that hoe-ass nigga the Grim Reaper, and after she filled me in on everything, I see why that nigga was pissed off.

13

GRIM REAPER (NO ONE'S SAFE)

"Please, I need to see a doctor," the woman said as she lay on the small mattress that was on the basement floor, but I just ignored her as I walked upstairs to the living room, where I grabbed the phone off the table and dialed Susie's number over and over, only to get sent straight to voice mail. And that only pissed me the fuck off. First her father went missing, and that muthafuck had all my money from the last drop we did. Then I send her to check shit out, and now I could barely get her ass on the phone, I thought to myself as I paced back and forth while redialing her number, and this time she answered. "Where the fuck is my money at?" I yelled through the phone as I listened to her on the other end tell me she was still at the hospital with her father and that he would be clear to leave the hospital soon. But something was telling me that she was lying.

I could hear it in her voice that something was wrong, I said to myself right before reminding her that I wouldn't hesitate to kill her or Rose if I found out she was lying. After hanging up the phone on Susie, I placed another call.

"Yeah," the person on the other end said as he answered the phone.

"Don't yeah me, muthafucka," I went on to say as I lit a cigarette.

"What do you need? I'm busy right now, and I can't talk," he said into the phone.

"Well, make time. I need you to tap into the system down in Miami and see if a man by the name of Emmanuel has checked in to any of the hospitals down there. I have a feeling some shit's not right, and I need to find out if he's really hospitalized or not," I said and then waited on his response.

"All right. You're going to have to give me a little bit of time," he said and then asked me for his last name.

"Muthafucka, does it look like time is our friend right now?" I yelled into the phone. "You got just as much riding on this shit as I do, so I suggest you get on it now," I said before giving him Susie's father's last name and then hung up the phone while taking a seat at the table.

"What the fuck," I yelled as I threw the ashtray up against the wall out of frustration because shit on my end wasn't going as planned, I thought to myself, and my phone began to ring, causing me to snap out of my thoughts. "What?" I yelled as I answered the phone and then began to smile ear to ear as I listened to my daughter Rose tell me that Malik had a shipment coming in next week, I thought to myself as I continued listening to everything she was saying. And then I began putting my plan into full effect.

Detective Brown

"I promise to get you out this situation, even if I have to die trying," I said out loud to myself as I sat behind my office desk while holding a picture of my wife in my hand as I tried my best to fight back the tears that were trying to fall. Never in a million years did I ever think my life would take a turn for the worse the way that it had. Not only was my wife and unborn child missing, but I had lost my partner and best friend, I said to myself as I swallowed the lump in my throat and I thought about Brian and all the memories we had.

I remembered when we first got in the police academy—how happy we both were. It seemed like it was just yesterday that I was sitting up laughing and kicking it with him. I could honestly say I was going to miss him, and no matter how this shit turned out in the end, I planned on killing everyone involved in his death as well as my wife's kidnapping. But until I got her back, I had to play by the rules, I said to myself as I stuffed the picture of my wife back in my wallet. "I need a drink," I said to myself as I stood up and snatched my jacket off the back of my chair before walking out of my office and down the hall toward the elevator, which I took all the way down to the garage and then stepped off and began walking toward my car.

"Aye, I was just about to come and talk to you," Derick said as I walked through the parking garage while taking a deep breath before coming to a complete stop.

"I'm kind of busy. Can this wait?" I asked in an irritated voice.

"Not really," he went on to say, causing me to straighten up my posture. "Did you know that Brian was building a case against Malik Green?" he asked, causing my heart to drop at the sound of that.

"I knew that he had gotten an anonymous tip on him a few months back, but he dismissed it."

"You didn't think that was important information to tell?" he asked, pissing me the fuck off.

"No, I didn't, because as you already know, Malik Green has been dismissed for any charges and checked out to be a legit businessman," I said in a stern voice.

"Well, I don't think he legit at all, and I damn sure don't think you do," he went on to say.

"Well, it doesn't matter what the fuck I think, now, does it? We all know what the streets say about him, but what the fuck can we do if there's no real evidence to build a case on him? Not to mention I was just kicked off his case and told not pursue it anymore. And I'm sure you heard about that. Now, if you don't have any hard evidence to bring him down, then I suggest you stop coming to me with this bullshit, because I'm not going to lose my job behind what you think," I said before walking away and toward my car before i said or did something i wouldn't regret later, and I pulled off toward the nearest bar.

Once I reach the bar, I went inside and ordered a beer and two shots of Hennessey. I wasn't in there a good forty-five minutes before the chief of police was calling and demanding that we meet up ASAP. After he gave me his location, I left and headed his way. When I pulled up, I noticed it was an abandoned building, I said to myself as I walked inside, where I came face to face with his fat ass, and I could tell by the way he looked and the vibe he was giving off that something wasn't right, I said to myself as I walked closer to him. "What's up, chief?"

"What's up is that I hear you've been running around town getting yourself mixed up in some shit that's has nothing to do with you," he said, causing my face to turn up. "Yeah, I know all about the shit you've been doing," he yelled. "You can't be that fucking stupid, and whoever it is that you're working with knows that this shit is way bigger than Malik Green. You have no idea what you have gotten yourself into, all because you want to make some extra cash on the side. Now, here it is. Brian is missing. No, fuck that. He's dead. And I'm sure you know that by now. I've overlooked the petty-ass shit that you and Brian were doing in the street for the past few years, stealing and robbing from the local drug dealers. Yeah, I know all about the dirty-ass shit that y'all were doing. But I never said a word because every cop and detective has done some dirty shit. But this right here I cannot overlook. This is way over my head. What you're doing is going to get me, you, and everyone else that's tied into this situation killed. Now, I brought you out here because I'm not sure if the station is bugged or not, but as of today, you will resign and turn over your badge. I can't jeopardize my life or my family's life for you. Now, this conversation will stay between me and you, but as of now. I need your badge and your gun," he said as I stood there taking in everything he had just said before taking off my badge and my gun.

"I appreciate you not ratting me out," I said as I looked at my badge one last time.

"We all make mistakes, David, but I advise you to leave this shit alone before you end up like Brian," he said as he held his hand out for my badge and gun, I thought to myself right before raising my gun and shooting him twice in the chest and watching his body fall to the ground. "What the fuck are you doing?" he yelled as he held his chest while breathing heavily as I stood over him with the gun still pointed at him.

"Whatever I have to do to save my family," I said right before pulling the trigger and shooting him in the head.

14

CINNAMON (A FEW DAYS LATER)

I can honestly say, since the tragic incident I've never been happier in my life. Ever since the last conversation Malik and I had, everything between us had been great. I was in a better mood. I now had a new physical therapist, since Malik's rude ass ran the last one off. I was getting dick down three or four time a day, and the best part was that Malik agreed to leave the street in exchange for us getting married in less than five months. Only thing left to do was plan our wedding, which I'd been working on day and night since he demanded that we get married year to date, I said to myself as I looked over the emails the wedding planner had sent to me.

When I met with her a few days ago, I told her I wanted a royal wedding and that I didn't care how much it cost, but it had to be perfect. Looking at some of the ideas she sent me, I now saw why Malik had picked her to plan our wedding. Her vision was better than what I had expected it to be, I said to myself as I looked through the rest of the emails with a smile because just a few weeks ago I thought I would never be happy again after being shot and losing my unborn child. But I see now that it was all a part of God's plan. And although I could never replace the baby I had lost, I was sure ready to give my future husband another baby. I just hoped I wouldn't get pregnant before the wedding. I wanted to look good in my wedding dress, which was being custom made. Speaking of dresses, Stonie's ass still hadn't replied to any of my text messages, and this bitch was my maid of honor. I needed her to be getting fitted for her dress, I said to myself right before getting up and walking over toward the dresser, where my purse, car keys, and cell phone were sitting, and then I headed downstairs and out the door. Once I was inside my Benz truck, I dialed Chyna. On the third ring, she answered.

"I know you're not calling me after standing me up the other day," she said through the phone, and I began to laugh out loud.

"I sent you a text, and I know you got it because it said you read my shit, you stupid hoe," I went on to say as I pulled away from my home and toward my condo.

"Yeah, whatever, bitch. Are you going to Markese's surprise party tonight?" she asked.

"Yeah, I'm going. I just have to find me something to wear. Speaking of that—" I was about to say, but she cut me off.

"Yes, bitch, I'm going to get sized today for my dress. I got your text message. Don't turn into no damn bridezilla on a bitch," she said, and we both began to laugh out loud.

"Fuck you, Chyna, and it's too late for that, bitch. I'm already in that mode, and Stonie's ass is about to feel it now. I've been calling and texting her, but she hasn't replied or called me back."

"I know. Me neither, and when I went to get my car the other day, I called her and knocked on the door, and I know for a fact she was there because her car was parked outside," Chyna went on to say, and for the next forty-five minutes, we talked about the wedding and everything I had planned so far—that was, until I pulled up to my condo and parked next to Stonie's Range Rover.

Once I was inside, I walked up the stairs and spotted this bitch sitting on the couch in the dark watching basic-ass TV because there was no cable or internet. "Why the fuck are you sitting in the dark?" I asked her as I cut a few lights on so that I could see. "What's wrong?" I asked, because from the looks of things, she had been crying. Her eyes had black circles underneath them like she hadn't been sleeping in days, and her eyes were bloodshot red. She looked like me about a week ago—horrible, I said to myself as I took a seat next to her.

"I was going to call you back, Cinnamon. I just needed time to myself," she said in a low whisper. But at this point, I didn't even care that she hadn't returned any of my calls. I wanted to know what was wrong with her. I was just about to ask her what the fuck was going on when I spotted what seemed to be an ultrasound picture on the table, I thought to myself as I reached out to pick it up. And my heart damn near stopped when I read the name across the top: Miracle Jones, which was Stonie's real name. Her mother named her Miracle because the doctors had told her she would never be able to have kids, but she still ended up getting pregnant with Stonie years later, I said to myself before looking back up at Stonie, who now had tears falling down her face. "You're pregnant?" I asked, and she nodded her head up and down. "Why didn't you tell me?" I asked with excitement as I reached out to hug her. And I could tell by the way she felt in my arms that she needed that hug, I thought to myself as I listened to her cry for a minute before she finally gathered up the strength to talk.

"I wanted to tell you, but you had just lost your baby, and I didn't want to mention the fact that I was pregnant," she said, causing my heart to feel a sense of sadness because I would never ever want my cousin to feel like she had to hide her pregnancy to spare my feelings. I had come to the realization that if it was meant for me to still be pregnant, I would be. In just the short amount of time that I had been pregnant, I had realized how precious it was and now hoped that she would feel the same.

"I don't know, Cinnamon. I've been going through a lot, and the fact that Markese—" she started to say.

"Hold up. Wait a minute. I knew you and Markese had fucked around before, but damn not that heavy, where you would let that nigga get you pregnant," I said, cutting her off.

"Well, he definitely isn't fucking with me anymore, after I told him I wanted an abortion," she said, causing my face to turn up.

"What the fuck you mean you want an abortion?" I asked, a little pissed off at hearing that.

"Cinnamon, you don't understand. I can't have a baby by him. Not to mention I just found out he has another bitch pregnant too. What the fuck do I look like, being pregnant at the same time as that bitch?" she asked as I sat there staring at her like she had lost her fucking mind.

"You're right. I don't understand! Do you hear yourself, Stonie? You're up here talking about how you want an abortion. Do you know what the fuck I would give to still be pregnant?" I yelled. "No. Fuck that shit! Do you know it's women out there who can't even have kids, and your selfish ass is talking about chopping yours up, all because another bitch is pregnant at the same time as you." I began to yell louder. "This type of shit happens every fucking day. Get over it. And if you didn't want a baby by that nigga, then why were you letting him run up in you raw? That doesn't even make sense," I said as I tried to fight back the tears that were trying to come out. "You really got me and life fucked up right now. That innocent baby hasn't done anything wrong, and it deserves a chance at life like every other child," I said as I wiped away the few tears that were now falling down my face as I stood up to leave. "I knew you were a coldhearted bitch, but got damn, Stonie, this shit's on a whole other level. And I'm not even trying to judge you, but hey, do what's best for you. But understand this: karma is a bitch, and I'm rooting for her to fuck you up the worst way," I said while snatching my purse off the couch. "Oh, and I suggest you get sized for your dress, because if you miss my wedding, you won't have to worry about karma fucking you up, because Ima do it myself," I said as I turned away to leave.

"You know, Cinnamon, it's easy for you to say that when have a nigga who gives you the world and that's not out here fucking everything that walks," she said, stopping me in my tracks right before I reached the steps.

"Fuck you, Stonie," I went on to say before walking down the stairs and out the door, where I jumped in my car and pulled off as I continued to release a few more tears as I thought about my unborn child who never even had a chance at life. And her baby did, and she didn't even want it. Shit like that made me question why God gave babies to women like her, I said to myself as I continued to drive until I was pulling back up at my house.

Stonie

I'm not ashamed to admit that I never thought that this situation would have such a big impact on my life. A few days after the argument me and Markese had, I went to the emergency room because I was experiencing pains to the point where I couldn't sleep. When I got there, they gave me an ultrasound to see exactly what was going on, and I'd be lying if I said seeing my baby didn't make me want to change my mind about getting an abortion. It's one thing to pee on a stick and know that you're pregnant, but to actually see it and hear the heartbeat only made it more real for me.

After finding out everything with the baby was OK and that I was just dehydrated, I was given fluids and then released. I went back to Cinnamon's condo and contemplated on what I wanted to do. I felt like God was trying to tell me something, because from the moment I saw my baby, I couldn't help but to start picturing what he or she would look like. For the first time since finding out that I was pregnant, I was beginning to feel different about the situation. But still I couldn't see myself having a baby by a nigga who had another bitch pregnant. Every time I thought about that, it pissed me off even more, and thoughts of abortion popped right back up. And just when I thought I had made my mind up, Cinnamon's ass popped up and made me feel less than I was already feeling.

I couldn't blame her for everything, she said, because it was the truth that woman lose babies every day. And some women can't even conceive or carry a child. And my cousin was one of those women who had miscarried her baby, and I saw firsthand how that affected her whole life. I felt like shit knowing that I had made my cousin cry. I was so caught in my own bullshit that I never considered how other woman felt. Not only did I have the nigga who I loved mad at me, but now my best friend, who knew me better than anyone one, was pissed off at me. The last thing I wanted to do was make her mad, especially when she had just become happy again, I thought to myself as I picked up the picture of the ultrasound and began looking at it, and a few tears began to fall down my face. And I began to ask God to forgive me for all the reckless shit I'd been doing since I'd been pregnant, and if it was his will, then please allow me to birth a healthy baby.

I didn't know where this road was going to take me or why I had ended up pregnant by Markese, of all people, but I was hoping that all things would work together, because whether Markese and I ended together or not, I would always love him for helping me love again and for giving me my first child, whom I planned on naming Chance whether it was a girl or boy. That would be the name, because I was damn sure taking a chance on keeping him or her, I said to myself as I reached inside my purse and pulled out a notebook and pen and began writing Markese a letter.

Once I was done, I hopped in the shower and got dressed. Since Mariah was the one who had run her big-ass mouth, she would be the one to deliver this letter to Markese. I was just hoping like hell he would read it and forgive me, I said to myself as I grabbed my purse along with the ultrasound and headed out the door while calling Mariah at the same time.

"Hello," she answered as I got inside the car.

"Where you at? We need to meet up right now," I said as I pulled off to meet her where that was.

Rose

"Come on, Ma. Pick up the phone," I said out loud to myself as I paced back and forth in the restaurant bathroom hoping that my mother would answer the phone. For the past few days, I hadn't been able to reach her or my grandfather, and I was beginning to get worried. It wasn't like them not to answer the phone. Not only that, my father had been acting real different. I couldn't explain it, but I felt like he knew something and wasn't telling me, I said to myself as I took a deep breath before walking out of the bathroom and running right into Malik.

"I was just looking for you," he said as he came to a complete stop. "Are you all right?" he asked in a concerned voice.

"Yeah, I'm fine. Just some family problems, that's all."

"Aw, OK. I'm just making sure. But look, you can take the rest of the day off, as well as the weekend. I have some people coming in to remodel the place. And by the way you look, I can tell you could use a few days off," he said, but I knew better than that, seeing that I'd peeped that he had another shipment coming in tomorrow, and he probably didn't want anyone there when he brought in his drugs. I couldn't understand why I was feeling like I should tell Malik about what my father was doing. Something was telling me that he was not the person my father making him out to be, but until I knew that my mother was safe, I just had to keep going with the plan and hope like hell everything would work out in the end, I said to myself.

"OK, well, I guess I'll see you Monday morning," I went on to say before walking toward my office, where I gathered all my things, and then headed out.

Once I got to my car, I headed back to the hideout spot where we all had been hiding for the past month and a half. The whole ride there, I tried calling my mother but still got no answer, I thought to myself as I pulled up to the run-down building we had been staying in. With all this damn money my parents claimed to have, why the hell were we staying here? I asked myself as I walked inside the building and toward the door where we lived and began walking inside. But before I could even shut the door, I was hit over the head from the back, and seconds later everything went black.

Yvette

They say all storms don't come just to fuck shit up, but to clear ways for a new path. But if you ask me, no matter how many times you start a new beginning, you will still be left with old scars. I guess they're reminders of what you never want to see again, or maybe they're left there to remind you of what couldn't destroy you. I can't speak for everyone who's dealing with a storm, but I know if I could forget all this shit and walk away without so much as a bruise or memory, I would. But that would be too easy, I said to myself as I hit the blunt while looking over at the phone, which wouldn't stop ringing, I thought to myself as I grabbed the .45-caliber off the table that I was sitting at. Then I stood up and began walking over toward the closet that I had these two muthafucks tied up in and opened it. Hell, the old man looked like he was already damn near dead, I said to myself right before placing a call to Porsha.

"What's it looking like?" I asked as I leaned up against the wall a bit.

"Come on, now. Besides a bunch of dead muthafuckas, it's looking a lot like Christmas," she said, making me smile ear to ear before getting serious.

"Thank you, Porsha. I couldn't have pulled this off without you." Because ever since she'd been here, I'd had eyes on everyone. I'd been in control of everything this whole time, which was why I wasn't tripping when Carlos's wife tried to pop up on me because she caught that shit the moment she landed in the States. Not to mention the lick she just hit that made my move across the chessboard one to remember. And with his queen in my possession, there was only one more move I had to make to get that checkmate, I said to myself, but I snapped out of my thoughts when she began to talk.

"Yeah, yeah, yeah. Don't mention it. I'll see you in a few hours. It's time we end all roads that can lead to destruction," she said before hanging up the phone and leaving me with another phone that wouldn't stop ringing, I said to myself before answering it.

"You sneaky-ass bitch," Big Malik yelled through the phone. "What, you thought I wouldn't find out this whole time you've been lying to me? I checked at every hospital down in Miami, and that old muthafucka hasn't checked into any of them. But since you think I'm game..." he said before the phone went quiet and another voice began speaking.

"Ma, please help me," the voice on the other end of the phone said before he began to speak again.

"You got less than twenty-four hours to bring me all my money and drugs before I kill her ass," he went on to say, and I laughed out loud at the comment he'd just made.

"You've always been a bitch ass nigga," I said, laughing harder this time. "Don't get quiet now," I said into the phone. "You should have known better than to come for my kids. I mean, come on now. I know you didn't think I was going to let that shit slide now, did you?" I asked, still laughing a bit.

"Do you really think I give a fuck about that bitch, Yvette?" he asked with a little laugh of his own. "You're doing me a favor by taking her off my hands. I haven't trusted a bitch since you fucked me over. You think you're hurting me by taking her?" he asked, still laughing.

"No, I don't! Me taking her has nothing to do with you. This is just payback for all the shit she tried to do to me years ago. I know you well enough to know you don't give a fuck about nobody but yourself," I said. "But I do know you will care once you see the way I've left your warehouse down in Miami," I said with a smirk as the phone went silent. "I mean, damn, after I showed you how to flip that shit and double your profit, all you have is a few million dollars and a couple of bricks that look like shit?" I asked in between my laughs. "Not to mention the half million dollars I took off this old-ass muthafuck who looks like he may have a breath and a half left in him. I mean, damn, I know my son's product is probably the only reason why you got the chump change you got now," I said while shaking my head. "You're pathetic, and you wonder why I fucked off the way I did. I deal with kings only. And you? You're just a fucking peasant. Just like back then, I pulled all the strings. And if you haven't realized by now, I'm still calling all the plays. Only thing different is you're on the bench now, and just like this bitch," I said as I raised the .45 to her face, "you're dead to me," I said and then pulled the trigger and shot her and her father in the head before hanging up the phone.

"Two down; two more to go," I said as I stood there looking at both their dead bodies before throwing the end of my blunt on them and closing the door.

15

GRIM REAPER "ALL BAD"

"Yeah, no one by that name has checked into any hospital in Miami. I even went as far as looking into hospitals in Fort Lauderdale as well, and there are still no signs of him," the person on the other end of the phone said before I hung up on him and began calling that bitch Susie.

"I knew It. I knew that bitch was lying to me. I heard it in her voice," I said out loud as I called her again but still got no response, I thought to myself as I heard someone trying to open the front door. And I immediately grabbed the Glock off the table and ran toward the door before it opened. And when it did, I hit my daughter Rose in the back of the head with the butt of my gun and watched her body fall to the ground as I stood over her, ready to hit her again. But she had blacked out, I thought to myself as I grabbed some tape that was not too far from where I was.

"Y'all wanna play with me?" I said as I began taping her hands behind her back. "I'll show you muthafucks," I said as I continued to tape her hands and feet.

Once I had her tied up like I wanted her, I placed her in a chair and waited until she woke up. After I had been sitting there for almost an hour still trying to call Susie, she finally woke up.

"Ahh," she started to say as she slowly opened her eyes.

"Where the fuck is she at?" I yelled as I stood up and grabbed her by the hair.

"I don't know," she cried as I held her hair in my hands. "Please. I don't know," she cried out and began to sob.

"You better hope like hell for your sake she didn't run off with my money, because once I find her, Ima make her watch me kill you before I kill her," I said while letting go of her hair and walking toward the table, where I began calling Susie again. And this time she answered. Well, at least I thought she did, I said to myself as I listened to Yvette on the other end begin to speak, and I grabbed the sawed-off from underneath table and began walking toward the door. Knowing Yvette, she could be anywhere, and she had Susie.

I knew it would only be a matter of time before she came here, I thought to myself before reminding her that I could give a fuck about that bitch. I damn near dropped dead when she mentioned the fact that she had just hit my warehouse down in Miami and that all the money Susie's father had from the last drop, she got that too, I said to myself right before hearing two gunshots go off, and then the phone hung up.

"Shit, shit, shit," I yelled as I punched a hole in the wall. "What the fuck!" I yelled louder as I began pacing back and forth before running downstairs to the basement, where I opened a safe and took out half a million dollars. "Get the fuck up," I said to the person who I'd just uncuffed from the pole that sat next to the small matches. "Walk up the stairs," I said as I pointed the gun at her, and moments later we were walking up the stairs, where I began taping her mouth and hands. "Listen to me very close. Ima untie you, but if you so much as blink the wrong way, Ima kill you. Do I make myself clear?" I ask my daughter Rose, and she gave me a head nod to let me know she understood before I cut her loose. "All right, now watch her. That's the only thing that's saving us right now," I said as I began grabbing all the weapons that I had hidden around the house as well as anything thing that could be traced back to me. Once I had everything I needed, we headed for the car, where I placed a call.

"Yeah," the person on the other end said as I pulled away from the spot I'd been staying at while looking for any signs of Yvette.

"I need a phone traced and every location and number it's dialed in the last forty-eight hours. After that we need to meet up, and if you so much as try to set me up, I promise you're going to regret it," I said before giving him Susie's cell number.

Malik

For the first time in a long time, a nigga was finally feeling free. After tomorrow night, I would be turning everything over to Markese and Choppa. I'd put in enough work over the years to sit back and enjoy life. I wasn't going to stunt, though. It was a bittersweet feeling knowing that I was about to leave the streets. I had never thought I'd see the day when I'd walk away from all this shit. I was going to miss every bit of it, but not more than my bitch or my family missing me if some shit were to go left later down the road. I would ask Markese, Choppa, and Zilla to do the same, but knowing them niggas, that shit wasn't going to happen. So the least I could do was step them up to win and plug them in with best Colombian drug lord who was still living to this day, I said to myself as I sat at my desk and made sure everything was good for tomorrow's shipment.

Once I had everything the way I wanted it, I headed out to find Amanda to let her know she was free to leave and that she could have the rest of the weekend off. And based on the way she looked, I could tell she needed it anyway, I said to myself as I watched her walk toward her office to get all her things before leaving. Once she was gone, I called Kim and had her come run the restaurant. When she finally pulled up, it was almost an hour later. After telling her I'd be gone until Monday, I headed toward my truck, where I placed a call to Markese.

"Yo," he answered as I hopped into my truck.

"You already know, fam. Same shit, different day. But look, Ima need you to get with Choppa later on and meet up with me. I'll let you know the location in few," I said as I pulled away from the restaurant while continuing to rap with Markese until I was pulling up in front of my spot and walking in.

After telling Markese I'd call him back, I headed upstairs to holla at Cinnamon. But to my surprise, shorty wasn't there. I was just about to call her and see where she was at when I heard the front door open and close, I thought to myself as I headed back downstairs. I was just about to ask her where the fuck she had been at when I noticed she looked like she had been crying. I ain't going to lie. A nigga's heart dropped when I saw that shit.

"What's wrong?" I asked, hoping like hell it wasn't shit I did.

"Nothing," she went on to say as she tried to brush past me, but I ended up grabbing her by her arm, causing her to stop.

"Then why does it look like you been crying?" I asked as I turned her around to face me, and I could tell she was about to give me the same answer as before.

"Nothing, Malik. I just had some words with Stonie, and it kind of hurt my feelings. That's all."

"Well, y'all need to work that shit out. You coming home crying and shit that ain't good, Cinnamon," I said while pulling her closer to me. "Besides, whatever it is, I'm sure it can be fixed. In the meantime, I got something that will make you happy," I said, causing her to smile.

"And what is that?" she asked.

"This dick," I went on to say, causing her to burst out laughing.

"Fuck you, Malik. You play too fucking much," she said while hitting me a few times.

"I'm just playing, baby. But I do got something for you. It's upstairs," I said as she stood there looking at me with a mug.

"I'm not playing with you. If I get all the way upstairs and you're playing, Ima be pissed off," she said before walking up the stairs to our room, where I watched her walk toward her walk-in closet.

"All right, I'm up here," she said as she came out of the closet but stopped in the middle of her tracks when she seen me standing there holding a box that had a ten-carat diamond ring that was shaped like an egg and had diamonds all around the band, I thought to myself as I watched her standing there with her hands covering her mouth.

"What's that shit you was saying, shorty? I don't hear you talking now," I said as I walked closer to her as she stood there, still speechless. "I don't know why I have to keep telling you you're going to be my wife,

Cinnamon. Ever since I met you, I've been knowing you're the woman Ima marry. And after all this shit we've been through, with the loss of our baby and you being shot and still staying with me, shit…how I'm feeling, we can get married right now. I don't know too many women like you. Shit, come to think of it, I don't know one woman like you. That's why it will always be you. I know you may be happy with the ring you got, but shit, I'm not. And besides, this one means a lot more to me. And until you get the actual wedding ring, I need you to wear this one for me," I went on to say. I grabbed her left hand and removed the seven-carat one and replaced it with the ten-carat, and I watched her stare at it for what seemed like a lifetime before she jumped on me.

"I love you so much, baby," she said while damn near squeezing the life out of me. "Oh my God. I can't believe you got me this big-ass ring. Like, for real, baby, I don't need or want another one. This one is perfect," she went on to say as she kept looking at the ring. "Shit, I'm going blind just looking at it," she said before getting quiet. "I'm serious, Malik. I don't want another ring. I just want you. I was OK with my last ring, but this one is even better, and the fact that it's shaped like an egg shows me you put a lot of thought into it."

"Hell, yeah. Just like Ima keep putting my seeds in yo eggs," I said, making her laugh. And for the rest of the day, we worked on that second baby until it was time for Markese's surprise party.

Narrator
After everything Cinnamon had been through, you would think she and Malik would have a happy ending. I mean, why wouldn't you, after that big-ass ring he'd just given her with the promise of leaving the streets? You would think God would bless this union and spare them from any more heartbreak. But what's done in the dark must to come to light before you can make anything right, and the fucked-up part was that she looked the happiest she had ever been since the incident as she stood in front of the mirror, Versace down matching her man's, as they both prepared to leave for Markese's birthday bash, still in a daze from all the excitement about the wedding. Cinnamon's joy and happiness made Malik feel as if his life

was back on track and that he had everything he'd ever wanted. Except for the loss of their child, he couldn't have been any happier as they drove toward the club, where they met up with Zilla, the mother of his child, Chyna, Dominique, and Mariah to surprise Markese. They all gathered around the room dressed in over a half million dollars' worth of designer and gold while waiting on Choppa's cue to let them know he and Markese were on the way up and for everyone to be ready. And moments later the door opened, and everyone screamed "Surprise!" as they threw confetti up in the air.

"I knew y'all niggas was up to something," Markese said as he walked through the room with a smile, dapping all the men and giving all the women hugs.

"You know I wasn't about to let you bring in your birthday alone," Malik said as he popped a bottle of Ace and held it out for Markese to take it.

"I appreciate it," Markese said as he hugged Malik tight and told him he loved him, and for the next hour, everyone popped bottles left and right, blunts were passed around, and food was brought in—that was, until Mariah asked Cinnamon to go to the bathroom with her, and they both left the party and headed toward the bathroom. On the way there, a short, brown-skinned woman who wasn't all that good looking kept looking at Cinnamon, to the point where she had to stop and ask that bitch what the fuck she was staring at.

"I'm not the one you should be worried about," she said as her friend walked up, and that's when it dawned on cinnamon that the light-skinned thick chick was the same bitch she had seen Malik with when she first met him, and the brown-skinned one was the same one with her when she overheard them at the nail shop.

"Why the fuck would I be worried about you or any other bitch?" Cinnamon asked with a mug.

"What's going on?" the light-skinned chick asked with a slight mug.

"Girl, nothing. This bitch walking around here like she's that bitch, not knowing she's out here looking dumb. Malik was just with you a little over a week ago," she said, causing Cinnamon's heart to drop.

"Don't listen to them hating-ass bitches," Mariah started to say.

"Who's hating? I don't have shit to hate off of, especially when I was just with him about a week ago," the light-skinned one started to say right before Cinnamon ran up and gave her a clean two-piece, causing her to stumble and her friend to try to jump in. But Mariah was on her ass like white on rice hitting her with a left as Cinnamon dragged the light-skinned girl to the floor by her hair while trying to stomp her with her red bottoms as security tried to pull them apart, but Cinnamon's grip was so tight that they were having a hard time pulling them apart.

"Aye, somebody get Malik out here. This is his girl and his sister fighting," one of the security people yelled as they continued to try to break Mariah and the friend up without causing any injury to the both of them. And moments later, everyone came running out from the private room. You would have thought a war had broken out once Chyna saw Cinnamon standing over the girl, still holding on to her hair as she ran up and began trying to stomp the girl out. That was, until Dominique grabbed her. And even then, she was still kicking and trying to break loose as Malik tried to get Cinnamon off the girl, who was now bleeding.

"Grab her," Malik yelled to the security person, who had step out of the way so that Malik and his team could get Cinnamon and Mariah.

Once Malik got Cinnamon off the girl and her face was revealed, he knew right then and there that anything he and Cinnamon had was about to be over.

Cinnamon

I vowed to myself a long time ago to never fight over a nigga or ever let a bitch make me feel like she got one up on me, but Malik wasn't just any nigga to me. He was the man I planned to marry in less than five months, the nigga I almost lost my life over, not to mention my unborn child's life. So when this bitch mentioned the fact that she was just with my nigga a little over a week ago, it sent me over the edge. It wasn't so much what she said but more how she said it that led me to believe it was true. And the fact that this bitch had the balls to try me in a club full of people pissed me off even more, I thought to myself as I held her hair in my hands as I listened to Malik and Choppa tell me to let go. But I wasn't trying to hear shit that they were saying, I said to myself as I felt Malik pick me up and Choppa grab my hands, forcing me to let go of her hair as security grabbed her so I couldn't get a hold of her again.

"Let me go!" I yelled as tears began to run down my face, and I kicked and hit Malik everywhere that I could. "I asked you! I asked you did you have anything to tell me. All you had to do was keep it real!" I yelled as loud as I could as he tried to hold me down, but I somehow broke loose and began hitting him in the face to the point where Markese, Choppa, and Zilla had to hold me back. "After everything I've been through, you do this shit to me?" I cried even harder as he tried to walk up but stopped when I began trying to kick him. "What type of nigga are you?" I asked with a slight laugh. "You couldn't even control this weak-ass bitch. The least you could have done was fuck with a bitch who can keep her fucking mouth shut!" I yelled again.

"Just listen to me, Cinnamon," he tried to say, but I cut him off.

"I'm not listening to shit you have to say! I can't believe this shit," I said as I walked back and forth, with Zilla and Choppa still covering me and Markese covering him. "I should have left your ass when I lost my muthafucking baby. You're a fucking clown to me. I would call you a bitch-ass nigga, but even that title's too good for a nigga like you and couldn't express how I really feel about you. You're a fucking fraud, and you're dead to me. You want to be free?" I asked, looking him dead in his eyes with tears still falling from mine. "Well, here's your walking papers, nigga. You're free," I said right before turning toward the stairs to leave, because I wasn't about to wait on no damn elevators to take me downstairs. "What the fuck are y'all looking at?" I asked as I brushed past the people who were standing around watching like they had never been through this shit before, I said to myself as I listened to Chyna call my name, but I keep walking until I reach the door.

"Cinnamon," she kept yelling until she caught up with me, and when she did, I just broke down in tears as she hugged me tight.

"I just don't understand," I cried out loud as she hugged me and cried with me.

"I know it hurts, but right now you can't be walking down the street barefooted in the middle of January," she said as she wiped a few of my tears, and for the first time since the fight, I looked at my arm, and one of the gunshot wounds was bleeding.

I had such an adrenaline rush that I hadn't felt anything until now. "I have to get out of here," I said to Chyna, who spotted a cab coming toward us and flagged it down as she reached into her purse and pulled out her credit card.

"Here. Use whatever you need, and don't worry about paying me back. I'll make sure to get your purse and anything else you left," she said as I began getting inside the cab.

"Thanks, Chyna, but I don't need this. I have money stashed at the condo," I started to say, but she stopped me.

"I know you don't need it, but just take it anyway," she went on to say before giving me another hug and telling me she loved me and to stay strong. And moments later, I was pulling off and heading to my condo, where I wondered the whole ride there why God was putting me through so much hell. I must have thought about that the whole ride there, because I didn't even notice we had pulled up until the cab driver said something.

After paying him, I stepped out of the car and began knocking on the door, since I didn't have my keys or purse. After I had been knocking for about five minutes straight, Stonie answered the door, and I could tell by the way she looked that she wasn't expecting me to look the way I did, I thought to myself as I walked up the stairs ignoring her questions as she asked why I looked the way I did. And when I finally reached the bathroom, I could see why she had so many questions, I said to myself as I looked in the mirror and began shaking my head as I listened to Stonie in the other room going off on the phone. I was sure whoever it was she was talking to was filling her in on what had just gone down, I said to myself as I locked the door before taking my clothes off and hopping into the shower, where I stayed until the hot water turned cold. And by the time I got out, I had my mind made up. Not only was I going to leave Malik alone, but I planned to move away from Chicago as well. This city had caused me more heartbreak and hell than I'd ever had to experience in my whole life, I thought to myself as I lay in bed with just a towel wrapped around my body as I looked at my engagement ring that I just gotten a few hours ago, and I began crying some more.

I guess it's true when they say God will save you from the unknown. I should have peeped that shit a month and a half ago when everything went left for me, but like they say, love truly is one of the strongest drugs out there. And the love that I had for Malik was an overdose that could have destroyed me if God hadn't saved me, I said to myself as I took off the ten-carat ring and held it in my hands as I thought about what I was going to do with it. A part of me wanted to give it back, but then another part of me felt like it was owed to me after all the bullshit I'd been through.

After all, this ring would be the only thing I'd keep. All the clothes, jewelry, and cars—Malik could have that shit. I planned to start fresh. Besides, I had never been a dumb bitch. I was half a million dollars up thanks to him. All the money he'd given me, I'd stashed and invested it. I was just hoping like hell I would never need it for something like this, but fuck, it was what it was, and now that it was over, I planned to move somewhere where the sun would always shine even when it rained.

16

DETECTIVE BROWN (JUDGMENT DAY)

"It is with sad news that our chief of police was murdered a few nights ago. His funeral will be held this weekend in honor of his legacy," one of the state representatives was saying as I stood in the back and listened to the speech they were giving for him, and a few tears began to fall, not because I felt bad for what I'd done but because it could have easily been me in a few hours stripped from my life as well as my wife and unborn child, I thought to myself as I looked over at his wife and children crying, as one of the family members held his wife in their arms, I thought to myself as I gave them one last look before turning to walk out of the room.

"Aye, David," Derick called out, stopping me in my tracks. "You all right, man? I saw you could barely hold up in there," he asked as I wiped my eyes with the back of my hand.

"Yeah. It's just fucked up what happened to him. He had just called me a few hours before he was murdered, saying he wanted to talk about Brian," I said as I shook my head while trying to sound as sincere as possible.

"Yeah, I feel that. But luckily, we have a team that's trying to look into every camera that's on the streetlights, stoplights, and buildings to see who was in the area at the time of his death," he went on to say, causing me to lose the last bit of breath I had, knowing that I could be exposed once again.

"Well, I hope they find the bastards who did it," I lied. "But look," I said, moving in closer to him so that no one would be able to hear me, "I know I told you to leave the Malik case alone, but I've been doing some thinking, and you were right," I said while taking a deep breath. "I got word that he's bringing in one of the biggest shipments ever tonight. I've been watching him for a few days, and it checks out. I plan on taking him and his entire team down tonight, but i can't do it alone," I said, looking at him for a response.

"Just tell me when and where. I got three men itching to get some type of excitement," he said before we both took off down the hall toward my office, where he called in three other men to help get the job done.

"What I am about to say should stay in between these walls," I said to the men who had just entered the room. "Tonight we're going to take down Chicago's most feared kingpin," I said while posting Malik's picture against the wall. "This is Malik Green," I said as I began posting some more photos on the wall. "And this man right here is Markese Green, his right-hand man, also his brother. This man is Corteze Miller, known on the streets as Choppa. He's very dangerous and will not hesitate to shoot or kill anyone who poses a threat to him. He did four years for armed robbery a while back. He could have gotten away, but his accomplices got caught and ratted him out. Shortly after, the trail all of our witness and their entire families were slaughtered," I said while shaking my head as I flashed back to the crime scene. "Last but not least, this is Zach, known on the streets as Zilla. He's Corteze's little brother. He's also dangerous and has had his own run-ins with the law. These four men must be handled with extreme caution. Do not hesitate to shoot if needed. I would like to bring them in alive, but if things go a different way, do not be afraid to make that call, because I guarantee you they won't be. Suit up, wear you vests, and prepare for the worst, although we're hoping for the best," I said before fully going over the plan with everyone. Once we all had an understanding and the office was clear, I said a prayer and then placed a call.

"Yeah," the person on the other end answered.

"Everything's good. The plan is in motion."

Markese

The last conversation my mother and I had, had me looking at shit a lot differently, I said to myself as I sat on the couch looking at the envelope Stonie had Mariah give to me last night before shit broke out in the worst way, I said to myself as I opened the envelope and pulled out a letter and began reading it.

> *I hope this letter reaches you. I don't know where to start, so I guess I'll start it off by thanking you for being a friend, one that I never thought in a million years I would grow to love the way that I do. I'm a firm believer that all things happen for a reason. My reason for meeting you was to open my heart, which had been cold for so many years. If you had asked me a few months back, I would have told you I never planned on falling in love with you the way that I have. With all my rules, you would think that I would have dodged this shit called love. I tried so hard to fight the feelings that I have for you, even to the point where I was willing to get rid of my biggest blessing all in fear of love, when in reality I needed your love the most. I know that I can't change things between us, and I also know I can't be upset that you have another child on the way. I would never want the mother of your other child to feel as if her child doesn't matter, and knowing that I'm about to become a mother, I would never want to feel that way. I have made two mistakes that I will have to live with for the rest of my life. One is putting my unborn child in danger, and the other is losing the man I needed more than I knew, the man I never asked for but who came unexpectedly and changed my life as well as my world for the better. And for that I will always love you. I hope we can work past our differences and become friends again despite all the shit that I've done, because in seven months, we're going to become parents. And I refuse to hate the man who gave me the chance to love again. You have almost seven months to think about forgiving me, and I will to let you have all seven of those months because I know the majority of this is*

my fault. Nevertheless, I want you to know that I never once looked at you the way that you thought I did. I just knew that you could do better than this street life shit, but that's not for me to say. I just hope you don't allow it to get in the way of being a father, because both of your children are going to need you to take care of them, I hope to hear from you soon.

I will always love you,
P.S. Stonie

"Damn," I said out loud to myself as I read the letter before pulling out what was left inside the envelope and began smiling as I looked at the ultrasound of the baby. All this time I had been fucking with Stonie, and I never once asked shorty what her real name was, I said to myself as I read the name across the top, and I continued to stare at the picture with a smile, despite the ill feelings I had for shorty at the moment. I knew deep down I couldn't be mad at Stonie, and the fact that shorty opened up and told me how she really felt about me made me feel some type of way, knowing that I felt the same way about her, I said to myself as I placed the picture and the letter back in the envelope, as I heard voices begin to fill the room.

"Y'all niggas ready to end this shit?" Zilla asked, walking into the living room with Malik and Dominique right behind him.

"Shit, I been ready," I said as I stood up and gave Zilla, Dominique, and Malik some dap.

"You good, fam?" I asked Malik as I gave him some dap.

"Hell nah. That nigga ain't good. You saw the way Cinnamon was knocking his shit back last night," Zilla said as he took a seat.

"Yeah, I'm straight. I can't worry about that shit right now. I tried talking to shorty this morning, but she wasn't tryna hear shit I was saying. I'll deal with that shit later. Right now, I have to worry about bringing in this shipment and ending all this for good," Malik said while taking a seat.

"Fasha," I said right before Choppa came down the stairs with his dreads hanging over his face with no shirt on and a chopper in his hands.

"Y'all niggas ready to dirt this hoe-ass nigga and snatch his badge?" Choppa asked while standing on the last step pointing the chopper, and we all shook our heads because this nigga would dirt anybody, I said to myself as I watched him come take a seat next to me. And for the next few hours, we went over the plan step by step until it was time for me and Zilla to go grab the fake shipment, I said to myself as I threw him a bulletproof vest because anything could happen or anyone could be waiting on us, I thought to myself as I jumped in the truck.

"I feel for any nigga that think they're about to run up on this truck," Zilla said as he placed the two .40 Glocks with extended clips on his lap.

"Shit, you already know how I'm coming," I said, referring to the Draco and the .40 Glock I had on me, and then I pulled off toward the route.

Once we were in route, I hit Malik to let him know shit was good for him to move out. The route we were taking was about forty-five minutes away from the restaurant, so you know I was clutching the whole ride there, wishing a muthafucka would pop out. And just when we thought the coast was clear, five police cars came out of nowhere and surrounded the truck before we could even pull all the way into the restaurant, I thought to myself as I looked over at Zilla, who was putting the guns in a compartment underneath the seat as I pulled over and watched as the policemen surrounded the truck with theirs guns out.

"Put your hands on the steering wheel!" One of the policemen yelled as he pointed his gun at me through the window before opening the door and pulling me out right along with Zilla.

"Check the back," Detective Brown bitch-ass said as he walked up on me and began searching me. "You can wipe that smirk right off your face," he said as he pushed me up against the truck.

"Detective Brown," one of the men yelled. "Come take a look at this," the man yelled again as me and Zilla looked at each other, and moments later we heard Detective Brown going off.

"Shit, shit, shit," he yelled from inside the truck before coming back toward me and Zilla. "Where the fuck is the shipment?" he yelled.

Grim Reaper

As I waited on the call saying Malik and his crew had been taken down, I loaded up all the guns I would need to handle Yvette's sneaky ass and anybody that was with her, I thought to myself as I looked up at the time while wondering where the fuck this nigga was at. And right on cue, I heard loud bangs on the door, I thought to myself as I grabbed the Glock off the table before looking to see who it was. Once I saw who was on the other side of the door, I opened it.

"You set me up!" he yelled as he burst through the door and tried to grab me, but I pointed the .40 Glock at him before he could take another step.

"What the fuck are you talking about?" I asked as I placed the gun to his head.

"You set me up, muthafucka. That's what! You had me following Malik and his team—for what? A truck full of fucking canned goods?" he yelled as my face turned up a bit.

"Wait, what?" I asked, still confused.

"You heard me, muthafucka. There wasn't shit on that truck, so either you played me, or they played us," he yelled again as I stood there with a confused look as I tried to put two and two together.

"Shit," I said out loud, and I continued to think.

"You can't be fucking serious," he went on to say as he let out a slight laugh. "All this time, Malik was playing us. And your dumb ass couldn't even see that," he said, laughing louder this time as he continued to talk. "And if Malik didn't know I was tied with you before, he does now," he went on to say right before I heard another knock on the door. "Who the fuck is that?" he asked as I looked through the peephole before answering the door. And if looks could talk, well, let's just say this nigga was confused when he saw Derick walk through the door. "What the fuck is he doing here?" Detective Brown asked as I shut the door and locked it.

"I mean, I couldn't be the only muthafucka getting played around here. I paid Derick to keep a close eye on you. I knew if he pressed you enough, you would eventually ask him for help with Malik, seeing that he already body bagged Brian. Now, what I didn't expect was for Malik to pull this stunt. But since he did, I just have to go with plan B," I said while shrugging my shoulders. Then I looked over at Derick, who was leaning up against the wall. "You got that address?" I asked because he was the one I had paid to track down Susie's phone.

"Yeah. I got it right here," he started to say as Detective Brown tried to run up and attack him.

"You muthafucka," he started to say as he charged toward him, but I shot him before he could reach him, causing him to fall to the floor and for Derick to kneel down over him.

"You see, David, if you and Brian would have cut me in a long time ago, we wouldn't be here today. You see, this man right here..." he said, pointing up to me, "he was locked up with my brother. And in exchange for paying a lawyer to have him released early and, of course, a nice bag, I gave him you two muthafucks and all the dirt that he could use to blackmail y'all—and to put you away for good. With all the resources you could have used, I still can't believe you let shit get this far," he said while shaking his head. "I would have done it myself, but shit, I actually like my job. And since you two muthafuckas were already doing dirty shit, I didn't think you would mind," he went on to say with a little laugh of his own. "It's sad it has to be this way," he said before standing up.

"My wife—where's my wife?" he asked. I walked down the hall and grabbed her, and his eyes lit up at the sight of his pregnant wife right before I put a bullet in her head and watched her body drop.

"Damn, that was cold," Derick said before shooting Detective Brown in the head.

"It had to be done," I said in a nonchalant voice. "Now, let's go kill the rest of these muthafucks," I went on to say before grabbing the duffel bag full of weapons and then headed out to end Yvette and any roads that led back to her.

Malik

You wanna talk about luck? Shit, if I didn't have bad luck, a nigga wouldn't have none at all. Just when I planned on leaving the streets and starting over, I get caught up behind a nothing-ass bitch. I'm not the one to point fingers or blame the next muthafucka for my mistakes, but damn, I wasn't expecting shit to come out the way it had, especially since I didn't fuck shorty, I thought to myself as I flashed back on what happened the night before and then began shaking my head. I had never seen Cinnamon more hurt in my life except when she lost my seed. And even then, that was a different type of hurt. I could see in her eyes how disappointed she was at me, and the fact that I'd just upgraded her engagement ring hours before really made shit look worse than it really was, I said to myself as I took a deep breath.

I couldn't even blame shorty if she did up and leave a nigga alone, but I damn sure wasn't about to let her walk away without a fight, I said to myself as I pulled up to her condo and parked while taking another deep breath before stepping out and knocking on the door. I can't even lie. A nigga was nervous as hell as I stood there waiting on her to open the door. And moments later the door opened, and if looks could kill, hers was saying she wished she would have killed me last night, I thought to myself as I walked in and shut the door while she took a seat on the steps not too far from me.

"Before you say anything, just don't, because I could give two fucks about what you have to say. I didn't open the door to hear you out but for you to hear me out," she said, and I stood there listening to everything she had to say as tears began to fall down her face. "I thought long and hard last night about what I was going to do," she went on to say as she wiped a few tears away. "I thought about fucking you up. Setting the house on fire. Shit, I even thought about killing yo ass. But what the fuck is that going to do? I'm still going to be in love with you. I'm still going to be hurt, and I'm still going to miss you, and that's just something I will have to deal with over time. I want so bad for things to be the way they were when we first met, but that can't happen, not even after the shooting. Things will never be the same, Malik. In almost a year of us being together, I have experienced so much love but had to endure just as much pain, and at this point, I can't keep ignoring the signs, because there are only two things that will happen. We both will end up dead, or Ima end up more heartbroken than I already am. I love you to death, Malik. I do," she cried. "But I love me more." And with that she went on to say, as she dug into her pocket, "As much as I want to keep this ring, I just can't," she said as she stood up while stepping off the steps. "Thank you for everything—the good, the bad, and the ugly, because it made me stronger," she said as I reached out and grabbed her and then pulled her close to me.

"Just hear me out, Cinnamon," I tried to say, but she cut me off.

"Let me ask you this," she said as she reached out and grabbed my face, forcing me to look at her. "Were you with her a week ago, like she said you was?" she asked. I took a deep breath and rubbed my hands across the top of my head as I thought about the response that I was about to give her, then said fuck it.

"Yeah, I was, but…"

"But what? There is no *but*. If I did the same thing to you, would you want to hear me out? Would you be so easy to forgive me?" she asked. And for the first in my life, I didn't have the answer to that question, because I knew if the shoe was on the other foot, I'd be ready to body bag Cinnamon and that nigga. I wouldn't be thinking about giving her no second chance. But I couldn't tell her that, I said to myself as I stood there looking at her. "That's what I thought," she said before taking a step back and opening the door. "Take care, Malik, and I really hope you find yourself before it's too late," she went on to say as she held her engagement ring out for me to take. But instead I told her to keep it before walking out to my car, where a nigga had to pray to God that once I ended all of this shit, he would heal Cinnamon's broken heart and send her back to me, because I'd be damned if I watched another nigga have my bitch.

I'm not even going to stunt. For the first time in my life, I felt my heart break, and no nigga alive can say seeing the woman he loves walk out of his life wouldn't break his heart too. But I couldn't deal with the situation like I wanted to. I still had to worry about bringing in my last shipment and dirting these hoe-ass niggas, I said to myself as I pulled away and headed toward Choppa's condo to go over the plan for tonight's shipment. Once everybody had the plan down pack, me, Choppa, and Dominique went one way, and Markese and Zilla went another way. Once we got conformation that Markese and Zilla were on the move, me and Choppa headed to the drop while Dominique kept an eye out for everybody. Once we pulled up to the warehouse, we were supposed to meet the connect. I sent my mother a text, and moments later the doors opened, and we were driving in where a bunch of niggas in black suits stood with big-ass choppas, Tecs, and Glocks in their hands.

"Damn. Look at that chopper right there," Choppa said as we pulled in and parked.

Once we were inside, the doors closed, and we both stepped off the truck and over toward my mother, where both me and Choppa were searched and stripped from our guns that we had on us, I thought to myself as I looked over at my mother like, "What the fuck is this about?"

"Don't worry. It's nothing personal," a man said in a thick accent as he walked up smoking a cigar. "Your mother is known to be very mischievous," he said, looking at my mother while winking at her. "I'm Carlos. And you would be Malik?" he said while taking a seat on the edge of the table. "I've heard a lot about you, and I like the way you run your operation. I would have extended this offer to you long ago, but your mother..." he said, looking over at her. "Let's just say it would have been a war—one that I'm not prepared for, and I'm always prepared for war," he said. "But enough about what I think. Let's get down to business," he went on to say. He snapped his fingers, and one of the men in suits brought over a few bricks with a knife. "It's all yours," Carlos said, and I walked closer to the table and cut into one of the bricks so I could taste the product before placing it in a kit and watching it turn. "See? The purest it comes," Carlos stated as I sat the small bottle back down.

"I agree," I said as I waved for Choppa to start bringing the duffel bags over. "In the first two bags, it's all hundred-dollar bills. Two bags are all fifties, and the last two bags are twenties," I said while sitting the bags in front of him.

"Good," he said as he took the cigar out his mouth before blowing the smoke out.

"It's a hundred and five keys there," he said, pointing over to the product. "Consider the extra five as a welcome to the family," he went to say before speaking in Spanish, and moments later, a few of his men began loading our truck with all the product. "It's nice doing business with you, and I hope we can continue," he said while extending his hand out for me to shake it. "I'm trusting that all the money is there. I don't have time to sit and count this shit. I have to get out of the States before the feds pick up that I'm here, you know?" he said in a nonchalant voice as I shook his hand while letting out a slight laugh.

"Yeah, I know," I went on to say.

"And as for you…" he said, looking over at my mother. "Tick tock," he went on to say as a few of his men began picking up the bags of money, and moments later they were all walking out and leaving me halfway happy knowing that all I had to do now was dead the rest of these muthafucks, I thought to myself as me and Choppa grabbed our Glocks off the table.

"All right. Now it's time to handle our real issues," my mother said as we began walking toward the truck.

"Hell yeah. You know I'm ready," Choppa added while grabbing his chopper from the back.

"All right, but let's take this product back to the spot first," I said as we headed for the underground trap. But before we made it all the way there, Dominique was calling, saying Markese and Zilla were and zill being taken to Cook County, and everything checked out with Detective Brown's bitch ass. "I knew it," I said out loud as we pulled up to the barn. "Give me a minute. You still got eyes on that nigga?" I asked, and once he told me yeah and that he was on his way to us, I hung up.

"What happened, fam? Everything straight?" Choppa asked.

"Nah. Markese and Zilla just got whipped," I said, and Choppa began shaking his head.

"See? I told you. You should have been let me snatch that nigga's badge," Choppa said as we stepped off the truck.

"Well, today's that day. Let's get this shit off the truck and underground," I said as me and my mother walked toward the latch that led to the underground tunnel as Choppa opened the doors to the truck. But before I could get all the way underground to get the carts for the product, I heard Choppa spraying the chopper and yelling, I thought to myself as I pulled the .40 Glock with the extended clip from my waist and took off toward the truck, where I spotted a nigga on the floor fighting for his life before I shot him in the head alongside another nigga who was on the other side of the truck, I thought to myself as I bent down and shot him in both his legs, causing him to drop his gun as I took off running toward the other side to see who it was, but before I could off that nigga, a bullet came from behind me and hit him in the head, causing the rest of his body to drop, I thought to myself as I turned around and spotted my mother standing behind me, as I stepped over the nigga she had just killed to get to Choppa. But before I could, I heard Choppa yelling, "It's another one, fam. It's another one." And on cue, me and my mother dropped low to see who was on the other side of the truck.

"This ain't got shit to do with you, son." I heard what sounded like that nigga the Grim Reaper, I said to myself. A moment later, I heard two shots go off, and Porsha yelled, "Y'all good?" I thought to myself as I walked around the truck to where Porsha was standing over my father's body, and I turned him over so that he would be facing me and my mother, who was now walking up.

"Like I told you before, this is chess, not checkers," my mother said as she knelt down over him with a smile right before he cocked back and spit on her, causing her to smirk. "Since you're already dead, Ima let that shit slide," she said while wiping the spit off her shirt as she stood up, leaving me to finish him off, I thought to myself as I stood over his body while watching him fight for his life before I pointed the Glock at him.

"Like you said, pops, a nigga that has a lot to lose will always think twice. Maybe you should have tried that," I said before pulling the trigger and emptying the rest of my clip as well as all of the hurt a nigga been holding in for the past month and a half, I thought to myself before taking off to see about Choppa, who was now lying in Porsha's lap in the back of the truck with the chopper still in his hands.

Cinnamon (six months later)
"I can't explain something I don't see that feels deeper than the sea and will hit you like a wave. Even the oceans weren't prepared to believe, and all the angels in heaven waited front row to see an age even decades couldn't beat a flame. Only God could stand to see two twin flames who were always meant to be." I smiled as read the poem I had

had just written while I waited for my plane to land in Chicago. Out of all the poems I had written, this by far was my favorite one. It described the way I felt, even six months later.

I felt more in love with Malik than I did the day I decided to leave him and move away from Chicago. I will say that I was glad to hear, after everything that had happened, that he had finally left the streets and turned legit. Hearing that made my heart smile. And as much as I wanted to reach out to him, I just couldn't. Not even after months of him calling and sending messages through Stonie and Chyna. I still didn't reply. I felt the only way to truly forgive him would consist of me cutting off all ties with him. I was shocked to receive a million-dollar transfer to my account from his. I guess that was his way of paying me back. I'm not going to say that it wasn't owed to me after everything that I'd been through, but honestly, I didn't want his money. What I wanted was something that he could never give me, and that was for everything to go back to the way it was when we first met, I thought to myself as I listened to the pilot say we had landed in Chicago, and I began grabbing all of my things to get off the plane so that I could meet up with Chyna.

I hadn't seen Stonie or Chyna since I up and left Chicago, but today was Stonie's baby shower, and no matter how I felt, I wouldn't miss this for the world. I had made sure to make Chyna promise me she wouldn't tell Stonie or anyone else I was coming. I wanted to surprise Stonie, especially since she had been begging me ever since I'd moved to come and visit me down in Florida. But every time she asked me, I told her no. Not because I didn't want to see her, but because I needed time to myself and time to heal from everything life had put me through. I had gone from being the happiest woman in the world to losing the biggest blessing of my life to almost losing my life, and sadly, I had lost the man who would always have my heart whether I liked it or not. When you have taken as many losses as I had, all you want to do is try to heal, I said to myself as I spotted Chyna looking for me as I walked up behind her.

"Damn, you fly-ass shit," I said as she turned around and jumped on me.

"Oh my God," she kept saying as she hugged me. "I missed you so much," she said as she held on to me tight.

"I missed you too," I said, and I let out a few laughs as she continued to hug me before letting me go.

"Damn, that Florida weather been doing you right," she said as she stood there looking at me with a smile. "What you been eating? Dick? You getting thick-ass shit," she said, causing me to laugh out loud.

"Nah, ain't no dick, bih. I'm just living my best life," I said as we walked toward her car.

"I know that's right," she went on to say as we jumped in her Benz and pulled off.

"Did you get my gifts I had sent for the baby shower?"

"Yeah. I got all twenty-two of them," she said, causing me to roll my eyes while laughing a bit, because she was being dramatic, as usual.

"I only sent like sixteen, so shut the fuck up," I said before getting serious. "You didn't tell anyone I was coming, did you?" I asked, and she gave me a look that said, "Bitch, you tried it."

"Don't ask me no dumb-ass question like that," she said, and for the rest of the ride until we reached the place where Stonie was having the baby shower, I caught her up on my new life in Florida. That was, until we pulled up to the event, and for the first time in a long time, I had butterflies, I said to myself as I helped Chyna get all the bags out of the trunk before we walked inside. "Damn, Stonie really went all out," I said to myself as I looked at all the pretty pink, purple, and white decorations she had all over the place before walking toward the other room, where everyone else was, and for a minute the room got quiet as everyone stared at me.

"What? What's wrong?" Stonie asked, and she turned around and spotted me standing there with bags full of gifts, I thought to myself as I watched her take off running toward me.

"You, stupid bitch!" she yelled as she hugged me tight while crying. "I thought I would never see you again," she said in between her cries as she lightweight choked me.

"I moved away. I didn't die," I said as I let out a slight laugh. "And you know I wouldn't miss this day for nothing," I said as we pulled away from each other, and I began rubbing her belly. "Gosh, you got big," I said as she wiped her tears away.

"I know, right? I'm so ready for this shit to be over," she went on to say before cussing Chyna out for not telling her I was coming.

After exchanging words with Stonie's crybaby ass, I went and spoke to Mariah and the rest of the family, and they were just as happy to see me as I was to see them. I was just thinking that Malik wouldn't show when I heard his voice.

"Come on now, fam. You knew I wasn't going to miss this shit," I heard him say as I stood not too far at the candy table with my back turned, hoping like hell he wouldn't walk over toward me. But hell, we're talking about Malik, I said to myself as I felt the presence of somebody standing behind me.

"Now, I know you ain't think I was going to let you go that easy. Now, did you?" he asked as I turned around to face him. And for a moment, I was speechless as I stood there staring at him.

Malik
A year and a half later
When you get hit with as many unexpected blows as I have, even you would be surprised to make it out of that shit alive. I know everybody was thinking shit was going to crumble, but this was chess and not checkers. I knew all along what I was up against from the first time my truck got hit. I knew it was an inside job, and the information my mother put me on cleared Kim and pointed me right to Amanda, or should I say Rose. I knew if I wanted shit to play out the way I needed it to, I had to play dumb and allow her to breathe in order to trap my father. I also knew Detective Brown was partners with that nigga Detective Brian Knight, the first fed we had to dirt. And just like Rose, I played him like a violin too. But what I didn't know was that he was tied in with my father until he slipped up and gave it away. That was when I put the plan in effect to catch him as well. My biggest regret is not killing that hoe-ass nigga before shit went left.

I could have taken my father out a long time ago, but I was trying to play that shit out the best way I could. With a case still pending against all of us and a missing detective who was working a case to take me down, not to mention his partner, who was out to catch me slipping, every move I made counted. I knew everyone who was tied in with my father, just like I knew about his warehouse down in Miami that Dominique and my Auntie Porsha hit. I mean, after all, I am an eye-for-an-eye type of nigga, so he had to know I was coming to collect sooner rather than later. I wasn't going to stunt, though I was bit salty I didn't get to body bag that nigga Detective Brown.

Shortly after being run up on, I had Dominique pinpoint Amanda and Detective Brown's car. When I pulled up on the scene, he was already dead, alongside a pregnant woman. When we ran through the house, we saw that Rose, or Amanda, or whatever the fuck she wanted to go by, was tied up. After she told me her part of the story and claimed that she knew nothing about us being brother and sister, I kinda felt bad that she had gotten played the way that she did. But that still didn't take away the fact that she had tried to take me and my family down, whether she knew or not. She was the shit's, and that I couldn't let that slide, so I offed her ass too. As for my father and Detective Brown—well, let's just say we set them up and made it look like Detective Brown and my father were in on some dirty shit. And thanks to Dominique, he set Detective Brown's house up with all kind of dirty shit, but not as dirty as the death of his own partner, which we pinned on him, and come to find out the niggas my father was with when he ran down on us were the feds too, so it all panned out like a deal gone bad and cleared us from having anything to do with their murders. And shortly after that, Markese and Zilla were free, and my lawyer hit Cook County with a lawsuit that paid us very well. Not as well as moving them 113 bricks, though.

I made it clear after that I was out of the game, and to my surprise, Markese and Zilla both agreed they were done too. So you can only imagine how that made a nigga feel. Not only had I cleared my name, I had made more money in two months than I had in the past years, and my family was finally free. I had everything I wanted except for the woman I needed. After popping up at Cinnamon's condo right before the deal went down, I tried for two months straight to get her back, but shorty wasn't going and eventually changed her number and moved away. I knew it was real when she left everything of hers behind, including the engagement ring, which she left Stonie to give to me. I ain't going to lie. A nigga was sick behind that loss, but I couldn't blame anyone but myself. But deep down I knew that no matter what, one day I would see her again. Seeing Markese throw in his jersey and settle down with Stonie and Dominique not letting Chyna go nowhere, I knew it was only a matter of time before I'd see shorty again. Besides, I had Dominique keeping tabs on her. Hell yeah, a nigga was stalking.

I knew Cinnamon's whereabouts all the way down in Florida just like I knew she was flying back to Chicago. I told Cinnamon from jump she was going to be my wife, and I meant that shit. So you know when I saw her at the baby shower, I wasn't about to let her get away from me again. Of course, she tried to play like she didn't want a nigga, but I saw past that shit. After months of working on us, she finally gave in and took a nigga back, and I kept my promise and made her my wife. Now she is carrying my son, who I planned to name after Choppa, I thought to myself as Cinnamon, Markese, Stonie, Zilla and his family, Mariah, Chyna, Dominique, and I stood on the yacht as we talked about our memories and said our goodbyes to Choppa. Yeah, my nigga didn't make it, and to this day, that shit hurts me more than anybody will ever know.

Choppa was more than just a friend to me. That nigga was my brother and still is. I would give all this shit up to have him back. That lil nigga's probably in heaven causing hell right now. He always said it was fed or dead, but I'd rather my nigga be doing fed time than to be dead any day. I knew I couldn't blame myself for his death, but somehow I did. But one thing about Choppa was, he'd rather die fighting back than not at all, and I knew he would be happy to see us all get out of this shit alive, I said to myself as I watch baby Zilla dump Choppa's ashes in the ocean.

"Are you OK, baby?" Cinnamon asked me as she turned around to face me.

"Yeah, I'm straight," I said as she placed my hands on her stomach so I could feel the baby kicking.

"You know, baby, Choppa's going to cause hell when he touches down, right?" I asked her as she wrapped her arms around my neck.

"He's already giving me hell," she said with a smile. As I looked over at Markese, two little girls, and baby Zilla, who was causing hell then, I smiled and vowed from here on out that it would always be God, family, money till I died! And as far as my mother—well, let's just say she's finally free.

EndLess CrossRoads
Yvette

I was always taught to handle shit accordingly, and after my last experience with Big Malik, I now know that I couldn't allow my past to ever show its face in my future again, I said to myself as I sat in a chair across from Carlos's wife and waited for her to fully wake up. You see, I'm not one to take threats kindly, nor am I ever going to allow this bitch to one day expose who I am, because whether she likes it or not, Carlos will always be mine. And now that Mariah knew who her real father was, things between Carlos and me had changed for the better. But there was still one loose end I had to tie up before I could agree to be his wife, I said to myself as I watched her begin to wake and look around the room in confusion as to where she was at. That was, until she laid eyes on me.

"I would advise you not to say a word," I said while looking over at all thirty teeth of hers that I'd pulled out while she was passed out, I thought to myself as I watched her look to her left at the row of teeth. "While you were knocked out, I took the pleasure of pulling out all of your teeth and wiring your gums with explosives. So the moment you open your big-ass mouth to talk, boom!" I said, and I laughed out loud. "I know you didn't think I was going to let that shit slide," I said as I sat up a bit like the queen that I am. "I mean, come on now. You know I'm too petty for that shit. Had you not opened your big-ass mouth up, we wouldn't be here right now. I let shit slide in the past off the strength of Carlos. And before you get to thinking too hard…" I said as the door opened and Carlos walked in looking sharper than a tool box, "don't," I said as he walked over and planted a kiss on my cheek. "You see, this is a queen board, and like you said before, the queen must protect the king, no matter what," I said as Carlos moved behind me.

"Come on, baby. Make this shit quick. We have to meet Mariah and the kids," he went on to say in that thick accent I loved so much, I said to myself as I stood up and walked closer to her. "Now you can see for yourself that you only matter because I allowed you to. And with that," I said while pressing a button and turning on the bomb that was wired to her mouth, "all roads end with you," I said with a smile before turning to face my king. "Let's go meet the kids. I'm sure they're wondering where we are," I said as I walked toward Carlos and took his hand.

"By the way, you look beautiful ma'ma" he went on to say as we walked toward the door, and moments later, the bomb went off.

"Not as beautiful as Endless CrossRoads," I said as we continued to walk as if we hadn't just heard that bomb go off, I said to myself as I hopped on the chopper to meet my kids on the yacht.

The End

In Memory of Anthony Lloyd
02/08/1994-09/24/2013
I love you, little brother, and I'll see you at the CrossRoads!

Made in the USA
Columbia, SC
20 June 2024